JUNE THOMSON, a former teacher, has published over thirty novels, twenty of which feature her series detective Inspector Jack Finch and his sergeant, Tom Boyce. She has also written seven pastiche collections of Sherlock Holmes short stories. Her books have been translated into many languages. June Thomson lives in Rugby, Warwickshire.

By June Thomson

a&b

The Secret Documents of Sherlock Holmes

JUNE THOMSON

Allison & Busby Limited
12 Fitzroy Mews
London W1T 6DW
www.allisonandbusby.com

First published in 1997.
This paperback edition published by Allison & Busby in 2014.

10 9 8 7 6 5 4 3 2 1

ISBN 978-0-7490-1657-9

Typeset in 11/16 pt Sabon by Allison & Busby Ltd.

The paper used for this Allison & Busby publication
has been produced from trees that have been legally sourced
from well-managed and credibly certified forests.

Printed and bound by
CPI Group (UK) Ltd, Croydon, CR0 4YY

Contents

I should again like to express my thanks to June Thomson for her help in preparing this fourth collection of short stories for publication.

Aubrey B. Watson LDS, FDS, D. Orth.

Foreword

by
Aubrey B. Watson LDS, FDS, D. Orth.

Those of you who have read the three earlier collections[1] of Dr John H. Watson's hitherto unpublished accounts of certain inquiries undertaken by Mr Sherlock Holmes will not need reminding of the curious circumstances under which they were acquired. However, for those who are not familiar with the facts, I supply the following brief explanation of how these papers came into my possession.

They were first obtained by my late uncle, also a Dr John Watson, although he was a doctor of philosophy, not of medicine, and his middle initial was F not H.

However, because of the similarity of his name to that of Mr Sherlock Holmes' friend and companion, my uncle had made a study of the work of the great consulting detective and his near namesake, Dr John H. Watson, and

[1] These collections are *The Secret Files of Sherlock Holmes* (1990), *The Secret Chronicles of Sherlock Holmes* (1992) and *The Secret Journals of Sherlock Holmes* (1993). Aubrey B. Watson.

was considered by many to be an expert on the subject.

It was for this reason that in July 1939, my uncle was approached by a Miss Adeline McWhirter who claimed to be a relative of Dr John H. Watson on his mother's side of the family. She had, she said, inherited the despatch box containing Dr Watson's handwritten accounts of some of Mr Holmes' inquiries which, for various reasons, had never been published and which he had placed for safe keeping in his bank, Cox and Co. of Charing Cross[2]. Finding herself in straitened circumstances, Miss Mc Whirter had reluctantly decided to sell both the box and its contents.

After a careful examination which convinced him of their authenticity, my late uncle bought them and was planning to publish the manuscripts when war was declared a few months later in September 1939. Afraid for their safety, he therefore made copies of the Watson documents before depositing the originals in the strongroom of his own bank in London.

Unfortunately, the bank suffered a direct hit during the bombing of 1942 which reduced the papers to charred fragments and so damaged the despatch box that the words painted on the lid, 'John H. Watson, M.D. Late Indian Army', were indecipherable. My late uncle was therefore faced with a dilemma for he was left with nothing to prove the existence of the originals apart from his own copies.

Unable to trace Miss McWhirter to verify his account

---

[2] Dr John H. Watson refers to this despatch box in 'The Problem of Thor Bridge'. Aubrey B. Watson.

and fearful of his reputation as a scholar, my late uncle decided not to publish the Watson papers after all and, on his death, the whole collection, together with his own footnotes and several short monographs he himself had written on various aspects of the canon, passed to me under the terms of his will.

As I am an orthodontist and therefore have no academic reputation to consider, I have, after much careful thought, decided to offer the documents for publication although I cannot vouch for their authenticity. Readers must decide that for themselves.

I have in places added footnotes of my own in order to bring up to date those already supplied by my late uncle. Readers will also find in an appendix one of his monographs, that concerning the vexed question of the true identity of the King of Bohemia.

The Case of the Ainsworth Abduction

I

Although I know, even as I take up my pen to commit the following account to paper, that there is little chance of it being published, at least not for several years, I have nevertheless decided to record the events in case a future editor might wish to place it before the general public.

It began one morning in September, a few months after my marriage to Miss Mary Morstan and my return to civil practice.[1] I was on my way home from an early visit to one of my patients in the vicinity of Baker Street and, having not seen my old friend Sherlock Holmes for several weeks, I decided to call on him at my former lodgings.

I found him, surrounded by test tubes and retorts, busily engaged in a chemical experiment which had filled the room with the most noxious fumes.

[1] Dr John H. Watson, who had met Miss Mary Morstan during the 'Sign of Four' case in September 1888, married her sometime before March 1889, the date of the inquiry into the scandal in Bohemia. Not long before his marriage, Dr Watson bought a medical practice in Paddington. Dr John F. Watson.

'It is a test I am carrying out into coal tar derivatives,' he explained, having greeted me cordially. 'Unfortunately, I have not so far succeeded. But I shall persevere with the task until I discover a satisfactory solution.'[2]

'If you do not asphyxiate yourself first, Holmes,' I remonstrated, crossing the room to fling open the windows.

'My dear fellow,' he replied, 'I should much rather die in the cause of chemistry than suffocate with the boredom of idleness.'

'You have no cases on hand then?'

'Not at this precise moment. However, I am expecting a client to call shortly although what his business is remains a mystery. You may if you wish read his telegram which is on the table.'

Picking up the sheet of paper, I glanced over the message which read: WILL CALL ON YOU TODAY AT 11AM ON URGENT BUSINESS STOP AINSWORTH.

'It is hardly informative,' I agreed. 'Perhaps the matter is too delicate or too complex to explain in a telegram.'

'Or my prospective client is too miserly to spend more than a few pennies on sending it. We shall soon find out. It is a quarter to eleven now. Will you wait for his arrival, Watson, to find out what this urgent business is about? Or have you more pressing affairs of your own?'

---

[2] Mr Sherlock Holmes evidently continued to be interested in coal tar derivatives because, during the Great Hiatus, he carried out research into the same field of chemistry at a laboratory in Montpellier in France. *Vide*: 'The Adventure of the Empty House'. Dr John F. Watson.

'I shall be delighted to stay,' I replied. 'My practice is fairly quiet at the moment.'

'But evidently flourishing,' Holmes remarked. On seeing my surprise, he continued, 'There is no mystery, Watson. As soon as you walked into the room, I noticed you were wearing new boots which, judging by their quality and the distinctive pattern of stitching along the uppers, were bought at Eastgate's of Brompton Road.[3] Anyone who can afford their prices must be well on the way to success. And now, my dear fellow, come and sit down in your old armchair and tell me what you have been doing since I last saw you.'

There was, however, little time for private conversation. Hardly had we sat down and Holmes had filled and lit his pipe than the front door bell rang and his client was shown into the room.

He was a large, florid man, very broad across the chest and with features to match his girth for the heavy chin, beetling eyebrows and broad, fleshy cheeks, mottled a dark purplish-red in colour, seemed exaggerated beyond normal. His presence, too, was larger than life as was his voice, both of which seemed to fill the room to overflowing.

'Mr Sherlock Holmes?' he boomed, fixing both of us in turn with an impatient glare from his bright blue eyes.

'I am Sherlock Holmes,' my old friend replied.

[3] T. Eastgate was a manufacturer of fashionable ladies' and gentlemen's boots and shoes with retail premises in Buckingham Palace Road and Brompton Road. The firm was by appointment to His Majesty, the King of the Belgians. Dr John F. Watson.

'Then who the devil is he?' our visitor demanded, turning that choleric stare in my direction.

'That gentleman is Dr Watson, a colleague of mine,' Holmes explained coolly.

'I came to consult you, not some other d-d fellow!' came the riposte.

I half rose from my chair in preparation to leave the room, having no desire to cause any unpleasantness between Holmes and his prospective client. As I did so, Holmes gestured to me to remain seated before addressing his visitor in a cold, clipped voice.

'Either Dr Watson remains in the room or you must leave, sir. He has my complete confidence and I have no intention of conducting any business in his absence. The choice is entirely yours.'

For a moment, I thought the man would explode with rage. His chest swelled up like a turkey cock's and his mottled complexion turned an even brighter red while his blue eyes were positively blazing. However, he managed with difficulty to contain his anger and, nodding curtly to me as if giving me his permission to stay, he acquiesced grudgingly.

'Very well, Mr Holmes. I agree.'

'Then pray be seated, Mr Ainsworth, and explain what urgent business has brought you here.'

'Not Mr Ainsworth,' he retorted, lowering himself into the armchair which Holmes had indicated and which he entirely filled with his enormous frame. 'I am Sir Hector Ainsworth. As to my business, sir, before I begin to explain that, I should first like to know your fees. I am not a rich man.'

I saw Holmes suppress a small smile at this confirmation of his client's parsimony. However, it was with a serious expression that he explained his terms, adding that these did not include expenses.

Sir Hector puffed out his cheeks and looked much taken aback.

'That is a great deal of money, Mr Holmes,' he remarked.

'On the contrary, my fees are considered reasonable and, under certain circumstances, I am prepared to charge only by results. Should I fail, you will pay nothing.[4] If, however, you think these terms excessive, I advise you to take your business elsewhere,' Holmes suggested suavely, rising to his feet as if he considered the interview over.

'No, no! You mistake me, sir!' Sir Hector blustered. 'I am prepared to accept your fees. I am not used to London prices, that is all. Why, the cab driver who brought me here from Paddington station charged me sixpence – yes, sixpence, sir! – for the journey. It is outrageous! Of course, I refused to tip the fellow.'

'Your business with me concerns money?' Holmes inquired in an attempt to bring his client back to the point.

'Money? What the deuce made you think that?' Sir Hector demanded, swelling up once more with fury at

---

[4] In 'The Problem of Thor Bridge', Mr Sherlock Homes remarks: 'My professional charges are upon a fixed scale. I do not vary them, save when I remit them altgether.' Dr John F. Watson.

Holmes' interpretation. Then recalling whatever business had brought him to Baker Street, he once more subsided.

'Well, yes, Mr Holmes, money does come into it although I cannot for the life of me imagine how you came to such a conclusion. It concerns my daughter Millicent, my only child and therefore my sole heir. She is already in possession of a small capital sum, left to her by her mother, my late wife. But under the terms of her will, my daughter cannot touch either the capital or the interest until she marries or reaches the age of thirty, whichever occurs first.'

Sir Hector paused here as if his account were over and he were waiting for Holmes to reply.

'I do not see the point,' he began.

'Not see the point! Why, it is as plain as the nose on your face, sir! The scoundrel who has abducted my daughter intends to marry her by force and then seize hold of her money! That is the point, Mr Holmes! I am surprised a man of your much-vaunted intelligence fails to grasp it.'

Holmes' lean features flushed with anger but he controlled his impatience and, when he spoke, his voice was admirably calm and steady.

'I think, Sir Hector,' said he, 'that you should start at the beginning. When exactly was your daughter abducted?'

'Sometime last night. I was told of her absence by her maid who, going to wake her this morning, found her bed empty.'

'Do you know who has abducted her?'

'Of course I do!' Sir Hector boomed in reply. 'It is the assistant groom, a miserable little runt of a creature called

Weaver, Albert Weaver. Once I lay hands on the man, I intend horsewhipping him to within an inch of his life! That is your brief, Mr Holmes. You find my daughter and return her to my care. At the same time, you hand Weaver over to me to deal with as I think fit.'

'So that you may horsewhip him?' Holmes suggested, both his tone and expression perfectly serious.

The irony was lost on Sir Hector who nodded vigorously.

'Exactly, sir! I am glad you have at last grasped the point. Now is there anything else you need to know?'

'A few more facts, Sir Hector. Where does Weaver sleep?'

'Sleep? What the devil has that to do with the case?'

I saw Holmes' jaw tighten before he said in a voice as cutting as a steel blade, 'If I am to take on the inquiry, then I must decide which questions are relevant. I repeat: Where does Weaver sleep?'

'Over the stables, where grooms are usually accommodated. The head groom and the stable boys also have rooms there.'

'How did Weaver gain access to the house last night? Were there any signs that he had broken in?'

Sir Hector seemed strangely disconcerted by this question and for several long moments remained uncharacteristically silent. Then he said with obvious reluctance, 'Not that I am aware of although I understand from the cook that when she came downstairs at six o'clock this morning, she found the back door unlocked and unbolted.'

'So someone inside the house must have let him in?' Holmes suggested with sweet logic. As his client again remained silent my old friend continued, 'Sir Hector, it pains me greatly to have to put this question but it must be asked. Has your daughter indeed been abducted or has she in fact eloped?'

The effect of this question on Sir Hector was not as extreme as I had expected. There was no eruption of anger although his eyes nearly bulged out of their sockets. However, when he spoke, it was with the exultant tone of a man scoring a point in an argument.

'Elope, sir? With a groom? My daughter has too keen a sense of family honour to do any such thing. Besides, if she had eloped, why would she leave all her clothes behind? Answer me that, Mr Holmes.'

'You mean she took nothing?'

It was Holmes' turn to be disconcerted.

'Not a stitch!' Sir Hector retorted with undisguised triumph. 'I myself questioned her maid most carefully on that very point.'

'How curious!' Holmes murmured, half to himself.

I doubt, however, if Sir Hector heard this comment for, his anger once more roused, he was holding forth in his usual overbearing manner.

'That is not to say nothing was taken. Oh, no, sir! The infernal scoundrel, Weaver, helped himself to my gig and the pony to go with it as well as my daughter's horse which I gave her on her twenty-first birthday. Nice little mare; cost me a fortune. And that's not to mention the tackle.

Saddle, bridle, the lot, gone from the stable! And now, Mr Holmes, is that the last of your tomfool questions? Or is there something else you need to know?'

'Only a description of your daughter.'

Sir Hector seemed curiously nonplussed by this request. Screwing up his eyes as if trying to focus on some far-off image he only dimly perceived, he was silent for several moments.

'There is no point in beating about the bush, Mr Holmes,' he said at last. 'My daughter Millicent is no beauty. In fact, to put it bluntly, she is a very plain young woman; takes after her late mother. Age, twenty-two; dark hair; tall, about my height and built like a grenadier.'

Although I had to bite my lip and turn away to look studiously out of the window, Holmes received this information with perfect gravity.

'And what of Weaver, the groom?'

'I've told you already, he's a miserable little runt of a man; a former jockey; clean-shaven; sandy-coloured hair. Age? I have never troubled to ask the fellow but I suppose he must be about twenty-six. As for Jemima . . .'

'Jemima?' Holmes sounded perplexed.

'My daughter's mare, Mr Holmes! She's a chestnut; white blaze on the forehead; jumps like a cat. Now is that all, sir? Then I assume you will want to make inquiries at Elmsfield Hall, my place of residence. Here is my card, giving details of my address. The nearest station is Elmsfield, a small market town a few miles from Reading.

18

I suggest you catch the 12.45 train from Paddington which I myself intend taking.'

'I am afraid that may not be convenient, Sir Hector,' Holmes replied firmly. Turning to me, he continued, lowering one eyelid fractionally although the rest of his face remained perfectly sober, 'I should much appreciate your assistance on such a complex case, my dear doctor, but I believe you have some urgent business of your own to attend to first. At what time will you be free?'

I was much surprised at Holmes' unexpected invitation as well as amused by the manner in which it had been made. Joining in the spirit of the game, I pretended to ponder on the proposition for a few seconds before replying.

'I should be finished by one o'clock.'

Sir Hector, torn between exasperation at Holmes' refusal to accept his own arrangements but mollified, as I have no doubt Holmes intended, by my old friend's reference to the complexity of the case, broke in impatiently.

'Then I suggest you catch the 1.25 train instead. I shall send the carriage to meet it. Good morning to you, gentlemen.'

Shaking hands energetically with both of us, he seized up his hat and stick and went stamping out of the room.

Holmes waited until he heard the street door slam shut behind him before bursting into laughter.

'What an extraordinary man, Watson! 'Pon my word, I declare I have rarely met such a peculiar client. As for the case, that presents a most unusual dilemma. Has

Lady Millicent been abducted or has she eloped? And if she has eloped, why has she taken no clothes with her except, I assume, what she was wearing at the time? But what were they? Hardly just her nightgown, one supposes. And why take her horse? If she and Weaver intend a runaway marriage, I would have thought it would have been more of an encumbrance than a blessing. By the way, my dear fellow,' he continued in an offhand manner, 'I was right, was I not, in assuming you would be willing to accompany me this afternoon?'

'I have only two routine visits to make on patients, neither of whom is seriously ill. I am sure my neighbour, Jackson,[5] will make them for me. It is a reciprocal arrangement and I obliged him only a fortnight ago.'

'And Mrs Watson will not object?'

'Not at all, Holmes. She often urges me to take more time away from the practice.'

'An inestimable woman!' Holmes murmured. 'You are indeed fortunate, my dear fellow. However, to return to the case in hand, I shall meet you, shall I not, at Paddington station to catch the train as planned? It will be much pleasanter to travel by ourselves without having to suffer the fatigues of Sir Hector Ainsworth's overpowering presence.'

'I shall indeed be there,' I assured him.

It was only after I had taken my leave and was on

[5] Jackson, also a doctor, was a next-door neighbour of Dr John H. Watson's when he was living in Paddington. *Vide*: 'The Adventure of the Crooked Man' and 'The Adventure of the Stockbroker's Clerk'. Dr John F. Watson.

my way home by hansom that it struck me how cleverly Holmes had so arranged matters that he had not only secured my companionship but at the same time had managed to dispense with Sir Hector's. But any small doubt I might have felt at his skilful manipulation of the situation was more than compensated by the thought that I would once more accompany him on an investigation and I felt an immediate quickening of my pulse at this prospect.

II

Those arrangements which I needed to make to cover my absence were soon completed. Jackson agreed to act as my locum and my dear wife welcomed the news that I was to enjoy a few hours of leisure in the countryside in the company of Holmes. It was therefore with a light heart that I set out to walk the short distance to Paddington station[6] where I met my old friend.

I found him in excellent spirits. In the intervening hours since we had last met, he had looked up Sir Hector Ainsworth in his encyclopaedia of reference[7] and regaled me on the journey with this information as well as other titbits of gossip he had picked up from an

[6] In 'The Adventure of the Engineer's Thumb', Dr John H. Watson remarks that his practice was 'no very great distance from Paddington station'. Dr John F. Watson.

[7] There are several references to Mr Sherlock Holmes' encyclopaedia of reference which he had compiled himself and which contained useful information on a variety of subjects. *Vide*, among others: 'A Scandal in Bohemia' and 'The Adventure of the Priory School'. Dr John F. Watson.

acquaintance who moved in aristocratic circles and on whom he had called briefly on the way to the terminus.[8]

'Sir Hector is evidently extremely wealthy, Watson, having married Henrietta Bagworth, the heiress to Sir Montague Bagworth, the shipping millionaire, who was known to his intimates as Monty Moneybags. Gossip has it that the daughter was an amiable woman but so exceedingly plain that her father paid Sir Hector a huge sum to take her off his hands. However, the unfortunate Millicent seems destined to remain a spinster, Sir Hector having failed to offer a large enough dowry to tempt a prospective bridegroom. I understand the impoverished Duke of Chester once persuaded his eldest son to pay court to her but, having met her, he promptly took to his heels and fled the country for Bechuanaland where I understand he still remains.'

'Poor woman!' I interjected, thinking of my own domestic happiness.

'I quite agree, my dear fellow. We are fortunate not to belong to the aristocracy where marriage, specially for women, is more a question of money, looks and breeding than the softer emotions. Although Lady Millicent may own one of the necessary attributes, breeding, and is likely to inherit another, money, at her father's death, I fear she fails so miserably on the third that no man will look at her with the exception, it appears, of Albert Weaver,

8 Later in his career, Mr Sherlock Holmes was to make use of Langdale Pike, a 'human book of reference upon all matters of social scandal', for a similar purpose. *Vide*: 'The Adventure of the Three Gables'. Dr John F. Watson.

the groom, and I suspect even in his case it may be the prospect of her fortune which has attracted him rather than the lady herself.'

'But abduction, Holmes! That is a serious matter!'

'Of course it is, my dear fellow, if, as I remarked before, Lady Millicent has indeed been abducted. But that remains to be seen.'

We passed the rest of the journey discussing a report in the morning papers of a burglary which had taken place at Lord Packburton's and in which his entire collection of Far Eastern exotica had been stolen until we alighted at Elmsfield, a small market town, where we found Sir Hector's carriage awaiting us. After a journey of about three miles through pleasantly wooded countryside, we arrived at Elmsfield Hall.

The house was an imposing Queen Anne mansion, its magnificent stone facade, with its many-tiered windows, surmounted by a large triangular pediment. Yet despite its grandeur, there were signs of neglect, caused no doubt by Sir Hector's miserliness. Grass was sprouting between the flagstones of the terrace, and the lawns and flowerbeds, which extended in front of the building, looked ill tended.

We were greeted at the door by an elderly butler whose mournful expression put me in mind of an undertaker's mute.

His lordship, he informed us, as he showed us into the drawing room, had been called away to attend to some business with a tenant farmer, but had left instructions that we were to be given any assistance we might require.

'I should like to speak to Lady Millicent's personal maid,' Holmes said.

'Very good, sir,' the butler replied.

When he had left the room, Holmes remarked in a jocular manner, 'I am much relieved we are spared Sir Hector's presence, Watson. Without it, I am sure we shall make better progress. Let us hope his tenant keeps him fully occupied for the rest of the afternoon.'

He broke off as there came a knock at the door which, on his calling out 'Come!', opened and a young, fresh-faced country girl entered the room.

'You are Lady Millicent's maid?' Holmes inquired and, having received her assent, he added. 'And what is your name?'

'Polly Noakes, sir,' said she, dropping a little curtsy.

'Then come and sit down, Miss Noakes,' Holmes said, conducting her to one of the armchairs where she perched herself on its edge, clearly ill at ease at finding herself seated in the drawing room, usually the exclusive prerogative of the gentry.

'And now, Miss Noakes,' he continued, assuming his most amiable manner as he sat down opposite her in a comfortable tête-à-tête designed to make her feel at home, 'there is nothing to be afraid of. Dr Watson and I are merely inquiring into Lady Millicent's disappearance. I am sure you want to help us all you can.'

'Yes, sir,' Polly Noakes replied faintly.

'Excellent! Now I understand it was you who found

your mistress was missing when you went to wake her this morning.'

'Yes, sir,' came the same faint answer.

'And she had taken none of her clothing with her?'

This time she answered with a little nod of her head.

'Then what was she wearing when she left?'

It took Polly Noakes a few seconds to grasp the significance of the question and then her brow cleared and she piped up, 'Her riding habit, sir.'

'Indeed? I am most grateful to you, Miss Noakes, for you have solved one of the minor mysteries of the case,' Holmes said with grave courtesy. 'Now tell me what you know about your mistress and Albert Weaver, the assistant groom.'

'Not much, sir,' the girl said, blushing bright pink at Holmes' compliment and appearing to gain a little more confidence from it. 'They used to go out riding most mornings for an hour or so, her ladyship on Jemima and Weaver on Sir Hector's big black horse, Samuel. Then, in the afternoons, they usually practised jumping in the paddock.'

'"Usually"?' Holmes inquired.

'Well, sir, for the past week, the arrangements have been turned around, so to speak. The training lessons were held in the mornings and they went riding in the afternoons.' She hesitated for a moment and then added more boldly, 'The last five afternoons they were gone for more than an hour. It was more like three. It was a terrible rush, sir, to get Lady Millicent out of her riding clothes and into a gown in time for tea in the drawing room at five o'clock.'

'Did your mistress give you any explanation for this change in her routine?'

'No, sir; and it wasn't my place to ask.'

'Quite so. Then tell me, Miss Noakes,' Holmes said, leaning forward in his chair and regarding her with great interest, 'as you are clearly a young lady of remarkable powers of observation, have you noticed anything else out of the ordinary over the past five days, however trivial?'

Colouring up again prettily, she replied after a moment's hesitation, 'Only the tickets, sir.'

'What tickets?'

'I don't know, sir. I found them in the pocket of Lady Millicent's riding habit when I was brushing it down ready to put away. One lot was pink, the other yellow.'

'Do you still have them?' Holmes inquired, his voice carefully casual.

'Only the last ones, sir, those I found yesterday afternoon. The others, the pink ones, I left out on the dressing table but Lady Millicent must have thrown them away. I can't remember when I found those. It could have been Tuesday or Wednesday.'

'Never mind about that. You still have those you found yesterday, the yellow ones?'

'Yes, sir. They're where I left them. Would you like me to fetch them?'

'If you would be so good.'

As soon as she had left the room, Holmes turned to me.

'I believe, Watson, we may be close to finding an

answer to our dilemma – is this affair an abduction or an elopement? I always find it most significant when someone alters their normal routine, as Lady Millicent has evidently done recently. Perhaps these tickets will explain not only why such a change was made but also what Lady Millicent and Weaver were doing every afternoon for the past five days which took up several hours of their time.'

He broke off as Polly Noakes re-entered and handed to him two little oblong slips of yellow paper.

'Thank you, Miss Noakes,' Holmes said gravely. 'You have been most helpful.'

Bobbing a little curtsy, she began to leave the room but turned back at the doorway, her face flushed and her eyes bright with unshed tears.

'She is all right, isn't she, sir? Lady Millicent, I mean,' she asked in an anxious tone. 'She's been a good mistress to me and I wouldn't want her to come to any harm.'

'I am certain we shall find her safe and well,' Holmes assured her.

As soon as the door closed again behind her, Holmes, with me at his shoulder, began eagerly to examine the two tickets she had given him. They were small, little more than two inches long and one and a half inches wide, and both had torn perforations along the left-hand side. The paper of which they were made was of a thick, coarse quality and on each was printed in heavy black ink a letter and a number, B24 on one and B25 on the other, while a single letter A had been handwritten on each in the top right-hand corner.

'What do they remind you of, Watson?' Holmes inquired.

'Halves of theatre tickets?' I suggested. 'The other halves were torn off at the door.'

'No, not a theatre,' Holmes said musingly. 'At least, not a usual one. Theatre tickets are invariably printed with the name of the theatre and the title of the play as well as the place where the seats are to be found in the auditorium, the dress circle, for example, or the stalls. Besides, the paper is too coarse. But they certainly appear to be tickets to somewhere or for something. The question is: what? And why the two different colours, yellow for one set and pink for another?'

'Could they be raffle tickets then? I remember my wife buying some at a Christmas charity fair in aid of the Association for Bible Studies in Poplar. They were very similar in size and each book of tickets sold was a different colour.'

'A possibility,' Holmes conceded. 'But why the handwritten letter A in the top right-hand corner? And why should Lady Millicent have bought tickets for at least two raffles on separate days? Such a theory hardly explains either why she and the groom were absent for nearly three hours unless . . .'

Before he had time to complete the sentence, the door burst open and Sir Hector came striding into the room, dressed on this occasion in tweeds, his boots and gaiters liberally spattered with mud. Something had clearly annoyed him for, barely acknowledging our presence, he plunged immediately into an angry tirade.

'I apologise for not being here to greet you. I was called away by one of my tenant farmers. It was urgent, he said. Do you know what the fellow wanted? To complain about a leaking roof! Expected me to pay for the repairs as if I am made of money! Fix it yourself, I told him. There's plenty of spare tarpaulins in the stockyard. The man's a fool, sir! An utter buffoon!'

To my astonishment and also Sir Hector's, Holmes greeted this last remark with a little outburst of his own.

'Of course!' he exclaimed, striking his hands together. 'What a fool I have been not to see it before!'

'See what?' Sir Hector expostulated. 'Are you referring to my tenant? But you haven't met the man!'

'No, not him, Sir Hector. I was speaking of Weaver.'

'The assistant groom? But why . . . ?'

'There is no time now to explain! Dr Watson and I must return immediately to London.' Hurriedly shaking his client by the hand, Holmes added, 'Do not trouble to send for the butler, sir. We will ourselves call at the stables and order the carriage. I shall write to you as soon as I have news of your daughter's whereabouts.'

'And when do you suppose . . . ?' Sir Hector began.

We failed to hear the rest of the sentence. Holmes had bundled me out of the room. Having let ourselves out at the front door, we dashed round to the stables where we found the carriage already prepared for our return journey, the coachman idling away the time by smoking a small cigar and chatting to one of the maids.

At our precipitate arrival, he flung aside the cheroot and leapt upon the box while the young woman fled inside the house. Within minutes, we were seated inside the carriage and bowling along the road to Elmsfield station.

I was naturally curious to discover the reason behind our sudden departure for I could see nothing in the situation to warrant Holmes' decision to return immediately to London. However, although I questioned him directly on this very point, he refused to give me an answer, merely remarking with an infuriating smile, 'All in good time, Watson. At the moment, I have nothing more than a hypothesis which needs some facts to support it. As soon as I have those, you will be told everything.'

My exasperation was increased when, on arriving at Elmsfield station, he insisted I went ahead of him through the ticket barrier while he, for some equally inexplicable reason, turned back towards the entrance.

'But there is a London train due at any moment!' I protested. Indeed, as I spoke, I could hear the engine approaching and could see its plume of smoke rising above the rooftops.

'Then hold it for me, Watson,' said he coolly as he walked away.

He caught the train with seconds to spare. As I stood at the open door of a first-class carriage, fuming with impatience, I saw him come running like a stag on to the platform, waving an arm at the guard who had his flag raised and his whistle at his lips.

'I suppose,' said I sarcastically as the whistle blew and

he bounded into the compartment beside me, 'that you will also refuse to explain what business was so urgent it nearly made you miss the train.'

'Not at all, my dear fellow,' said he with a mischievous twinkle in his eye. 'I was anxious to verify one of the facts I referred to earlier. My hypothesis is now taking shape very nicely. In fact, Watson, I think I may say with every confidence that this little affair is almost over.'

III

I heard nothing from Holmes over the next two days and had begun to think that, despite his confident assertion that the case was as good as solved, he had come to some unforeseen impasse when the door bell rang.

It was about one o'clock and, my wife being away visiting an old school friend of hers, Mrs Isa Whitney,[9] I had, after eating lunch alone, retired to my consulting room for a quiet half-hour spent reading the *Morning Post* before setting out on my afternoon calls.

Thinking the visitor might be a patient, I was in the act of folding up the newspaper and tucking it away out of sight when Holmes came bursting into the room.

---

[9] Kate Whitney, wife of Isa Whitney, one of Dr John H. Watson's patients, was 'an old friend and school companion' of Dr Watson's wife, Mary. It was on Mrs Whitney's pleading that Dr Watson went to the Bar of Gold, an opium den in Upper Swandham Lane, to find her husband, an opium addict, and became involved in the disappearance of Mr Neville St Clair. *Vide*: 'The Adventure of the Man with the Twisted Lip'. Dr John F. Watson.

'Watson!' cried he. 'I am delighted to find you at home. Fetch your hat and stick, my dear fellow. We are going out.'

'Where to, Holmes?' I asked, a little taken aback at his unexpected appearance.

'To Clapham.'

'Why to Clapham?'

'To solve the riddle of the Ainsworth case,' he replied impatiently as if I should have been aware of his intentions.

'But I have patients to call on,' I protested.

'None of whom are of any great importance,' he retorted. Seeing my surprised expression, he burst out laughing. 'You were not quite quick enough in hiding the *Morning Post* under that pile of medical journals. A portion of its front page is still visible. The conclusion is therefore obvious. A doctor who has time to read the newspaper can have no urgent cases on hand. So do hurry up, there's a good fellow, and send for that accommodating neighbour of yours. I have a hansom waiting at the door.'

Knowing it was useless to protest that I had been merely enjoying a few moments of leisure before setting off on my professional rounds, I hastily scribbled a note for my neighbour, Jackson, and also for my wife who might return home before me, then I seized my hat and stick and followed him outside to the cab, hoping he might enlighten me on the journey.

But he was as secretive as before and refused to confide in me what evidence he had acquired in the past two days which had led him to make inquiries on the south side of the river.

'Wait and see, Watson,' was all he would reply, adding

with barely suppressed amusement, 'We are catching a train which later this afternoon will take us to a destination where all your questions shall be answered.'

I could make nothing of this enigmatic remark apart from supposing that Clapham Junction was in some way connected to the case although I could not see its significance. Lady Millicent had left Elmsfield Hall by gig. As far as I knew, there was no suggestion that a train journey had played any part in her abduction or elopement unless Holmes' investigation had proved otherwise.

He was in a particularly effervescent mood that afternoon and spoke so entertainingly on a variety of subjects that I gave up puzzling over the conundrum and became so absorbed in his sprightly conversation that I paid little heed to the route we were taking.

It was therefore much to my surprise that, when the cab at last drew to a halt and we alighted, I found myself not at Clapham Junction but on the avenue which runs alongside Clapham Common, one of those large open tracts of grass and trees which have made the southern suburbs of London so popular a place of residence for those who can afford to escape from the close confines of the city centre.

I was also surprised to see that part of this large area was given over to a fair. Stalls had been set up upon the grass as well as amusements of every kind, including swing boats and a helter-skelter, while, over to the right, a large tent had been erected, gaily decorated with flags and bunting.

'Where exactly are we going, Holmes?' I asked when he had finished paying off the cabby.

'There!' he said, flourishing his stick at the tent. 'To the circus.'

I must confess I was considerably annoyed by this remark. While it was true I had no seriously ill patients to attend to, I considered it thoughtless of Holmes to have taken me away from my practice for so trivial a reason as a visit to the circus. But I had no opportunity to express my exasperation. Holmes had gone striding ahead and by the time I caught up with him he had already plunged into a narrow passageway left open between a double row of hoopla stalls and coconut shies. The crowds of people and the clamour of the stallholders, urging passers-by to try their luck at rolling a penny or to visit one of several freak shows, exhibiting midgets, fat ladies or human skeletons, made conversation impossible.

It was only when we reached the booth selling tickets to the circus that I understood his reason for bringing me to so unlikely a destination.

'Do you see now, Watson?' he asked with a smile, showing me the tickets he had just purchased.

They were two slips of coarse, bright blue paper, perforated down the centre, each half printed with a large letter C and consecutive numbers, fourteen on one and fifteen on the other. Each was also marked with a large letter A in the top right-hand corner.

'They are just like those Lady Millicent's maid found in the pocket of her riding habit!' I exclaimed.

'Exactly, Watson!'

'But what on earth made you realise they were circus tickets?'

'It was a chance remark of Sir Hector's. If you recall when we met him at Elmsfield Hall, he referred to his tenant as a buffoon. The word set into motion a sequence of other words, from buffoon to clown, and from clown to circus. I am afraid I was teasing you when I spoke about catching a train to our destination. It was that train of thought I had in mind.

'The word "circus" also reminded me of something which I had glimpsed briefly outside Elmsfield station when we took the carriage to Elmsfield Hall. That was why, when we returned to the station, I sent you on ahead. I wanted to look more closely at the billboard on the wall outside to make quite sure I had remembered correctly, as indeed I had. What I had glimpsed so briefly but which had nevertheless lodged in my mind was a large, garishly coloured poster for Molesworth's Circus which had been visiting Reading during the previous week.

'That fact and the discovery of the tickets in Lady Millicent's pocket convinced me that she, in company with Weaver, had visited the circus on at least two occasions for its afternoon performances. As the ticket seller has just confirmed, different coloured tickets are issued each day, blue, yellow, pink and so on. They are also marked A or E to indicate whether they are for the afternoon or evening performance. That is to prevent members of the public who have attended one of those performances from using them to re-enter the tent without paying after the interval on another day or indeed to prevent anyone finding a discarded half ticket from doing the same.

'It took me a little time to find out where Molesworth's Circus was now performing and to make a few preliminary inquiries before calling on you this afternoon.'

'But what possible connection can Lady Millicent have with the circus?' I asked.

'The performance has already started. Shall we enter and find out?' Holmes replied, leading the way towards the entrance where a man dressed in a red uniform, lavishly bedecked with gold braid and silver buttons, tore our tickets in half before waving us inside.

Much of the interior of the large tent was taken up by tiers of wooden benches, arranged in a horseshoe shape round the circus ring which was separated from the audience by a low barrier. On the far side was another opening, hung with heavy red velvet curtains through which the performers entered. Above this entrance, a small group of musicians, consisting of brass and percussion players who were dressed like the ticket collector in red uniforms, was installed on its own velvet-hung balcony.

As we entered, these musicians were accompanying the antics of a troupe of clowns with a cacophony of braying trumpets, banging drums and clashing cymbals which, mingled with the shouts of the clowns themselves and the delighted shrieks of laughter from the audience, was quite deafening.

We found our seats and settled down to watch the rest of the afternoon performance which, I must confess, in my impatience to discover what part Lady Millicent could possibly play in this unlikely setting, I found only mildly enjoyable although Holmes seemed hugely entertained by all the acts, even the dancing dogs and the lady fire-eater.

It was the fifth act on the bill which was evidently the one we had come to see for, as the ringmaster announced it, I felt Holmes stiffen beside me in anticipation.

'And now, ladies and gentlemen and all you dear, delightful children,' the man was declaring, 'it gives me great pleasure to introduce to you an entirely new act, never before seen in this country – the beautiful, the bewitching, the breathtaking Vittoria, the circus belle, and her magnificent mount, Jemima!'

With that announcement and to a roll of the drums and a fanfare from the trumpets, the curtains at the back of the ring parted and in trotted a chestnut horse, its head adorned with pink and white plumes and its harness jingling with tiny silver bells. On its back, which was covered by a magnificent crimson and silver saddle cloth, was standing the slight figure of a young woman, dressed in pink-sequined tulle, her long golden hair adorned with plumes matching those of the horse.

Horse and rider were accompanied by their own ringmaster, a tall, well-built man, wearing a large black moustache, curled up at the ends, a blue satin coat, white breeches, leather boots and a gold top hat. He was brandishing a long whip which he proceeded to crack. At these signals, the young woman leapt on and off the horse as it cantered round the ring, or turned somersaults on its bare back to loud applause.

For several moments, I was too bewildered to grasp the

significance of what I was seeing. Surely Lady Millicent, whose own father had described her as no beauty, could not possibly be this dainty, graceful figure, as pretty and as fragile-seeming as a Christmas tree fairy, which glittered pink and silver under the gas flares?

It was the sound of Holmes' delighted shout of laughter which brought me to an understanding of the situation and I immediately joined in his merriment.

When he had recovered sufficiently to speak, he murmured in my ear, 'Come, Watson. We have seen enough. Let us meet Vittoria the circus belle and her assistant as they leave the ring.'

Having emerged from the circus arena, we made our way past the guy ropes to the far side of the tent where the artistes' exit was positioned under a canvas awning close to a row of caravans in which I assumed the various performers were housed.

Our arrival was well timed; hardly had we reached this exit than we heard the sound of muffled applause and a final flourish of drums and trumpets which suddenly became louder as the velvet curtains were drawn back to allow Vittoria, the horse and the attendant ringmaster to leave the ring.

They emerged at a walking pace, Vittoria dismounting and leading the horse forward by the bridle. Both looked hot and tired, especially Vittoria. Seen at close quarters and in the cruel light of day, she no longer presented the delicate, ethereal figure which had pirouetted so gracefully under the lights. The pink and white porcelain complexion could now be seen as nothing more than a thick layer of grease-paint, rouge and powder while the eyes and mouth were also artificially enhanced. In short, she looked less like a Christmas fairy and more like one of the clowns. Even the sparkling dress had been reduced to a crumpled mass of cheap net covered with garish spangles.

'Lady Millicent Ainsworth?' Holmes inquired politely, stepping forward and raising his hat.

I should, of course, have been prepared. Even so, it still came as something of a shock when, instead of the circus belle responding to Holmes' inquiry it was the moustached and booted attendant who spoke up.

'Who the devil are you, sir?' he, or rather she, demanded, frowning heavily and tapping the handle of the whip against the side of her leg in an ominous manner.

'I am Sherlock Holmes and this is my colleague, Dr Watson,' Holmes explained. 'Your father asked me to inquire into your disappearance.'

'Holmes, the private detective?' Lady Millicent countered, looking him up and down with considerable disfavour. 'I have heard of you, sir. You make your living by thrusting your nose into other people's business, do you not? Well, since you are here, I suppose I had better speak to you although I warn you now that I have no intention of returning to my father's house and, as I am of age, there is nothing either you or the law can do to make me.'

'I was not intending to do anything of the sort,' Holmes said pleasantly, a smile on his lips although I suspected that his amusement arose as much from the similarity between Lady Millicent and her formidable father as from a mere desire to placate her.

'Then you had better come with me,' the lady retorted, striding ahead of us to one of the nearby caravans. We followed obediently, first Holmes, then myself. Vittoria, alias Albert Weaver, in his bedraggled finery brought up the rear, having handed over the horse, Jemima, to one of the circus assistants.

The interior of the caravan was surprisingly comfortable. At Lady Millicent's invitation, Holmes and I sat down on a long cushioned bench, which no doubt served double duty as a bed, and watched while Lady Millicent and her erstwhile groom divested themselves of their circus identities.

In Lady Millicent's case it was simply a matter of discarding her gold silk hat and stripping off the large, curly moustache, after which she emerged more or less as what I imagined was her usual self, a heavily built, strong-featured young woman whose self-confidence and imperious manner suggested an upbringing in which she was more used to giving orders than obeying them.

The transformation of Weaver from circus belle to male companion was more dramatic. Off came the blonde wig, revealing short-cropped, sandy hair. Off, too, came the pink and white complexion with the aid of a damp towel while a masculine looking, dark blue dressing gown, flung over the tinselled skirt and bodice, completed the metamorphosis – apart, that is, from his lower limbs which were still encased in pink silk tights and matching satin slippers.

'Whisky!' Lady Millicent was exclaiming, pouring generous measures into four glasses which she handed round before sinking down on to another padded bench facing ours and drinking deeply from her own glass with evident pleasure.

'Well,' she said, setting down the tumbler and fixing Holmes with a piercing glare, 'what have you to say for yourself, Mr Holmes? Do you propose informing my father where I and my fiancé are to be found?'

'Fiancé?' Holmes repeated. 'So you intend to marry?'

'As soon as we can get a special licence.'

It was Albert Weaver who spoke, casting a fond glance in Lady Millicent's direction and enfolding one of her large hands in both of his. Although they made an unlikely couple sitting there hand in hand, it was quite evident from their exchange of smiles and air of affectionate intimacy that they were indeed very much in love.

'Then I must congratulate you and also beg your pardon,' said Holmes. 'I was told by your father, Lady Millicent, that you had been abducted.'

The remark was greeted by peals of merriment from the happy pair.

'I am afraid,' said Lady Millicent at last, having regained her composure, 'that my father is apt to exaggerate, Mr Holmes. With him everything is either black or white, good or bad, especially when it most closely touches him or his concerns which are money and his family pride. No doubt he described himself as a poor man? Ah, I thought so! Poverty is one of his particular bugbears. Although he is now wealthy, he was not always so fortunate. Before he married my mother, he had, as the saying goes, hardly two brass farthings to rub together. On my marriage, I will inherit a small amount of capital from my late mother's estate, not a large sum but enough to provide me with an annuity of £200 a year which at present my father has control of. I am convinced that the loss of this income and the prospect of my marrying Albert, who, in my father's eyes and those of his aristocratic acquaintances, is hardly the ideal husband for a baronet's daughter, persuaded him to believe I could not possibly have left of my own free will but must have been abducted, even though I left a letter on his desk explaining my intentions.'

'Your father mentioned no letter,' Holmes replied.

'That does not surprise me. No doubt he saw it and, suspecting what it contained, chose not to open it but put it away somewhere unread. He is like an ostrich which hides its head in the sand rather than face an unwelcome truth. But I am surprised he persuaded you I had been abducted. Look at me, Mr Holmes! I am hardly a helpless maiden who was carried off by force over Albert's shoulder! If anyone had done the carrying, it would have been me, not him.'

There was another burst of laughter in which all of us joined. When it had died away, Holmes remarked, a little defensively, I thought, 'It was only the fact you left your clothes behind which puzzled me and persuaded me to take up the case. I see now the reason for it. In your new life, you hardly needed skirts and gowns. Your riding habit and your circus costume provided all your necessary garb, at least for the time being.'

'That was partly the reason. I also left them because I wished to take with me as few reminders as I could of my old life and because I did not want to be accused of owing my father anything. For that same reason, I have waived all rights to my income for the next two years which will more than pay for the gig and horse we took with us, as I have also explained in my letter. Albert and I want to be beholden to no one except ourselves.'

'May I ask you something personal, Lady Millicent?' Holmes inquired.

'Ask away, Mr Holmes, although I do not promise to answer your question,' said she with unaffected frankness.

'What made you decide to join the circus?'

'You had better answer that, Albert. It was your decision,' Lady Millicent replied, giving her fiancé's hand an affectionate pat at which he smiled at her fondly before taking up the account.

'When I was a young lad, Mr Holmes, I worked for a circus, looking after the animals,' Weaver began. 'That's when I first learnt to love horses. There was a couple of artistes, a husband and wife team. Ted and Rosie Hubbard, known in the business as the Marvellos, and their horse Wonder, who performed in the ring. The first time I saw them, my sole ambition was to have my own equestrian act like theirs one day. They were a kind couple and sometimes let me use their horse so I could practise some of the tricks, like leaping on and off when the horse was cantering, or turning somersaults on its bare back. But in order to buy my own horse, which I'd need before I could set myself up as a circus entertainer, I had to have money and the pay was not nearly enough. So, when I saw a post advertised at Newmarket for a stable boy to train as a jockey, I took it. I was there for eight years and was able, once I was properly trained, to earn a fair amount, especially when I rode a winner, and to put a little aside.

'But I missed the circus life. It's like the sea, sir. Once you've got it in your blood, you're never happy on dry land. Anyway, the stable went bankrupt and I found myself out of a job. There were no vacancies at the time at any of the other stables and, as I still hadn't saved enough to buy my own horse, I applied for the post I saw advertised for an assistant groom at Elmsfield Hall, intending to keep it only long enough for me to save up a little more money.

'The rest I think you may guess, Mr Holmes. I met Lady Millicent, and,' he added, casting a shy, sideways glance at his fiancée who beamed broadly back at him, 'we fell in love. I confided in her my ambition to join the circus as an equestrian performer which she heartily agreed with. It was then we decided to set up as a pair, like the Marvellos, me doing the riding and her acting as my ringmaster. By great good fortune, her horse, Jemima, was just the mount I'd been looking for, gentle, obedient and handsome to look at. We started training her every day in the paddock and then, when Molesworth's Circus came to Reading, we introduced ourselves to the owner, showed him our act and he offered us a place amongst his artistes.

'My only regret, Mr Holmes, is having to sneak away in the night but there seemed no other way out. Sir Hector would never have given us his blessing.'

'I take your point,' Holmes agreed drily. 'And so you intend to marry and remain in the circus?'

'For the time being, Mr Holmes. Eventually we will have to retire but by then I hope we will have saved enough to open our own riding school somewhere in the country. When we do, we may be considered respectable enough even by Sir Hector's standards for us to write to him and let him know where we are. Until then, sir, we would be grateful if you said nothing to him.'

'Your secret is safe with us,' Holmes assured him, getting to his feet and holding out his hand in turn to the two of them, Lady Millicent wringing his with so much vigour that I saw Holmes wince inadvertently.

Outside, he clapped me on the shoulder.

'Well, Watson,' said he with a chuckle, 'you have the happy ending which, as a sentimentalist, you always look for. Wedding bells will chime and the bride and groom will live happily ever after; at least, one sincerely hopes so. You and I, however, are not so fortunate and must bear our loss with as much stoicism as we can muster.'

'What loss, Holmes?' I asked, a little puzzled by his remark.

'I will have to confess defeat to Sir Hector and waive the fee I might have charged him while you, my dear fellow, will have to forgo the pleasure of publishing an account of the case.'[10]

[10] Dr John H. Watson makes a passing reference to the case in 'The Adventure of the Sussex Vampire' in which Vittoria, the circus belle, is listed under the letter V in Mr Sherlock Holmes' volume of reference. Dr John F. Watson.

The Case of the Boulevard Assassin

I

As I see from my three massive volumes of notes for the year 1894, the months following Holmes' miraculous escape from death at the hands of his arch enemy, Professor Moriarty, were a particularly busy time for my old friend.[1] For some of those adventures, such as the cases concerning Mr Jonas Oldacre, the Norwood builder, and Professor Coram of Yoxley Old Place, I have written and published complete accounts.[2] For various reasons, others have remained unrecorded. Among these is one

---

[1] On 4th May 1891, Mr Sherlock Holmes apparently plunged to his death over the Reichenbach Falls in Switzerland during a struggle with Professor Moriarty, the international arch criminal. However, although the Professor was killed, Holmes survived and spent the next three years travelling in Tibet, Persia, the Sudan and France, returning to London to resume his practice in April 1894. *Vide*: 'The Adventure of the Final Problem' and 'The Adventure of the Empty House'. Dr John F. Watson.

[2] These cases were later published respectively under the titles 'The Adventure of the Norwood Builder' and 'The Adventure of the Golden Pince-nez'. Dr John F. Watson.

particular inquiry which, because of its sensitive political nature, cannot as yet be set before the public although I remain hopeful that, at some later date, I shall be allowed to publish this account of it.

It was, I recall, one afternoon in late October when a special messenger arrived with an urgent letter from Mycroft Holmes, summoning us to meet him without delay at the Diogenes Club.[3] Should this narrative ever appear in print, those readers who are already familiar with my other published adventures will not need reminding that Mycroft Holmes held a unique position in the government. Although ostensibly employed as an auditor, he was, in fact, a highly regarded ministerial adviser whose specialised knowledge on a variety of subjects had made him so influential in deciding matters of national policy that, as Holmes once pointed out, there were times when he was the British government.

'Your brother does not explain what this meeting is about?' I inquired, full of curiosity, for Mycroft Holmes had introduced my old friend to several of his most interesting cases.[4]

'No, not a word, which makes me suspect that it is a <u>matter of some</u> importance,' Holmes replied. 'But rather

[3] The Diogenes Club was situated in Pall Mall, opposite Mr Mycroft Holmes' lodgings. *Vide*: 'The Adventure of the Greek Interpreter'. Dr John F. Watson.

[4] As well as advising Mr Sherlock Holmes on certain cases, Mr Mycroft Holmes also introduced his brother to two investigations, those concerning Mr Melas ('The Adventure of the Greek Interpreter') and Arthur Cadogan West ('The Adventure of the Bruce Partington Plans'). Dr John F. Watson.

than waste time speculating, Watson, let us find out the facts from the fountainhead itself.'

We took a cab to the Diogenes Club in Pall Mall where we found Mycroft Holmes already comfortably installed in the Strangers' Room, the only part of the premises where conversation was permitted. As we entered, he waved a plump, languid hand towards two armchairs which were drawn up facing him.

'You will forgive me for not rising,' said he. 'I have had the most exhausting day.'

I have remarked before on the physical differences between the two brothers, a dissimilarity which always struck me whenever I saw the two of them together. Holmes' thin, sparse frame and energetic manner were in direct contrast to Mycroft's portly figure and air of massive indolence. It was only in the keenness of his glance that one was made aware of the intellectual power contained in that large head and unwieldy frame.

'You are, of course, familiar with the name Sante Caserio,' he began, taking a pinch of snuff from a tortoiseshell box.

'The Italian anarchist who assassinated the French President a few months ago?' Holmes inquired, sitting forward in his chair and fixing his brother with a look of eager attention.[5]

---

[5] Monsieur Sadi Carnot (1837–1894), the fourth President of the Third Republic, was fatally stabbed by the Italian anarchist Sante Caserio at Lyons on 24th June 1894. He was succeeded as President by Jean Casimir-Perier (1947–1907) who resigned after only six months in office. An Italian anarchist was also responsible

'Exactly so,' Mycroft Holmes replied. 'The man was arrested and is at present being held in custody awaiting execution. It is not therefore Caserio who concerns us here. Rather, it is one of his colleagues, Alphonse Huret, better known under the pseudonym of the Boulevard Assassin, whom the French authorities are anxious to track down. That name, too, should be familiar to you.'

'Indeed it is!' Holmes exclaimed. 'I have been following the accounts of his exploits in the newspapers for the past few months. He has been blamed, has he not, for the death of Monsieur Boncour of the Justice Department, as well as attempts on the lives of two other important members of the French government?'

'Which is why I have sent for you, dear boy. In a week's time, Monsieur Claude Auriel, the Minister of Overseas Affairs, is due to arrive in London, ostensibly on a private visit to the Earl of Evesham, a relation of his by marriage, his daughter having married the Earl's youngest son. However, while he is here, Monsieur Auriel will, in fact, be engaged in secret talks with officials from our own Foreign Office in an attempt to settle some of the differences between our two countries.[6] From information received through a government agent inside the anarchist

---

for the assassination in Switzerland of the Empress Elisabeth of Austria in September 1898. Dr John F. Watson.

[6] France, Great Britain's former enemy during the Napoleonic Wars, was considered her main rival in the colonisation of Africa. In 1904, the relationship between the two countries improved when King Edward VII made a state visit to Paris which led to the signing of the *Entente Cordiale* in 1904. Dr John F. Watson.

movement, the French authorities believe that, while he is in London, an attempt will be made on Monsieur Auriel's life by Alphonse Huret who, now that Caserio has been arrested, is their chief assassin.

'I have therefore been specifically asked by a certain highly placed official in the French government to request your help in this matter. Since your success over that important affair three years ago, it is felt that you are the only person they can trust to bring about Huret's arrest.[7] For captured he must be before more members of the French government are assassinated. And that is not all, Sherlock. From our point of view, the continued presence of the Boulevard Assassin poses a threat to our own national stability. If Huret continues with his murderous career, it could well encourage other anarchists to turn their attention to the British government with heaven knows what consequences. Now, my dear Sherlock, are you prepared to take the case?'

'Of course,' Holmes replied without the least hesitation.

'I thought that would be your answer. If you succeed, as indeed you must, it will be another fine feather in your cap.'

'I am more interested in facts than feathers,' Holmes replied.

'Then let us get down to them. Knowing your habit of

---

[7] In the winter of 1890 and the early spring of 1891, Mr Sherlock Holmes was 'engaged by the French government upon a matter of supreme importance'. Although he wrote to Dr John H. Watson from Narbonne and Nimes, he apparently did not inform Watson of the exact nature of this business. *Vide*: 'The Adventure of the Final Problem'. Dr John F. Watson.

keeping cuttings of any interesting items of news in the daily papers, I assume you have at least a partial record of Huret's past career to which I can add further information passed on to me by my colleagues in the French Ministry of the Interior. The first attempt was made on Monsieur Delmar, head of the Secretariat of Cultural Affairs, when he was walking down Boulevard Haussmann. A shot was fired from a passing *fiacre* which fortunately missed its target. Monsieur Boncour of the Justice Department was not so lucky. At the beginning of September, he was killed by a bullet which was also fired from a moving vehicle, this time a hearse, which approached slowly down Boulevard St-Germain towards the terrace of the Café des Fleurs where Monsieur Boncour was enjoying a glass of cognac. Once the deed was done, the hearse gathered speed and disappeared amongst the traffic.

'The third attempt was made only a fortnight ago on the life of Monsieur Poujade, Chief Secretary to the Minister of Finance. He was shot as he left his apartment in Boulevard des Italiens. Again a vehicle was used, in this particular instance a small delivery van. Monsieur Poujade was struck in the shoulder and is still in hospital receiving treatment for the wound.

'All the vehicles were later found abandoned. They had been stolen and in two cases their rightful owners garrotted, presumably because they had seen the thieves and could identify them. However, other witnesses were able to give descriptions of the man who fired the gun. As these were not widely published in the English newspapers, you may not be acquainted with them. In the first attempt, he was described as a pale-faced, red-bearded man. In the second and fatal attack, he was wearing eyeglasses and a brown goatee; in the third, black hair and dark, bushy whiskers. I am sure you can draw your own conclusions from these details.'

'That Alphonse Huret is in the habit of wearing different disguises and appears to have a predilection for beards, suggesting he may have some distinguishing feature about the lower part of his face, perhaps a scar or some other easily recognisable mark,' Holmes replied. 'It therefore follows that we cannot be certain either of his exact appearance or of what disguise he may adopt for his next assassination attempt. As none of these descriptions refers to his height or build, I assume no one remarked on them.'

'In all three cases, Huret was seated inside the vehicle so that only his face was visible.'

'What of his accomplice, the driver of these various vehicles?' Holmes inquired. 'I assume Huret had one for he could hardly have managed the horses and at the same time aimed and fired his revolver. Have you no descriptions of him?'

'Very few, Sherlock, for he was always careful to keep his face averted and to wear a cap pulled well down over his face. And who takes notice of a cabby or a van driver? It was the man flourishing the gun who caught the attention of the bystanders. Only two witnesses could give any details about the driver's appearance and they merely stated that he was broad-shouldered and of a heavy build. I know it is little enough to go on and the task of tracking down Huret and his accomplice will be well nigh impossible.'

'Not impossible,' Holmes corrected him. 'Only exceedingly difficult. Looking for them among London's huge population will be like searching for two particular grains of sand on a seashore. But remember the old saying, Mycroft. If the mountain will not come to Mahomet . . .'

Although I failed to grasp the significance of the adage to this particular situation, Mycroft Holmes appeared to understand it at once. Smiling broadly, he completed the quotation.

'Then Mahomet must go to the mountain. How do you propose arranging such a meeting, my dear Sherlock?'

'By using a lure which Huret and his accomplice will find irresistible. In short, the victim himself. Or rather his double. What does Monsieur Auriel look like?'

'He is a tall, portly, grey-haired gentleman who wears gold pince-nez.'

'About my height, would you say?' Holmes asked with a negligent air.

Mycroft looked at him sharply.

'If your intention is to disguise yourself as Monsieur Auriel, then I am afraid there will be no opportunity for you to play the part. Monsieur Auriel will be staying in London for only a week. Because of the threat to his life posed by Huret, the authorities here and in France have strongly advised him not to appear in public. It has even been arranged for an official to visit him at the Earl of Evesham's residence in Park Lane rather than expect him to attend meetings at the Foreign Office. The risks of his being assassinated if he steps out of doors will be too great.'

'Then an opportunity must be created,' Holmes said coolly. With apparent inconsequentiality, he added, 'I believe the French soprano Celine Lefranc is currently appearing at Covent Garden opera house in *Aida*.'[8]

'Yes, that indeed is so.'

'Then what would be more natural than for Monsieur Auriel to attend a performance? Shall we say on the Wednesday evening following his arrival in London? I am sure the newspapers would be interested in printing a front-page report advertising this fact. There is the lure, Mycroft. The bait shall be myself disguised as Monsieur Auriel.'

'No! No! I cannot allow it!' Mycroft Holmes protested, throwing up his hands in horror. 'It is far too dangerous, dear boy. Huret is a professional assassin. As soon as you appear in public, he could strike at any time – outside the theatre or, heaven forbid, inside the auditorium itself. Besides, as you yourself have pointed out, we have no real idea of what Huret looks like. He could masquerade as anyone – a passer-by in the street, a

---

[8] *Aida* was composed by Giuseppe Verdi (1813–1901) and was first produced in Cairo in 1871. Mr Sherlock Holmes and Dr John H. Watson attended a Wagner performance at Covent Garden opera house after the successful conclusion of the Lucca case. *Vide*: 'The Adventure of the Red Circle'. Dr John F. Watson.

member of the audience, an innocent-seeming newspaper seller. The choice is endless. The police would not be able to guarantee you any protection at all.'

'You have forgotten one important factor which we know about the Boulevard Assassin and that is his *modus operandi*,' Holmes replied. 'All his attacks have followed a similar pattern. Without exception, he fires at his victim from a moving vehicle. Of course, such a method offers him the advantage of a quick escape. But, like his partiality for beards, there could be another reason. It is possible that he has some handicap or other – a club foot, say – which causes him to limp and which not only makes him instantly recognisable but also impedes his movements. Whatever the reason, I believe Huret will keep to his usual method, more so in this instance for he will not be operating in Paris but in London with which, I assume, he is less familiar.

'Allowing such an hypothesis is correct, we can then anticipate what form his actions will take. Having been alerted by the newspapers to Monsieur Auriel's visit to the opera, Huret will arrange with his accomplice to drive past Covent Garden opera house at the same time as Monsieur Auriel alights from his carriage outside the theatre. He will then aim his gun through the open window of whatever vehicle he and his accomplice are using on that particular evening. Their proposed victim, in this case myself, will present an easy target as I cross the pavement towards the entrance. Once the shot is fired, the driver will whip up the horses and they will escape into the evening traffic.

After abandoning the vehicle, they will then make their way on foot to whatever secret hideaway they are using.

'Alternatively, Huret may choose to strike after the performance is over although I think this is unlikely. Too many people will be leaving the theatre at the same time, making it much more difficult to pick out one individual from among the crowd.

'As for my own plans, I suggest I am introduced to Monsieur Auriel well before the proposed visit to the opera so that I may study the gentleman's appearance at close quarters, including any idiosyncrasies of gait or general bearing. Huret may have kept watch on his intended victim and become familiar with his physical characteristics. I leave it to you, Mycroft, to inform the Earl of Evesham and Monsieur Auriel of my intentions. By the way, I assume the police have been made aware of the situation?'

'Of course, Sherlock. I have personally warned Scotland Yard of Huret's imminent arrival and Inspector MacDonald has been assigned to the case.'

'MacDonald? An excellent choice! I have worked with him before and found him most intelligent and co-operative.[9] As soon as we return to Baker Street, I shall send him a telegram asking him to call on me this evening to discuss the arrangements. Well, Mycroft,' Holmes

---

[9] Inspector Alec MacDonald of Scotland Yard, originally from Aberdeen, sought Mr Sherlock Holmes' help with certain difficult cases, including the Birlstone inquiry ('The Valley of Fear'). Referred to as 'a young but trusted member of the detective force', he later achieved national fame. Dr John F. Watson.

concluded, springing to his feet, 'if there is nothing more you can tell me about the Boulevard Assassin, then Watson and I will take our leave.'

Mycroft Holmes struggled up from his own chair and extended a broad hand to each of us in turn.

'I see there is no point in trying to persuade you against the plan,' he remarked to Holmes.

'None whatsoever,' my old friend replied cheerfully.

'Then perhaps you, Dr Watson, may succeed where I have failed,' Mycroft said, turning to me and fixing me with his steel-grey eyes, a most sombre expression on his plump features. 'I beg you to try convincing him that his idea is a madness.'

'Your brother is right, you know, Holmes,' I said a little later when we were in a cab on our way back to Baker Street. 'The risk is enormous.'

'But the challenge is even greater,' he replied. 'Besides, my dear fellow, danger adds a little zest to life. Without it, we may as well all be amoebae stagnating at the bottom of a muddy pool. Pray do not over-concern yourself about my safety. I am not so foolish as to thrust my head into the lion's mouth without first taking a few precautions.'

'But what precautions can you take, Holmes? There are none that I can think of. As soon as you walk across the pavement towards the opera house, you will inevitably expose yourself to an assassin's bullet. You cannot protect yourself against that.'

'Then your memory is exceedingly short, Watson, for

you appear to have forgotten a certain Herr Dowe.'[10]

'Dowe? I know no one of that name.'

'Then perhaps you are more familiar with the word "brigandine"?' Holmes asked with a teasing air. 'Or the term "jack" may mean something to you?' Seeing my bewildered expression, he burst out laughing. 'Obviously not! Then, my dear fellow, you must wait as patiently as you can for Wednesday week when all shall be explained to you.'

'I find nothing at all amusing in the situation,' I retorted sharply, for I was exasperated as well as alarmed by his foolhardiness.

I wanted to add that by the following Wednesday evening, he might very well be dead. But the prospect of such an eventuality was so appalling even to contemplate that I dared not voice my fear out loud in case, by doing so, I might unwittingly bring about its actual occurrence.

Meanwhile Holmes, as if aware of these dark thoughts of mine, had turned the conversation to pleasanter matters, in this case the career of the French soprano Celine Lefranc, on which topic he expounded so engagingly that I almost forgot my apprehension over his safety.

I was reminded of it, however, on our arrival at Baker Street. As I alighted from the cab, Holmes remained seated.

'You go on alone, Watson,' said he. 'I have one or two small matters to attend to first.'

'What matters?' I asked.

---

[10] See the Herr Dowe footnote on page 85.

'I must send a telegram to Inspector MacDonald, asking him to call this evening at eight o'clock,' he replied, in a careless manner, as he tapped with his stick on the roof of the hansom to tell the driver to move on.

But as it drew away from the kerb, I heard him call up through the little trap door, 'The Tower of London, cabby!'

I was left standing alone on the pavement to ponder why Holmes had chosen of all places that unlikely destination unless, for some inexplicable reason, it was connected with Huret, the Boulevard Assassin, and Holmes' dangerous mission to bring about his arrest.

II

Whatever mysterious errand had taken my old friend to the Tower of London, it occupied him for several hours for it was nearly a quarter to eight before he returned, shortly before the arrival of Inspector MacDonald.

Despite my curiosity, I hesitated to question Holmes. There was a preoccupied air about him which inhibited any conversation and I busied myself with reading the evening paper, leaving him to sit, brooding and silent in his chair, his long legs stretched out in front of him, until Billy,[11] the page-boy, ushered Inspector Alex MacDonald into the room.

At the sight of MacDonald's tall, bony figure, Holmes' face immediately lit up and, jumping to his feet, he shook him warmly by the hand. Although, in the past, Holmes' attitude to the police had tended to be critical, the dour,

[11] Billy, surname unknown, is mentioned several times in Dr John H. Watson's accounts. He should not be confused with the other pageboy, also called Billy, who features in 'The Adventure of the Mazarin Stone'. Dr John F. Watson.

sandy-haired Aberdonian had won his respect, not least because of the man's intelligence and his frank admiration of Holmes' superior detective skills, even though he himself was not without talent in that direction.

Inviting MacDonald to sit down, Holmes immediately plunged into an account of his meeting with his brother Mycroft, his own suggestions as to how Huret might be lured to Covent Garden and the part he himself intended to play in bringing about the assassin's arrest.

'If I am correct,' he concluded, 'the attack will come soon after I have alighted outside the theatre. I therefore suggest that at least a dozen police officers in plain clothes are placed in the immediate vicinity of the opera house with instructions to look out for any vehicle which follows immediately behind mine. It will probably be a cab although that is by no means certain. Once my carriage has moved off, Huret's accomplice will urge his own horses forward to take its place outside the theatre, as if dropping off a passenger.

'It is at this precise moment that your men must act. Some of them will rush forward to compel the driver to stop while others will force open the door of the vehicle and arrest whoever is inside.'

Inspector MacDonald, who had been listening to this account with increasing unease, now spoke up for the first time.

'That is all very well, Mr Holmes,' said he, in his Scots accent, 'but I dare not risk it. You would not only be putting your own life in danger; there are also my own officers to consider. And what of the general public? Why, man, think of the outcry if some quite innocent bystander were killed by a stray bullet! No, no! I canna countenance such a dangerous scheme.'

'Then perhaps you can suggest an alternative,' Holmes said coolly, 'for Huret must be arrested. While he remains at large in London, he and his accomplice may decide to take the opportunity to murder our own Prime Minister or a member of his cabinet.[12] Think of the outcry if *that* were to happen, Mr Mac! And then there is your own reputation to consider. As the officer in charge of the Huret case, you would be held directly responsible by the Home Office.'

It was a shrewd and, I thought, unkind thrust which evidently went home for I saw the big Scotsman's jaw tighten and his sandy eyebrows draw together in a bushy frown.

'Aye, I take your point, Mr Holmes,' he said drily as he rose from his chair. 'Leave the matter with me. I shall come up with an answer before Wednesday. You may rely on me.'

Holmes waited until he heard the street door downstairs close behind MacDonald before he burst out laughing.

'I fall to see the joke,' I said a little stiffly. 'Surely you could have helped the man with the problem rather than <u>reminding him</u> in that manner of his responsibilities

[12] The Prime Minister in October 1894 was the Liberal leader Lord Rosebery (1847–1929) who was appointed to the office on 3rd March 1894 after the resignation of William Ewart Gladstone due to ill health. Dr John F. Watson.

should he fail? It is a very serious situation, Holmes, and MacDonald was right to point out the dangers.'

'Oh, tush, my dear fellow!' Holmes retorted. 'The good Inspector is far from stupid and, once he learns to use his imagination as well as his undoubted intelligence, he will make a very fine detective officer. All I did was give him a touch of the spur to force him over the jump. I do not doubt for a moment that he will find a solution. What amused me was the thought of what that solution will be. If I were, like you, a betting man,[13] I would lay odds of ten to one on his answer.'

'And what will it be?'

'The same as mine, of course. He will arrange to have the pavement at either end of Bow Street on the opera house side dug up and cordoned off, thereby forcing the passers-by to cross the road. By this means, he will restrict the number of pedestrians outside the theatre when Huret makes his assassination attempt. I suggest he will also introduce a number of his plain-clothes officers to cover that particular section of the street. At least, that would be my solution to the problem. If I am not mistaken, and I believe I have taken MacDonald's measure correctly, his will be exactly the same.' He gave a chuckle before

---

[13] As Dr John H. Watson admitted himself, he spent half his wound pension on betting on horses ('The Adventure of Shoscombe Old Place'). He also invested in stocks and shares. At one point, presumably because of his friend's straitened financial circumstances, Mr Sherlock Holmes kept the doctor's cheque book locked away in his own desk. *Vide*: 'The Adventure of the Dancing Men'. Dr John F. Watson.

adding, 'You realise, of course, Watson, that Bow Street police station is almost directly opposite the opera house? Should the need arise, Mr Mac will not have far to go to find recruits!'[14]

I saw little of Holmes over the next few days. He left the house soon after breakfast, not returning for several hours, on some occasions not until the late evening. From our brief conversations, I understood his time was taken up by official meetings, with Mycroft at the Diogenes Club, with senior officers at Scotland Yard and even more exalted personages at the Home Office and the French Embassy. He did, however, inform me that, at his specific request, I had been given permission to be present at the coming confrontation with Huret, a decision for which I was most grateful, having feared I might be excluded from their plans.

'And you will be pleased to know,' Holmes added with a smile, 'that our friend MacDonald has come forward with the very same scheme I suggested for ensuring the general public's safety. I should have wagered a guinea, Watson; I should be a richer man today if I had.'

Once Monsieur Auriel had arrived in London, Holmes spent several evenings at the Earl of Evesham's residence in Park Lane, dining in his company and that of the French Minister of Overseas Affairs.

Holmes returned from these dinner engagements

[14] Mr Sherlock Holmes visited Bow Street police station during his inquiries into the disappearance of Mr Neville St Clair. *Vide*: 'The Man with the Twisted Lip'. Inspector Bradstreet was on duty there on that occasion. Dr John F. Watson.

in a more loquacious frame of mind than from his professional appointments, laying great emphasis, for my sake but also, I felt, for his own, on the positive aspects of the assignment. The Earl, he declared, was most co-operative and had agreed to place his own carriage at Holmes' disposal. As for Monsieur Auriel, he was charming and also very appreciative of what was being done to ensure Huret's arrest. There would be no difficulty either in the matter of disguise. Monsieur Auriel had agreed to lend Holmes a set of his evening clothes for he was about Holmes' height, although much broader in build, a physical difference which could easily be disguised with a little judicious padding.

I assumed the French Minister of Overseas Affairs also walked a little stiffly with his chin thrust well forward for several times during the next few days, on entering the sitting room unexpectedly, I found Holmes pacing up and down in this particular manner as if familiarising himself with the gait.

It was not so easy, however, to judge my old friend's mood. Outwardly, he appeared busy and cheerful, if a little abstracted at times. But underneath that apparent composure, I detected a growing tension as of a watch spring being wound tighter and tighter, especially after the report appeared in newspapers of Monsieur Auriel's proposed visit to the opera on the coming Wednesday evening.

Like Holmes, I put on a cheerful countenance in order to hide from him my growing anxiety for his safety as the date of the Covent Garden mission grew nearer.

On the morning of that Wednesday, Holmes again left early, announcing he would be back by noon. After he had gone, I found the silence and the emptiness of the sitting room quite intolerable and, unable to settle to any task to fill the intervening hours until his return, I, too, left the house, calling first at my club in the hope that Thurston might be there and we could play a game or two of billiards to pass the time.[15] But I drew a blank. Thurston, I was told by another member, had gone down to the country to visit his married daughter. Emerging from the club just as a hansom was approaching, I hailed it and, on the spur of the moment, ordered the driver to take me to Covent Garden.

Even now, I am not sure exactly why I made this decision. Perhaps it was partly a need to see in daylight the setting where, later that evening, the momentous and perilous confrontation between Holmes and Huret, the notorious assassin, was to take place and, on a purely practical level, to reconnoitre the ground. I confess there was also a less rational motive, a superstitious urge to seek out some sign to suggest that the portents were favourable, although heaven above knows what I was hoping to find.

I alighted a short distance from Covent Garden and spent half an hour or so in the market itself which backs on to Bow Street, wandering aimlessly about under the great

[15] Thurston, Christian name unknown, was a fellow member of Dr John H. Watson's club and the only man with whom he played billiards. *Vide*: 'The Adventure of the Dancing Men'. Dr John F. Watson.

68

arched roof of glass and wrought iron, assailed on every side by the colours, sounds and odours of its busy confusion.[16] Here stall-keepers shouted out their wares, there porters carrying piles of baskets on their heads jostled a path through the crowds and everywhere there were urchins, scampering about like busy mice, running errands, pushing handcarts or simply gathering up any fallen fruit or vegetables which lay upon the ground. The savours of the place were as pervasive. Piles of oranges gave off their tangy scent, boxes of apples their sweeter fragrance, potatoes the homely aroma of country soil while from the litter of discarded cabbage leaves, bruised and trampled by hundreds of passing feet, rose a pungent green odour.

Eventually, tiring of this constant buffeting of my senses, I escaped outside and, having picked my way between the massed ranks of drays and wagons which crowded the cobbled forecourt, I emerged at last into the comparative peace and quiet of Bow Street.

I was reassured, as well as a little amused, when, having turned out of Floral Street, I saw that Inspector MacDonald's plan to ensure public safety was already being put into effect. At both ends of Bow Street on the opera house side, small gangs of workmen were digging

---

[16] Covent Garden market was London's main wholesale market for flowers, fruit and vegetables. Mr Sherlock Holmes visited it to interview Mr Breckenridge, a dealer in geese, although poultry was not usually sold there. Dr John F. Watson. NB Although the original buildings remain and are used today as a shopping arcade, the wholesale market was moved to new premises at Nine Elms, south of the river Thames, in 1974. Aubrey B. Watson.

up sections of the flagstones behind wooden barriers which effectively closed off that part of the pavement. Like all the other pedestrians, I was forced to cross over to the opposite side where I stopped to examine the imposing facade of the theatre with its six tall Corinthian pillars supporting the huge stone cornice and pediment.

At the sight of it, my amusement was immediately superseded by grave misgivings. It was in front of this building that the en-counter between Holmes and Huret would be played out, and I was considerably alarmed to see how narrow the stretch of pavement was between the kerb, where my old friend would soon be alighting from the Earl of Evesham's carriage, and the safety of the theatre's entrance. In a mere few yards, and in as short a space of time, the outcome of that encounter, whether for good or ill, would be decided.

I was in the act of turning away, sick at heart with apprehension, when I heard a voice at my elbow ask in a hoarse, wheedling tone, 'Buy some 'eather, sir? Lucky white 'eather only tuppence a bunch?'

Looking down, I saw a thin-faced young woman in a worn red dress, a basket on one arm and a small child clutching at her skirts, who was standing in the gutter and holding out towards me a small sprig of the so-called lucky flower.

Although Holmes has sometimes teased me for my sentimentality, I pride myself on my common sense which, under normal circumstances, does not lend itself to superstition. However, on this occasion, touched by the woman's plight and, I must confess, by the apparently propitious chance of meeting her when I was half hoping for some sign of good fortune, I took it as a favourable omen and, giving her a shilling, I tucked the sprig of white heather into my buttonhole. I confess that I was also prompted by a more negative impulse, fearful that, if I spurned the offer, the outcome of that evening's events might be adversely affected by my refusal, absurd though that may seem.

All the same, as I walked away, I could not help smiling wryly at my own foolishness and at the thought that, if anyone was in need of good fortune, it was not I but my old friend.

III

Holmes returned to our lodgings not long after my own arrival, bringing with him a large parcel wrapped in brown paper, the collection of which I assumed had been the purpose of his absence that morning. Whatever it contained was evidently heavy and also bulky but, when I inquired what it was, Holmes merely smiled enigmatically and replied, 'All in good time, Watson. You will see the purpose of it later.'

By 'later', I assumed he meant that evening outside the opera house.

It was the only reference he made to that coming event over the next few hours. Instead, we discussed a variety of topics, in particular the case of the aluminium crutch, a most curious investigation which he had undertaken during his early days in Montague Street before I met him.[17] He seemed in a reminiscent mood and, for the first

---

[17] Mr Sherlock Holmes refers to the 'singular affair of the aluminium crutch' in 'The Adventure of the Musgrave Ritual'. Dr John F. Watson.

time, gave me a full account of the inquiry, including the part played in it by Meadows, the notorious jewel thief, who for months had eluded arrest by disguising himself as Holmes.

At the end of his account, Holmes remarked with a chuckle, 'I may one day allow you to chronicle the adventure in your own inimitable style, my dear fellow, once our old friend Lestrade has retired from Scotland Yard. Until then, I fear the publication of the full facts would cause him too much professional embarrassment.'

Glancing at his watch, he rose to his feet, announcing in what I thought was too casual a tone, 'It is time I left, Watson, I told the Earl I would arrive no later than five o'clock.'

I, too, got up from my chair and for what seemed to me to be an eternity but was in fact no more than a few seconds, we stood facing one another in silence.

He was smiling but I thought I discerned under that debonair exterior the tension from which he was suffering, apparent in the over-bright eyes and the tautness of his jaw.

We shook hands without speaking. It was only when he was about to turn away that he remarked in a light-hearted fashion, 'Wish me luck, my dear fellow.'

Before I could reply, he had gone, taking with him the large brown paper parcel and a smaller packet containing a grey wig and a pair of gold-rimmed pince-nez, fitted with plain glass, which were his own contributions to his disguise as Monsieur Auriel. Moments later, I heard his footsteps descending the stairs and the slam of the street door behind him, followed by the sound of his familiar voice, high-pitched and imperious, calling for a cab.

I filled the long hours before my own departure as best I could, trying not to think of the coming events and their possible outcome. But never have I known time pass so slowly. Eventually, dressed in my evening clothes and carrying my stick and silk hat, I came out on to the landing outside my bedroom where, suddenly recalling Holmes' parting remark, I turned back to collect the sprig of white heather which, on my return earlier to Baker Street, I had hidden away in a drawer in case Holmes might see it and tease me for my foolishness. Retrieving it from its hiding place, I slipped it into my inside pocket before leaving the house to call a hansom.

IV

I had ordered the cabby to put me down in Long Acre from where I walked the short distance to Bow Street. Since my morning visit, the scene had considerably changed its character. Twilight had fallen and the lamps were lit, including those on the opera house which cast their brilliance over its stone facade, giving it the theatrical and unreal appearance of a piece of stage scenery. More prosaically, red lanterns had been hung on the wooden barriers closing off the excavated sections of the pavement to warn pedestrians, most of whom were thronging the opposite footway.

Even so, the area in front of the opera house was not entirely empty. A small group of bystanders had already gathered, quite apart from those individuals who were arriving on foot or by cab and carriage to attend the performance of *Aida* and who were being hurried inside the building by two uniformed commissionaires – MacDonald's officers, I suspected.

MacDonald himself, easily recognisable by his

height and sandy colouring, and looking remarkably distinguished in a cloak and evening attire, caught my glance and beckoned me to join him.

We shook hands as if the meeting were entirely fortuitous and then he drew me to one side.

'Now, Dr Watson,' said he with a twinkle, 'allow me to put you to a wee test. Look about you. Can you see my men? You will have to search hard for I flatter myself they are well hidden.'

'Let me see,' I replied, a little amused by the simplicity of MacDonald's 'wee test' for it was evident that most, if not all, of the bystanders and the apparently casual passersby on our side of the street would be plain-clothes officers. 'I suggest the commissionaires, the man over there waiting outside the theatre entrance as if for a companion, the newspaper seller a little way off and his two erstwhile customers who are so earnestly reading the *Evening News* under the street lamp.'

MacDonald gave a chuckle.

'Not bad! Not bad at all! You have picked out six from the total complement of twenty.'

'Twenty! Then where are the others? I see not one else who might be your officers.'

'Try the far side of the street, Dr Watson,' MacDonald suggested, nodding his head in that direction. 'Most of them are over there, walking up and down as large as life among the other pedestrians. There are more inside the police station, under Inspector Bradstreet's supervision. Now you're a former army man yourself, Dr Watson . . .'

'An army surgeon,' I corrected him.[18]

'Even so, you will appreciate the need in a situation such as this for organisation. With that in mind, I have planned this arrest as carefully as a military campaign. My men will make a pincer movement, thus confusing the enemy when they realise they are being attacked on two fronts.

'I have also posted two men at either end of Bow Street, each provided with a whistle. The one at the Long Acre end will give warning when the Earl of Evesham's carriage comes into sight, for we have already decided the route it will take along Shaftesbury Avenue and into Charing Cross Road. However, as we canna be certain in which direction Huret will come . . .'

'But surely his vehicle will follow behind the Earl's carriage?'

'Ah, but can we count on that, doctor? From all I've heard, Huret is as canny as an old fox. He must realise the English authorities will know about his exploits in Paris and, with Monsieur Auriel visiting London, might take precautions to protect him. At least, if I were in the man's shoes, that's the way my mind would be working. So in order to throw any possible hunters off his track, he may

---

[18] Having qualified as a doctor at St Bartholomew's hospital, London, Dr John H. Watson was trained as an army surgeon at the Royal Army Medical School at Netley, Hampshire and in 1879 was posted to India to join his regiment, the Fifth Northumberland Fusiliers. Soon after his arrival, he was transferred to the 66th Berkshire Regiment of Foot, later renamed the Royal Berkshire Regiment, and was sent to Afghanistan where he took part in the battle of Maiwand during the Second Afghan War (1878–79). Dr John F. Watson.

decide to approach from the Russell Street end. I know it is a long shot but it is better to be wise before than after the event. So my other lookout has orders to give a double blast on his whistle should any vehicle turn into Bow Street from that direction. Belt and braces, Dr Watson! As a practical man by nature and a cautious Aberdonian by breeding, that's the principle I always work on.'

'I take your point,' I began, impressed by MacDonald's forethought. I was about to add some complimentary remark about his own native intelligence when I was forestalled by the single blast on a whistle from the Long Acre end of the street, clear and loud enough to be heard above the hubbub of voices and the rumble of a passing four-wheeler.

At the signal, the scene immediately erupted like an overturned ants' nest. On our side of the road, the men whom I had identified as MacDonald's officers converged on the opera house, forming a double cordon to keep back any innocent passers-by. At the same moment, six other men joined them from the other side of the street, some emerging at the double from the police station, some pushing their way through the crowd of pedestrians. Among these I recognised a blind beggar who, moments before, had been standing in the gutter rattling his tin cup at passers-by. Some of the officers who had remained on the opposite pavement had, I noticed, placed themselves at the edge of the kerb, ready to rush forward as soon as the Earl's carriage drew to a halt.

MacDonald, too, had prepared himself for action, flinging aside his silk hat and throwing back his cloak to leave his arms free. I followed his example, abandoning my own hat but keeping a tight grip on my stick which, should the need arise, would serve as a useful weapon.

He had taken up his station at the front of the cordon and at the end nearest to the road where I joined him, noticing that six others were likewise positioned, including the commissionaires, the newspaper readers, the beggar and a loutish-looking individual who could quite easily be mistaken for a street ruffian.

I had no time to ponder on the consequences of the drama which at any moment was to be played out, nor even to examine my own emotions although I was aware of that feeling of heightened excitement mixed with an exhilarated and fearful anticipation such as I had experienced at my first taste of battle in Afghanistan, which sends the blood racing through the veins and the heart banging like a drum.[19]

Hardly had we taken up our positions than the Earl of Evesham's carriage came into sight, the pair of matched greys which drew it approaching at little more than a walking pace as they covered the last few yards to the theatre where they would be drawn to a halt. Indeed, the coachman was already reining them in while the groom, seated on the box at the rear of the carriage, was preparing to jump down and open the door to let the passenger

---

[19] Dr Watson is referring to the battle of Maiwand, 27th July 1880, during the Second Afghan War, at which he was wounded in the shoulder. He also apparently suffered a leg wound for he mentions such an injury several times in his published accounts. Dr John F. Watson.

alight, when the window in it suddenly shot down and a head was thrust through the opening.

Although the man's grey hair and pince-nez were momentarily and confusingly unfamiliar, the voice was instantly recognisable.

'Watson! MacDonald!' I heard Holmes shouting. 'The driver and the groom! Quick! Seize them, for God's sake!'

I have no clear recollection of the events which followed, only a confused impression of men throwing themselves forward, some clutching at the horses' bridles, others leaping upwards to wrestle the driver to the ground, while one of the commissionaires together with MacDonald and myself scrambled to seize the groom who, thrusting a hand inside his coat, had produced a revolver, its barrel glinting wickedly in the light cast by the theatre's lamps. Mingled with all this turmoil of movement was a clamour of noises, of men shouting and women screaming, of horses stamping and whinnying in terror.

It was by sheer good fortune that, when I raised my stick to bring it down on Huret's right arm, I struck my intended target and not MacDonald's head which was inches from it. I heard the man give a grunt of pain followed by the metallic clatter as the gun, struck from his hand, fell into the gutter where the newspaper seller kicked it swiftly out of reach. The next instant, Huret himself was down on the pavement, fighting like a wild beast in a frenzy of flailing arms and legs until MacDonald and one of the commissionaires, with a practised dexterity which spoke of years of experience, flipped him over to lie face downwards and the Inspector snapped a pair of handcuffs on his wrists.

'Excellent! Well done!' I heard Holmes exclaiming and I turned with something of a shock for, in the excitement of the events, I had quite forgotten his presence. He was alighting from the carriage wearing full evening dress although he had discarded the grey wig and the pince-nez. I noticed he was much broader in figure than usual, especially across the back and shoulders, and that he moved with considerably less ease.

'Let me see his face,' he was saying to MacDonald who was grinning broadly like a triumphant schoolboy who has just scored the winning touch-down. With the commissionaire's assistance, the Inspector forced the man to his feet so that he and Holmes stood confronting one another.

'Monsieur Alphonse Huret,' Holmes said softly, as if reminding himself of the man's identity.

It had never been in his nature to gloat over a fallen adversary and it was so on this occasion. For several long moments, the two men looked in each other's eyes, Holmes' face expressing nothing more than a polite interest much as one might show when introduced to a stranger.

As for Huret, I was struck more by the unremarkable nature of his features than by any overt sign of villainy although this should not have surprised me. As Holmes had once told me, the most winning woman he had ever known was hanged for poisoning three small children for their insurance money.[20]

---

[20] Mr Sherlock Holmes makes this comment in 'The Sign of Four'. Dr John F. Watson.

Huret was young, little more than in his mid-twenties, with a slight, almost boyish build. As for his face, it was long, especially about the chin, a peculiarity which, as Holmes had already predicted, might account for his partiality for wearing beards during his reign of terror as the Boulevard Assassin. His eyes were set well back in his head while the mouth was so thin as to be almost lipless. Even so, it was the type of countenance which one could sit opposite to in a railway carriage and, half an hour later, not recall a single detail about it, except perhaps its total lack of humour. He had fought like a mad beast to avoid capture but all that stupendous vitality was now dissipated apart from his black, deep-set eyes which still blazed, like live coals, out of their bony sockets.

It was his accomplice, the driver of the coach, an older man in his fifties, who showed the most emotion. His hands, too, had been secured behind his back and two of the plain-clothes men, the street ruffian and the beggar, had hauled him upright. He was still struggling against the restraints of the handcuffs and the men's grasp on his arms, his countenance distorted with fury as he screamed out in French against his captors. If one wished to look into the face of true villainy, it was there in his twisted features, the wide-stretched mouth and the expression of utter hatred which suffused even the flesh as if his rage had turned to black, bitter blood which coursed just below the surface, darkening the skin.

At a nod from Inspector MacDonald, the two prisoners were taken across the road to the police station,

Huret's accomplice first and then Huret himself, a small, inconspicuous figure who walked haltingly between his two tall captors, the left foot turned inwards at the ankle. For the first time, I was aware of that physical disability which Holmes had also prognosticated even before he had set eyes on the man.

MacDonald was saying, 'Why, man, it never crossed my mind they would seize the Earl's carriage to carry out when Holmes interrupted him.

'Explanations later, Mr Mac,' he said crisply. 'We must first make sure the real coachman and groom have come to no harm, unlike some of Huret's other victims.'

'Aye, of course!' MacDonald replied. 'I will see to that at once!' Without another word, he sprinted across the road and disappeared inside the police station.

'Pray God they are still alive,' Holmes murmured under his breath and then stood silent, head averted, as he waited for MacDonald's return.

Within minutes, he rejoined us and announced that a uniformed sergeant and a constable would be despatched to the Earl of Evesham's Park Lane residence to make full inquiries and to report to his lordship and the French minister on the evening's events. Indeed, as he was speaking, the two officers in question emerged from the police station and, having hailed a cab, were driven off at speed in the Long Acre direction.

'And now for the explanation,' Holmes said, leading the way across the road, 'for there is little else we can do until their return.'

V

After a short consultation with Inspector Bradstreet, who reported that the two criminals were safely locked up below in the cells and that he would personally arrange for an experienced man to drive the Earl's carriage back to its rightful place, we were shown into a small, whitewashed room at the rear of the building, plainly furnished with a deal table and some upright chairs.

No sooner had the door closed behind us than, to my great surprise, Holmes began to divest himself of his tail coat and white waistcoat, revealing a most extraordinary undergarment. It was like a sleeveless jerkin made of canvas but, instead of buttoning down the front, it was secured across the chest by several leather straps. The back was even more curious than the front for it was quilted into small, square segments, each one thickly padded and each containing some weighty object for, as Holmes unbuckled the straps and lifted the garment off his shoulders, it was evident it was extremely heavy, which would explain those awkward movements of his which I had remarked on earlier.

As MacDonald showed no surprise, I assumed he already knew of this strange garment and of Holmes' intention to wear it that evening so it was entirely for my benefit that Holmes offered an explanation.

'A bulletproof surcoat, Watson,' said he. 'I took the idea from the "Jack" or "brigandine", a padded linen jacket, reinforced by metal plates, which was worn by foot soldiers in the Middle Ages. There are some examples of it in the Tower of London's collection of weapons and armour, where I went to inspect them. More recently, in fact a mere five months ago, a certain Herr Dowe exhibited a similar bulletproof coat in London which used only padding.[21] I paid a tailor I know in Old Jewry to make my own version of it. As I assumed Huret would fire at me from behind, all I needed to protect was my back. I am of the opinion that such a surcoat would be useful to the police although its chief disadvantage is its weight.[22] It is also extremely cumbersome. However, in this case, it served a double purpose for it also gave me the portly

---

[21] In May 1894 Herr Dowe, a Mannheim tailor, demonstrated a bulletproof coat at the Alhambra theatre, London. Weighing only 12 pounds, it contained no metal only padding although the exact material used was a secret. It was said to resemble a 'carriage cushion'. Dr John F. Watson.

[22] Modern body armour was introduced on a small scale in the First World War but was very heavy. Lighter armour using steel, aluminium and fibreglass contained in a nylon garment was used in the Second World War. Modern bullet-proof jackets, comprising 16–24 layers of heavy-weave nylon cloth quilted together, are used today by the army, the police force and anti-terrorist forces. Aubrey B. Watson.

figure I needed as part of my disguise as Monsieur Auriel.

'My greatest mistake was to underestimate Huret's audacity and cunning. It never for a moment crossed my mind that he would use the Earl of Evesham's own carriage in his assassination attempt.'

'When were you aware of it?' I asked.

'Even before I set foot inside it. When the carriage arrived from the mews and drew up outside the Earl's residence, the groom got down from the box to open the door for me. It was then I noticed the man walked with a pronounced limp and the awful truth dawned on me. There was nothing I could do, of course, except continue to play the part of Monsieur Auriel and wait until we arrived outside the opera house to warn you of the true situation.'

'I am astonished,' MacDonald interjected, 'that the pair of them did not take you to some quiet side street and murder you there and then. Why, man, you were a sitting target!'

'A good point, my friend, but these anarchists are no hole-in-the-corner murderers, killing their victims by stealth, with no witnesses present. They are political assassins who glory in the act and the public alarm it arouses. They want their deeds blazoned across the front page of every newspaper to draw attention to their cause. Without that oxygen of notoriety they would wither away like noxious weeds starved of light and air.'

It was an hour before the sergeant and the constable returned from their inquiries in Park Lane and, in the meantime, the three of us discussed the case and its political implications although, as the minutes passed, Holmes withdrew more and more from the conversation, his thoughts quite clearly elsewhere: on the fate of the Earl's coachman and groom, I suspected.

It was therefore with anxious trepidation on Holmes' part, and also on mine and MacDonald's, that we saw the door finally open and Inspector Bradstreet enter. To our relief, he was smiling broadly so, even before he spoke, we knew that the news was good.

'Both men are alive but considerably shaken by their ordeal,' he announced. 'It seems the villains attacked them from behind as they were harnessing the horses, bludgeoning both of them senseless, which is probably why their lives were spared as they hadn't seen their assailants. They were then stripped of their uniforms and left bound and gagged in the stable.'

'Excellent news!' Holmes exclaimed, shaking Bradstreet heartily by the hand as if the Inspector himself were solely responsible for the men's safety.

Although I eagerly scanned the newspapers in the days immediately following the arrest of Huret and his accomplice, I was disappointed to find that little attention was paid to their capture apart from short reports which gave only the minimum of details.

Meanwhile, Holmes was as much occupied as he had been before the events with official appointments at Scotland Yard, the French Embassy and our own Home and Foreign Offices, none of which I attended. However, I was invited to accompany him to a meeting with his brother at the Diogenes Club a few days later.

As before, we gathered in the Strangers' Room where Mycroft greeted us warmly before pouring both of us a whisky and soda and replenishing his own glass.

'Congratulations, Sherlock, and you, too, Dr Watson, for I understand from our friend MacDonald that it was you who administered the *coup de grâce* to Huret. As for you, my dear brother, you cannot imagine how your praises are being trumpeted on both sides of the Channel. As well as removing two very dangerous men from society, the arrest of Huret and his accomplice has done much to improve our relations with the French government. In fact, I have here,' Mycroft added, producing an envelope from an inner pocket, 'a personal letter of thanks from the French President, Monsieur Casimir-Perier, which was sent over this morning in the diplomatic bag. I have also been asked to sound you out on your willingness to accept the Order of the Legion of Honour. Knowing your aversion to public awards, I feel obliged to find out what your answer would be before the offer is made.'

Holmes was silent for several moments before replying.

'As you so rightly remarked, Mycroft,' he said at last. 'I am reluctant to accept any official accolades. The work is itself its own reward without the need of a decoration to hang about my neck or pin on my lapel.[23]

---

[23] Mr Sherlock Holmes refused a knighthood in June 1902 ('The Adventure of the Three Garridebs') and also rejected Mr Mycroft Holmes' earlier offer for his name to appear in the next honours list with the words: 'I play the game for the game's own sake.' *Vide:* 'The Adventure of the Bruce Partington Plans'. Dr John F. Watson.

However, in this case, and this case only, I am willing to go against my principles and accept the honour.'

'Thank heaven for that, dear boy!' Mycroft exclaimed in relief. 'Had you refused, it could indeed have ruffled diplomatic feathers and caused considerable offence to our Gallic neighbours. I shall pass on your acceptance and you will no doubt shortly receive an official invitation to the Elysée Palace for the investiture.

'And now to more practical matters. The Home Office has received a request from its French counterpart to extradite Huret and his accomplice to France to stand trial for the assassination of Monsieur Boncour and the other murders or attempted murders they have carried out. I have recommended that the request should be granted as it, too, will help improve our relations with France. As some of our more vociferous anti-European backbenchers might protest at this should the full facts be made public, the arrest of Huret and his colleague has received as little publicity as possible. It could not be entirely passed over as too many people witnessed the event. However, as you have probably seen, an official statement has been given to the newspapers, not naming the assassins but merely referring to them as two dangerous criminals wanted by the French police for a series of armed robberies. A further statement will shortly be issued, explaining that, when they were arrested, they were on their way to commit a similar crime here in London, having stolen the Earl of Evesham's carriage as a cover for their activities. As for the notice of their extradition to France, that, too, will be dealt with as discreetly as possible.'

Turning to me with an apologetic smile, Mycroft Holmes added, 'I must therefore ask you, Dr Watson, not to publish an account of the case, popular though your narratives are with your many readers, myself among them. It would give too much ammunition to the Opposition to use against the government's front benches.'

I gave my word without any hesitation and so this account will be placed among my private papers.[24]

Only a few more facts remain to be recorded. Huret and his companion were duly extradited, tried and, having been found guilty, were later executed. In the meantime, Holmes travelled to Paris to receive the Order of the Legion of Honour. To my surprise and delight, he brought back with him a personal present for me from the French President, a silver-topped walking-stick engraved with the date of the Covent Garden adventure, a charming acknowledgement, I thought, of the small part I had played in the arrest of the Boulevard Assassin and his accomplice.

---

[24] Dr John H. Watson refers to the case in 'The Adventure of the Golden Pince-Nez'. Dr John F. Watson.

The Case of the Wimbledon Tragedy

I

It was on a hot July afternoon in the late 1890s[1] that Holmes became associated with the following investigation which was to present him with one of the greatest challenges to his remarkable powers of observation as well as his skill at deducing facts from apparently trivial evidence.

He was introduced to the case by a Mrs Woodruffe who had written to him requesting an interview. The letter itself did not indicate anything out of the ordinary. The handwriting was round, plain and legible while the address, Laburnum Lodge, Castlebury Avenue, Wimbledon, suggested the comfortable milieu of the middle-class suburbs. Nor were the contents of the letter at all startling. In it, Mrs Woodruffe merely stated that she wished to consult Holmes on a private matter and suggested the following

[1] The case is referred to in 'The Adventure of the Six Napoleons' which, although undated, is generally assigned to 1900. The Wimbledon tragedy must therefore have taken place before this date. Dr John F. Watson.

Monday afternoon at 3 p.m. for the appointment.

Holmes replied by return of post, confirming the time and date, and three days later Mrs Woodruffe duly arrived and was shown up to our sitting room.

Like her handwriting, Mrs Woodruffe, a lady of middle years dressed in decent black, was round and plain and had a shrewd, no-nonsense air about her. Having seated herself at Holmes' invitation in one of the armchairs, she came immediately to the point.

'I am housekeeper to Mr Abernetty, a wealthy widower, Mr Holmes,' she announced. 'It is a post I have held for the past five years, ever since the death of his wife. I would not have troubled you with what may seem to you an unimportant matter but, to tell the truth, I am much concerned about Mr Abernetty's well-being. I fear his life may be in danger.'

The remark was made with no attempt at dramatisation, simply being stated as a fact, and Holmes responded in kind.

'Indeed,' said he, settling back into his chair and regarding her with considerable interest. 'Pray explain your reasons.'

'Mr Abernetty has only the one living relative and she is connected to him merely by marriage as she is the widow of his late son, William, who died two years ago in a tragic accident. He was a very pleasant young man but sadly crippled after a childhood illness. However, that's neither here nor there, Mr Holmes. To return to the point, Mrs William Abernetty, as his daughter-in-law, is old Mr Abernetty's sole heir and on his death will inherit not only the house in Wimbledon and its contents but also, I imagine, a large capital sum. Before his retirement, Mr Abernetty was a very successful City stockbroker in the firm of Abernetty and Bland, where his son also held a position as a junior partner.'

For the first time, Mrs Woodruffe faltered and appeared at a loss as to how to proceed but, at an encouraging nod from Holmes, she took up her account again in a little burst of frankness which caused the colour to rise in her pleasant, homely features.

'I do not like Mrs Abernetty, Mr Holmes! I do not trust her! Every Friday she drives over from Clapham by cab to have lunch with her father-in-law and seems very solicitous over his health, giving me instructions about what he should and should not eat. In my own kitchen, too, as if she is in charge of the household! I understand it was because of her interfering ways that the last housekeeper, Mrs Sheldrake, gave up the post. You see, Mr Holmes, Mrs William Abernetty helped with the nursing of her late mother-in-law until her death and nearly drove Mrs Sheldrake mad with her orders. So she packed her bags and left immediately after the funeral without even waiting to give notice.

'But for all her fussing over Mr Abernetty, I've noticed that, whenever the old gentleman's taken ill, it's always on a Friday after one of Mrs Abernetty's visits.'

'Ill!' Holmes repeated, his eyes lighting up. 'What are the symptoms?'

'Gastric disorders. Sickness. Pains in his stomach.'

'I assume his doctor is called?'

'Oh, yes, sir; of course. On all four occasions I've sent the gardener's boy to fetch Dr Thorogood, Mr Abernetty's physician, who lives nearby.'

'And what is his diagnosis?'

'Acute indigestion. He advises a light diet and rest and prescribes a medicine to help with the pain. After a few days, Mr Abernetty recovers. But he's now in his seventies and, after each attack, he grows a little more frail. Oh, sir, I'm that concerned about him! He's a lovely old gentleman, very kind and courteous, and I'm worried to death the next attack will be his last.

'Mrs Abernetty even had the gall to suggest it was my fault the last time it happened. I'd made an apple pie for dessert and she said the cream I'd served with it was not quite fresh. Fresh, Mr Holmes! As soon as it was delivered, I put it straight into the ice-box.[2] It couldn't have been fresher if I'd made it myself with milk taken from the cow that very same morning.'

'Yes; quite,' Holmes murmured before adding, with apparent casualness, although I noticed he was studying her face with great attention, 'What happens to any food left over from the table after these visits by Mrs Abernetty?'

'It's taken to the kitchen, sir, and shared out between myself and the maid.'

---

[2] Although ice had been used for centuries for the preservation of food and the preparation of cold dishes, it was only in the early 1840s that two American firms, the Wenham Lake Company and Thomas Masters', began manufacturing refrigerators and ice-boxes, and the first artificial freezing mixtures were patented. The sale of ice-creams in the street was introduced in 1850. Dr John F. Watson.

'To any ill effects?'

'No, sir. None.'

'And who serves at table?'

'I do, sir.'

'Have you ever noticed anything suspicious?'

Mrs Woodruffe gave him a long, shrewd look.

'I believe I can guess what you are thinking, Mr Holmes, and God knows the same thought has crossed my mind more than once. Supposing Mrs Abernetty is adding something to the old gentleman's food? Nothing would be simpler. Mrs Abernetty supervises generally in the dining room, giving me instructions as to where the dishes should be set. But that is not proof, is it, Mr Holmes? I am sure, if old Mr Abernetty were to die, Dr Thorogood would put it down to natural causes and would sign the death certificate accordingly. He has no reason to suspect Mrs Abernetty. In fact, he was full of praise for the care she took of the late Mrs Abernetty. She twists him round her little finger like she does her father-in-law. And who else am I to turn to? The police? But where is the evidence? That's why I wrote to you, Mr Holmes. What should I do?'

Holmes rose to his feet and took several turns up and down the room, sunk deep in thought, while Mrs Woodruffe followed his every move with anxious eyes, bright with unshed tears.

Suddenly he swung about to face her.

'I agree you are placed in a very difficult position, madam,' said he abruptly, 'and at this stage, there is little I can do except offer you advice. When Mrs Abernetty arrives for luncheon next Friday, behave normally. Do nothing to make her think you suspect her. That is vitally important. At the same time, keep as close a watch on her as possible. Do these Friday visits follow any particular pattern?'

'As I said, sir, Mrs Abernetty arrives from Clapham by cab, usually at eleven o'clock, and stays for luncheon and tea. She always brings some embroidery with her and, if the weather is fine, as it has been lately, she and Mr Abernetty sit in the garden. Otherwise they remain indoors in the drawing room. After tea, at about six o'clock, the gardener's boy is sent to fetch a cab and she returns to Clapham.'

'And when do these gastric attacks usually occur?'

'In the early evening, after she has left.'

'Do you inform her of these attacks?'

'Not always, sir. It depends how ill Mr Abernetty is. If he's taken bad, as he has been on two occasions, then I send a telegram and she comes either that evening or the following morning. And the to-do she makes! Ordering calves-foot jelly and beef broth! I can't call the kitchen my own!'

Holmes rubbed a lean hand thoughtfully over his chin.

'As there is no way of knowing when the next attack will occur,' he said, 'I want you to preserve any food which is left over every Friday and also make sure that all plates, glasses and cutlery are left unwashed until the following morning when you are sure Mr Abernetty is in his usual health. Is that possible, Mrs Woodruffe? The servants will not consider this suspicious?'

'No, Mr Holmes,' she assured him. 'Since old Mrs Abernetty's death, the indoor staff has been much reduced. Apart from a cleaning woman who comes in daily, there is only the one maid who helps me in the kitchen and she will do as she is told.'

'You have an ice-box, I believe?'

'Yes, sir.'

'Then I advise you to keep as much of the left-over food in it as you can. In this hot weather, it will quickly deteriorate. Lastly, Mrs Woodruffe, should Mr Abernetty become ill, inform me immediately by telegram. I should also be much obliged if you would delay sending for Mrs Abernetty for as long as possible. Should the need arise – and let us pray heaven it does not – I should prefer to have time to make any inquiries that are necessary before she arrives. And now, Mrs Woodruffe, Dr Watson will show you downstairs and call a cab for you.'

'Do you seriously believe Mr Abernetty's life may be in danger?' I inquired, as I returned to the sitting room after carrying out this errand. 'His own doctor appears satisfied he has suffered nothing more fatal than indigestion.'

My old friend turned a most sombre face towards me.

'I sincerely trust you are right and I am wrong, my dear fellow. Nevertheless I detect a most unpleasant whiff of foul play about this case. How did Shakespeare put it? "By the pricking of my thumbs, Something wicked this way comes."[3] I could not have expressed it better myself.

[3] The quotation is taken from a speech by the second witch in Shakespeare's *Macbeth* Act 4, Scene 1. Dr John F. Watson.

Mrs Woodruffe evidently feels the same disquiet.'

'But that is hardly proof of intention to murder,' I pointed out.

'Never underestimate the power of intuition, Watson. It is a valuable weapon in the armoury of any detective, provided it is supported by the careful observation of material evidence. Indeed, it has long been my belief that the official police should pay considerably more attention to their own thumbs.[4] And we are not without other evidence to support such an intuitive assumption. There is motive. Mr Abernetty is a wealthy widower; Mrs William Abernetty is his only heir. Then there is opportunity. She could easily have added a little poison to his food. His symptoms could also point to some irritant toxin, possibly arsenic; not acute, I admit, but rather a long, drawn-out process of chronic poisoning carried out over a period of months but sufficient to undermine his constitution and lead eventually to his death.'

'But what of means, Holmes? Could Mrs Abernetty have access to arsenic?'

'Oh, that need prove no obstacle to a determined poisoner. Mrs Maybrick was accused of obtaining it by soaking fly-papers in a dish of water.[5] Mrs Abernetty

---

[4] In 'The Adventure of the Three Garridebs', Mr Sherlock Holmes comments on Inspector Lestrade's 'occasional want of imaginative intuition'. Dr John F. Watson.

[5] In 1889, Mrs Florence Maybrick was accused of murdering her husband, James Maybrick, with arsenic obtained in this manner. Although she was found guilty, the sentence of death was commuted to life imprisonment. Dr John F. Watson.

could have done the same. Or she could have bought it at any chemist's as a weedkiller, simply by signing the poison register under a false name.'[6]

'And in the meantime, what can we do?' I asked in some anxiety over Mr Abernetty's fate.

'Nothing, my dear fellow, except wait upon events,' said he, with a dismissive shrug of his shoulders.

However, I had good reason to believe that Holmes was not as sanguine about the case as he pretended. Over the next two days, his mood alternated between periods of contemplation when he would sit silently in his chair, his chin on his hand, and bursts of feverish activity when, leaping to his feet, he would hasten to the bookcase to consult one of his volumes on chemical analysis or rush precipitately from the house to hail a cab. From the stains on his fingers after these sudden excursions, I deduced he had been visiting his old haunts – the chemical laboratory at Bart's hospital, my own former Alma Mater.[7] But I said nothing, not wishing to intrude upon his thoughts.

At breakfast on the Friday morning, the day when Mrs Abernetty was due to visit her father-in-law for luncheon,

---

[6] The Arsenic Act of 1851 restricted the sale of arsenic to people over twenty-one. Details of every purchase had to be recorded in a poisons register and, before sale, the arsenic had to be coloured with either soot or indigo. Dr John F. Watson.

[7] Dr John H. Watson studied medicine at St Bartholomew's hospital and also served there for a time as a house surgeon. Mr Sherlock Holmes carried out his own experiments in the hospital's chemistry laboratory which is where Stamford, Dr Watson's former dresser, introduced the two men to one another, probably on 1st January 1881. Dr John F. Watson.

he was particularly withdrawn and silent, waving aside the dish of eggs and bacon and drinking instead several cups of strong black coffee. I was therefore considerably startled when, flinging down his napkin, he suddenly struck himself on the forehead with his open palm at the same time exclaiming, 'Oh, what a blind mole I am! I should be kicked from here to kingdom come!'

With that, he ran from the room. Moments later, he emerged from his bedroom fully dressed and went plunging down the stairs and out into the street where I heard him whistling urgently for a hansom.[8]

I assumed he had gone on some urgent business connected with the inquiry which I hoped would not occupy too much of his time in case a telegram arrived from Mrs Woodruffe, summoning us to Wimbledon.

The hours came and went. At one o'clock, when he had not returned, I had luncheon alone. By two o'clock, my anxiety had grown so acute that, unable to sit any longer reading the newspapers, I stationed myself at one of the windows where I stood gazing down on to the hot, sunlit street, searching for his tall, lean figure among the passers-by or for a cab which seemed about to draw to a halt outside our door. But still he did not come.

At half-past two, I noticed with sick apprehension a telegraph boy hurrying along the opposite pavement, looking up at the numbers on the houses, and I knew,

---

[8] Cabs could be summoned in the street by a special whistle, one blast for a four-wheeler, two for a hansom. Many Londoners carried a cab whistle on them for this purpose. Dr John F. Watson.

even before he crossed the road, that the message he was carrying was for Holmes.

Almost before he had time to ring the bell, I was down the stairs and had flung open the street door to seize the envelope which, as I had feared, was addressed to Holmes. Returning with it to the sitting room, I turned it over and over in my hands, hesitating to open it in Holmes' absence and wondering what news it contained although I feared the worst.

It was while I was thus occupied that I heard footsteps come bounding up the stairs and moments later my old friend came bursting into the room.

'Holmes, where on earth have you been?' I demanded, my exasperation at his long delay tempered with relief at his return. 'This telegram arrived only . . .'

Before I could finish the sentence, he had snatched the envelope from my hands, torn it open and hurriedly scanned its contents.

'Watson, fetch your hat and stick!' he cried. 'We must leave immediately. And let us pray heaven we arrive in time!'

It was only when we were in a hansom, rattling on our way to Wimbledon, that I had the opportunity to read the message.

It stated quite starkly:

COME AT ONCE STOP MR ABERNETTY GRAVELY ILL STOP DOCTOR WITH HIM NOW

II

Laburnum Lodge, we discovered when the cab drew up outside it, was a handsome red-brick villa, standing in considerable grounds. A brougham was already at the door: Dr Thorogood's, I assumed.

Holmes waited impatiently while I paid off the driver and, as I turned back to him, he said bleakly, pointing with his stick at the drawn blinds at all the windows, both upstairs and down, 'I fear we are too late, Watson. The deed has already been done.'

He set off at once at a rapid pace along a gravelled path which led round the side of the house towards its rear. As I hastened to catch up with him, he added over his shoulder, 'We will speak to Mrs Woodruffe first, Watson, before we make any other inquiries.'

A tearful Mrs Woodruffe answered our knock at the back door and showed us into a large kitchen where a little tow-haired maid, dressed in cap and apron, was seated at the table, her eyes round with shock. As soon as Mrs Woodruffe had dismissed her, Holmes at once plunged straight into his inquiries without any preamble.

'I gather Mr Abernetty is dead. When did this happen?'

'About forty minutes ago, Mr Holmes. He was taken so ill, sir, with stomach pains and sickness! He complained, too, of feeling dizzy and not being able to draw breath properly. I sent the gardener's boy at once for Dr Thorogood but poor Mr Abernetty died about ten minutes after he arrived.'

'I believe the doctor is still in attendance?'

'Yes, sir. He's in the morning room with Mrs William Abernetty as the blinds are down in the drawing room. She's supposed to be suffering from shock, or so she pretends,' Mrs Woodruffe concluded with some bitterness.

'Does he suspect foul play?'

'I don't think so, Mr Holmes. He said that as Mr Abernetty's had these gastric attacks before, it was only to be expected, considering his age. Do you want to speak to him?'

'No, not yet. First, I want to examine any evidence. You kept the food and dishes as I instructed? Where are they?'

'In here, sir,' the housekeeper replied, leading the way into a passage and opening a door which led into a cool, stone-flagged pantry, fitted with slate shelves. Laid out on trays upon these shelves were unwashed plates, glasses and cutlery as well as several covered serving dishes. Holmes lifted the lids of these in turn, revealing leftover vegetables and a ham, cooked on the bone, from which several slices had already been carved.

As Holmes inspected all of these with rapid attention, peering, sniffing and even tasting each dish with the end of one finger, Mrs Woodruffe continued, 'Because the weather was so hot, Mr Holmes, I served the ham cold, sir, with new potatoes and peas from the garden.'

'And for dessert?' Holmes inquired, turning away from these remains with evident dissatisfaction.

'A raspberry compote, sir, with whipped cream. The leftovers are in the ice-box.'

The box in question, a large metal container, stood nearby on a marble slab. Unfastening the catches, Holmes lifted back the lid to reveal its zinc-lined interior, packed with broken ice on which lay more dishes consisting of a bowl and a jug, holding the residue of the raspberry dessert and the cream, and a small glass dish containing a square piece of butter, decorated on top with a single sprig of parsley, from which a corner section had been removed.

Holmes stood for several long moments of silence, contemplating these remnants but making no attempt to touch or taste them. It was impossible to read his thoughts. His eyes were hooded and his lean features inscrutable. Then, closing and fastening the lid, he turned back to Mrs Woodruffe, shooting off at her a veritable fusillade of questions, some of which seemed to me to have little bearing on the inquiry.

'At what time precisely was the table laid?'

'At a quarter past twelve. Mr Abernetty liked to have luncheon served on the dot of half-past.'

'And when was it cleared away?'

'At two o'clock, sir.'

Holmes nodded, as if well pleased with her answer.

'When you laid the table,' he continued, 'what was placed on it first?'

'The plates and cutlery, Mr Holmes. Then the cold ham. I brought in the hot vegetables only when Mr and Mrs Abernetty were seated.'

'What about the condiments?'

'You mean the pepper and salt, sir?' Mrs Woodruffe asked. She appeared as bewildered as I at Holmes' interest in such a trivial detail. 'I put them out when I laid the cutlery.'

'And the butter?'

'I brought that in with the cold ham, sir.' Brushing aside this last remark, Holmes plunged on, pursuing some line of inquiry of his own, the purpose of which I failed to grasp at the time.

'Which way does the dining room face?'

'Face?' echoed poor Mrs Woodruffe, by now utterly confused.

'Yes, face,' Holmes repeated impatiently. 'Is it north, south, east or west?'

'South-east, I think, sir. I've never paid that much attention.'

'So it would get the sun for most of the morning and the early part of the afternoon?'

'Why, yes, sir.'

Apparently satisfied, Holmes moved on to another topic which seemed as inconsequential as all the others.

'Tell me, Mrs Woodruffe, did Mrs Abernetty bring her embroidery with her?'

'Yes, Mr Holmes. She has it with her now.'

'That is all I wish to know,' Holmes replied. Taking out his notebook, he scribbled a few words on a page which he then tore out, folded in half and handed to Mrs Woodruffe with the instructions: 'Give this to the gardener's boy and tell him to run as fast as his legs will carry him to Wimbledon police station where he is to hand the message to Inspector Willard and no one else.'

As she dropped a little curtsy and withdrew, Holmes took a last look round the pantry.

'To quote the bard again, Watson,' said he, 'as far as the investigation is concerned, this is a perfect example of a great reckoning in a little room.[9] It is quite extraordinary how Shakespeare manages so often to come up with the *bon mot*. And now that my inquiries are successfully completed, let us return to the kitchen and prevail on the excellent Mrs Woodruffe to provide us with some cooling refreshment.'

---

[9] The quotation is taken from Shakespeare's comedy *As You Like It*, Act 3, Scene 3, in which Touchstone speaks of a man being struck more dead than 'a great reckoning in a little room'. Many critics believe this is a reference to the murder of Christopher Marlowe, Shakespeare's fellow playwright, who, in 1503, at the age of twenty-nine, was stabbed to death by Ingram Friser in a Deptford tavern during a quarrel over the bill. Dr John F. Watson.

'Completed, Holmes?' I demanded, as I hastened to catch up with him. 'But how? What precisely have you found?'

'Evidence of murder, of course.'

'Where?'

'In those leftovers from luncheon which we have just examined.'

'But I saw nothing,' I protested.

'Ah, Watson,' said he, with a smile, 'there is the difference between us. You merely *see*, while I take the trouble to observe. And now,' he added, as we approached the kitchen door, 'we must once more wait upon events, in this case the arrival of Inspector Willard.'

I believe I have remarked before on Holmes' ability to make himself at home in any surroundings whether in the fetid confines of an East End opium den or the gilded splendours of a ducal mansion.[10] He showed the same easy familiarity in Mrs Woodruffe's kitchen, drinking a glass of that good lady's refreshing, homemade lemon cordial with evident appreciation before lighting up his pipe. I, meanwhile, sat at his side, seething with impatience to know what he had discovered which pointed so conclusively to Mrs Abernetty's guilt. It seemed to me it was something in the ice-box which had furnished that proof. But what exactly? It had contained nothing more <u>suspicious than</u> the remnants of the dessert served at

[10] In 'The Adventure of the Noble Bachelor', Mr Sherlock Holmes assures Dr John H. Watson that 'the status of my client is a matter of less moment to me than the interests of his case'. Dr John F. Watson.

luncheon and a dish of butter, leftover food which, had Holmes not insisted it be kept, would have been eaten by Mrs Woodruffe and the maid as their midday meal.

I tried in vain to resolve the problem by using a process of logical deduction such as Holmes himself would have applied to the case but I could find no rational solution. As Mrs William Abernetty could not have known that, on this occasion, the food would be set aside and not eaten as usual by the servants, it therefore followed that, if the food was indeed poisoned, the servants would also have suffered the same ill effects as old Mr Abernetty. But would his daughter-in-law have taken such a risk? One elderly gentleman dying of a gastric attack was one thing; similar symptoms shown by the servants was quite another. The suspicions of Dr Thorogood, complacent though he appeared to be, would surely have been aroused? Besides, thinking back to that initial interview with Mrs Woodruffe in Baker Street, I remembered Holmes had questioned her about this very point and she had replied that neither she nor the maid had ever suffered any sickness on those earlier occasions when Mr Abernetty had been taken ill.

And what of those other questions Holmes had put to the housekeeper on our arrival at the house? How could it possibly matter which way the dining room faced or whether Mrs Abernetty had brought her embroidery with her? Or, come to that, in what order the table had been set?

I confess I could make nothing of it and, giving up the attempt with a rueful shake of the head, I sat back in my chair, trying to contain my impatience as we waited for Inspector Willard.

He came about ten minutes later, his arrival heralded by two official sounding knocks at the back door. Holmes, who had been lazily blowing smoke rings at the ceiling, rose to his feet with a satisfied smile and let him into the kitchen.

He was a large man, broad of girth as well as of features, and so immensely tall that he had to duck his head in order to pass under the lintel. From the manner in which he greeted Holmes, shaking him warmly by the hand, I deduced that this was not the first time the two men had met, a conjecture which was borne out by his opening remark.

'Pleased to see you again, Mr Holmes,' said he heartily, 'although I gather from your message the news is not good. The lady in question, Mrs William Abernetty, is still on the premises?'

'She is in the morning room with the doctor, both of whom, I trust, know nothing yet of either your arrival or mine and Dr Watson's.'

At the mention of my name, Inspector Willard gave me a quick smile and a nod of his head, acknowledging my presence before turning back to my old friend.

'And what about evidence, Mr Holmes? As I said to you this morning, I can take the lady in for questioning on suspicion but I need proof of guilt before I can charge her.'

'Oh, the evidence is there, Inspector. Indeed, it is better than I dared hope. Have no fear; you shall shortly see it for yourself. And now, if Mrs Woodruffe will carry out the formalities and announce us, we will confront Mrs William Abernetty with that charge of murder.'

The housekeeper, who had listened to this exchange in silence but with an expression of relief and reassurance on her face, spoke up for the first time.

'Willingly, gentlemen,' she replied as, smiling gratefully at the three of us, she preceded us out of the kitchen, along a passageway and through a baize-covered door into the main hall. Here, she tapped on another door and, when a woman's voice bade her enter, she flung it open and announced in ringing tones, 'Mr Holmes, Dr Watson and Inspector Willard, madam!'

III

The room into which she showed us overlooked the back garden and was furnished as a small sitting-room with armchairs and an elegant little sofa covered in buttoned pink silk. Seated side by side on it, in an attitude of comfortable tête-à-tête which had been rudely interrupted by our unexpected arrival, were a man and a woman. The man, Dr Thorogood, was elderly and silver-haired, and had about him an air of smiling complacency as if well pleased not only with himself but with the young and beautiful lady whose company he was so evidently enjoying.

For she was indeed beautiful. From Mrs Woodruffe's comments, I had expected to find a hard-featured and overbearing virago. Instead, my first impression was of a young woman of perhaps three and twenty, delicately formed and exquisitely dressed in blue, a shade which complimented her eyes and enhanced the rich gold of her abundant hair.

We had evidently interrupted her in mid-sentence for she was leaning towards her companion in an attitude of womanly appeal, those blue eyes full upon his face, one hand resting lightly on his sleeve, the other clutching a lace handkerchief.

She had that attractive, mobile cast of features which readily conveys emotions; perhaps too readily, for as we entered I saw that expression of tearful appeal which, a second before, had been directed at Dr Thorogood turn to one of sharp suspicion.

'Who are you? What do you want?' she demanded, rising to her feet.

'Mrs William Abernetty?' Holmes inquired with the greatest civility as he walked towards her.

His voice and manner nonplussed her momentarily and her glance wavered. It was in those few seconds of uncertainty on her part that Holmes acted.

Before she, or indeed any of us, was aware of his intention, Holmes had stooped and picked up a tapestry needlework bag which was lying on the floor beside the sofa.

'How dare you, sir!' Mrs Abernetty exclaimed, making as if to snatch it back from him. But she was too late. Holmes had already retreated a few paces and, setting the bag down on a small table, had opened it and begun to unpack its contents.

First to emerge was an unfinished piece of *petit-point* embroidery, destined perhaps for a cushion cover or chair back. Next came a pair of scissors, several skeins of different coloured silk thread and a little felt booklet of needles. Last of all, he removed a black-japanned tin box about six inches square and three deep which, judging from the spray of pink blossom painted on its lid, may once have contained sweetmeats of some kind.

At the sight of it, Mrs Abernetty gave a shriek and sank down on to the sofa, the lace handkerchief pressed to her lips.

I confess none of us, not even Dr Thorogood, paid her the least heed; all our attention was fixed upon the box, the lid of which Holmes was in the act of opening.

Heaven knows what we expected to see. For my part, I had no idea and I was considerably bewildered, and even a little disappointed, when, as the lid came off, the contents were revealed. Lying inside it on a bed of crushed ice, most of which had melted, was nothing more than a small glass dish containing a lump of butter. Like the ice, it was much reduced by the heat and had spread itself into an oily and misshapen residue, the parsley sprig with which it had once been decorated lying near the bottom of the dish although it was still possible to discern that the butter had once been square and that a portion of it had been removed.

While the rest of us cried out in disbelief and astonishment, it was Mrs Woodruffe who made the only coherent comment.

'So that's where the dish went!' she exclaimed. 'I thought the maid had broken it and had thrown away the pieces although she denied it at the time.'

'When was this?' Holmes inquired eagerly.

'About a year ago, sir. It was one of a set of six. I even stopped a shilling out of the girl's wages to pay for it.'

She was interrupted by Inspector Willard whose broad, good-natured features expressed a complexity of emotions from baffled astonishment to a lurking suspicion that Holmes' revelation was nothing more than an elaborate hoax, the exact purpose of which escaped him.

'Now, see here, Mr Holmes,' said he in a tone of heavy reprobation, 'when I spoke of evidence, I had something more in mind than a lump of butter, even though I admit it's a strange object for a lady to carry about in her needlework bag.'

'Quite,' Holmes agreed drily. 'However, you have so far seen only half of the evidence, Inspector. If, Mrs Woodruffe, you would be so good as to bring the other dish of butter from the pantry, I shall explain the relevance of both to this inquiry.'

As the housekeeper left to carry out these instructions, Holmes lifted the dish from the box and held it out so that we could examine it more closely, an opportunity of which only the Inspector and I took advantage. Dr Thorogood, I noticed, looking pale and shaken, had taken himself off to the far side of the room where he sat down on an armchair, studiously avoiding the sofa where Mrs Abernetty was languishing, dry-eyed but still holding the handkerchief up to her lips. Placing his elbows on his knees, Dr Thorogood covered his eyes with one hand as if to shield them from some sudden and blinding light.

'You will observe,' Holmes was saying in that high, quick voice of his he always used when expounding some subject in which he was particularly interested, 'that the butter contains some tiny, dark grains which could be mistaken for milled pepper. In this instance, however, I believe that, on analysis, they will prove to be crushed laburnum seeds which contain a quinolizidine alkaloid, a poison known as cytisine.'[11]

'Laburnum!' Inspector Willard interjected. 'I know the tree – in fact, I have one growing in my own garden – but I've never heard it was poisonous. What put you on to it, Mr Holmes?'

'The name of the house, Laburnum Lodge. As Dr Watson will confirm, the realisation came to me suddenly this morning, like a bolt from above, and I drove straight over here to make sure the name was not merely a fanciful invention. But there is indeed a laburnum tree growing near the entrance to the drive. As Dr Watson will also attest, I have made a trifling study of poisons.[12] If given in small doses, cytisine causes nausea and abdominal pains which can be confused with a gastric complaint such as indigestion, as Dr Thorogood had diagnosed in the past when Mr Abernetty suffered from similar indispositions.

[11] Laburnum (*Cytisus laburnum*) is a cultivated tree which flowers in early summer. All parts of the tree are poisonous, especially the bark and the ripened seeds. Dr John F. Watson.

[12] Mr Sherlock Holmes is being unduly modest. According to Dr John H. Watson, Mr Sherlock Holmes was 'well up in belladonna, opium, and poisons generally'. *Vide:* 'A Study in Scarlet'. Dr John F. Watson

'However, I believe it was never Mrs Abernetty's intention to give her father-in-law a lethal dose which might have aroused suspicion. Instead, she fed him small amounts of the toxin over a period of time in order to so undermine his health that the final dose would be fatal.'

At this point in his exposition, there came a knock on the door and, at Holmes' invitation to come, Mrs Woodruffe entered, ceremoniously carrying the other dish of butter on a silver salver.

'"She brought forth butter on a lordly dish,"' Holmes remarked to me in a murmured aside. Seeing my bewilderment, he added with a touch of asperity, 'Jael and Sisera, Watson; the Old Testament, judges, Chapter 5.[13] Look it up, my dear fellow, look it up.'

Breaking off, he thanked Mrs Woodruffe and, taking the salver from her, placed on it the first dish, the one taken from Mrs Abernetty's bag, so that it was standing next to the one Mrs Woodruffe had just brought in from the pantry.

'Observe,' said he, pointing a long finger. 'While at first glance the two pats of butter might seem similar, both being roughly the same shape and placed on identical dishes, there are some significant differences. Only the one recovered from Mrs Abernetty's bag contains the dark

---

[13] After Sisera, the captain of the Canaanite army, was defeated in battle by the Israelites, he sought refuge in the tent of Jael, the wife of Heber the Kenite, who he thought was an ally. However, after offering Sisera hospitality, including 'butter on a lordly dish', Jael killed him by hammering a nail into his temple and then beheaded him. Dr John F. Watson.

grains I have already remarked on, and it has also softened to a greater degree than the other. There is one more piece of evidence which I took special note of as soon as I saw the second dish in the ice-box in Mrs Woodruffe's pantry. It was this which led me to suspect murder. Dr Watson, Inspector Willard, would either of you care to comment on it?'

The Inspector and I exchanged a baffled glance before we both shook our heads in unison.

'Then allow me to do so,' Holmes continued. 'Note the sprigs of parsley, gentlemen! The one on the pat brought in from the pantry has sunk into the butter no more than a quarter of an inch. But shouldn't it have sunk deeper? The temperature today must stand at over 80 degrees and, as the dining room faces south-east, it would have caught the full sun for the whole of the morning as well as part of the early afternoon. Had that butter remained on the table throughout luncheon, from twelve fifteen until two o'clock, the time when Mrs Woodruffe cleared it away, then in that hour and three-quarters I would have expected the butter to have become so soft that it would have begun to spread across the dish, causing the parsley to sink deeper into it.

'Let us now inspect the second pat of butter, the one discovered in Mrs Abernetty's bag which I have suggested contains crushed laburnum seeds. What do we observe about that?'

'The butter has melted and the parsley has sunk so deep into it that it is almost lying on the dish itself,' I replied.

'Exactly so, Watson! The inference is therefore obvious. It must be this second pat of butter which stood on the dining-room table throughout the meal.'

Straightening up, Holmes turned his head to look in Mrs Abernetty's direction, deliberately addressing his remarks at her.

'From this evidence,' he continued in an austere, clipped tone, 'we may deduce what happened in this house earlier today. After the dining-room table was laid and while Mrs Woodruffe was absent from the room, Mrs Abernetty substituted for the original dish of butter the one she had secreted in her bag, containing the crushed laburnum seed. After the meal was over and again in Mrs Woodruffe's absence, Mrs Abernetty then exchanged the two dishes, returning to the table the original from which she removed a portion of one corner to make it appear that part of it had been eaten in the course of the meal. As it had been kept in the tin containing ice, it was, of course, still relatively firm.

'Although Mrs Woodruffe remained in the dining room to serve the meal, she would not have noticed anything amiss as the dishes were identical and, at a cursory glance, so apparently was the butter.'

At this point, he broke off to address the housekeeper. 'I assume you noticed nothing?'

'No, sir, I did not,' she replied.

'Was it Mr Abernetty's habit to take butter with his meal?'

'Yes, Mr Holmes. He liked to put it on his vegetables,

especially new potatoes.' In a faltering voice which was close to tears, she added, 'Oh, sir, if only I had known!'

'You are not to blame yourself, Mrs Woodruffe. It was such a trivial difference that it was easily overlooked,' Holmes told her in a kindly voice. 'There are only two more questions I need to ask you and then you may go. Was a dish of butter usually supplied with the meal?'

'Yes, sir; always.'

'And was Mrs Abernetty aware you had an ice-box in the pantry?'

'Yes, Mr Holmes, she was.'

'When was it bought?'

'Last July, sir.'

'Was this before or after Mr Abernetty's first gastric attack?'

'About a week before, sir.'

'Thank you, Mrs Woodruffe. You may go now,' Holmes said gravely.

He waited until the door had closed behind her before resuming his account.

'I think,' said he, 'that what Mrs Woodruffe has just told us casts an even darker shadow over the events for it suggests that Mrs Abernetty first began to think about murdering her father-in-law a year ago. It was the purchase of the ice-box which gave her the idea of how it might be accomplished without rousing suspicion. The murder itself was carried out in careful stages over the following months. The motive, of course, was greed. As her mother-in-law and her husband were both dead, she was Mr

Abernetty's sole remaining heir. Indeed, I believe . . .'

Breaking off suddenly, he made a gesture of revulsion with one hand as if repudiating not only Mrs Abernetty but whatever black thoughts were troubling his mind.

'Come, Watson,' said he abruptly. 'Let us find somewhere more congenial for I confess I am sickened by the company which at present I am forced to keep.'

Although he did not mention her name or even look at her, all of us knew to whom he was referring, including the lady herself. I ventured a quick glance in her direction and saw her sitting upright on the sofa, her eyes still dry and those once mobile features as hard and as cold as marble, with such a dreadful fixity of expression that I was put in mind of a death mask.

Striding to the door, Holmes flung it open, pausing to direct one last remark at Inspector Willard.

'I shall call on you later at the police station,' he announced. 'In the meantime, I suggest you send the gardener's boy with a message to your colleagues for whatever officers you will need to bring about the arrest.'

IV

We left the house by the front door, Holmes walking rapidly across the lawn towards a large copper beech tree where he threw himself down on the grass in its shade, covering his face with an upflung arm.

For a few moments, I stood regarding him and then, recognising the all too familiar symptoms of depression and guessing he would prefer to be left alone, I walked quietly away.

There was one particular aspect of the case which, out of curiosity, I wanted to see for myself and, taking advantage of Holmes' absence, I strolled back towards the drive where my old friend had said he had observed a laburnum growing near the entrance.

It was a slender tree with delicate, fern-shaped leaves amongst which were hanging a few clusters of small, yellow flowers, tarnished a little by the heat and the lateness of the season. Many of the blossoms had already dropped to be replaced with bunches of narrow, green seed cases, very similar in shape to pea-pods. Lying beneath the tree among the litter of last year's leaves, I noticed many dried and empty pods and a scattering of small, round, black seeds which, as I picked one up and rubbed it between my fingers, felt as hard and as dry as a peppercorn.

If Holmes was right and Mr Abernetty had indeed died from cytisine poisoning administered by his daughter-in-law, then she had not had to look far to find the means for murder.

As I was pondering this aspect of the case, I heard the sound of running footsteps approaching along the gravel path at the side of the house and I hurriedly concealed myself behind a clump of rhododendrons. Seconds later, a young lad, presumably the gardener's boy, came into view trotting quickly down the drive to disappear through the gateway and along the road.

Within fifteen minutes, a four-wheeler cab, with the gardener's boy perched precariously at its rear, turned into the drive and drew up outside the house. Two people alighted, one a uniformed officer, the other a middle-aged lady dressed in black, most probably a matron employed by the police to escort female prisoners. My curiosity now thoroughly aroused, I remained where I was and was able therefore to witness the subsequent events.

The first person to emerge from the house was the bowed figure of Dr Thorogood, from his stance alone looking ten years older than the last time I had seen him. Getting into his brougham, he drove away, passing my hiding place at little more than a walking pace, as if both the horse and its driver were so utterly dejected that neither could summon up the energy to proceed any faster.

Not long afterwards, Inspector Willard's tall figure appeared on the porch, accompanied by the uniformed officer and the lady in black. Surrounded by this soberly dressed entourage, Mrs William Abernetty seemed as graceful and as resplendent as a bird of paradise among a flock of ravens, her blue dress and magnificent gold hair catching the sunlight as if the sun itself had conspired to enhance her beauty with its own radiance.

Unlike Dr Thorogood, I could see nothing about her to suggest either guilt or shame. With head held high, she spurned the matron's hand with a contemptuous gesture and climbed unaided into the cab where the others joined her. Seconds later, the four-wheeler came briskly down the drive, allowing me to catch a glimpse as it passed of her hard, stony profile, staring straight ahead.

As soon as the cab had turned into the road, I emerged from the shrubbery and set off across the lawn to find Holmes who was by now sitting upright, his back against the trunk of the beech tree and his arms locked about his knees. His mood seemed lighter and he greeted me cheerfully enough although his face bore that gaunt, careworn look which told me that his nerves were still stretched close to breaking point.

'They have all gone, Holmes, including Mrs Abernetty,' I announced.

'Yes, I heard the cab arrive and leave,' said he. 'Thank

God that woman's evil presence can no longer taint the atmosphere.'

'Evil?' I repeated, surprised at the choice of word which seemed a little excessive.

'Evil. Wicked. Monstrous. Choose whichever epithet you wish, Watson. None of them is adequate, for I believe she is guilty not of one murder but of three.'

Horrified, I fell silent and, seeing my expression, Holmes continued in a bitter, caustic tone.

'Oh, yes, my dear fellow, that beautiful creature whom no doubt you, like all the other men with whom she was acquainted, Dr Thorogood, her father-in-law and probably also her husband, thought so charming is a cold and ruthless killer, as deadly and as loathsome as a poisonous serpent. I began to suspect the extent of her iniquity this morning when I made a few inquiries about her, which was why I was so late returning to Baker Street.

'I spoke first to Mrs Sheldrake, the former housekeeper here who left so suddenly on the day of old Mrs Abernetty's funeral. You remember Mrs Woodruffe referred to her?'

'Yes, indeed, Holmes. How did you manage to trace her?' I inquired.

'Without too much difficulty although it took more than an hour. As she left without giving notice, I assumed Mrs Sheldrake had applied to one of the domestic agencies for another post. Fortunately, her name was unusual and, at the third such agency, I discovered her present address in Kensington where I interviewed her. One of her reasons for leaving the Abernetty household was her suspicions of Mrs William Abernetty and the part she had played in the old lady's death. It seems she saw Mrs William Abernetty coming out of her mother-in-law's bedroom early one morning. Later, when Dr Thorogood called to make a routine visit, old Mrs Abernetty was found dead in bed, of an apparent heart attack, as the doctor recorded on the death certificate.'

'Surely there is nothing suspicious in that, Holmes?' I protested. 'Mrs Woodruffe told us Mrs Abernetty had helped to nurse her mother-in-law.'

'Ah, yes, Watson! No doubt she did and carried out the task admirably, as Dr Thorogood evidently thought. There is, however, the towel to account for which, like the butter dish, was unaccountably missing.'

'I do not see.' I began but, ignoring me, Holmes bore on with his account as if, having steeled himself to begin it, he was compelled to continue in order to put into words those black thoughts which were still haunting him.

'Mrs Sheldrake noticed its absence when she was collecting up the laundry after old Mrs Abernetty's death. Although she could not explain why, she felt instinctively that young Mrs Abernetty had taken it and that it was in some way connected with her mistress's death. I believe her suspicion was correct for I am convinced the towel was placed over the old lady's face before the pillow was used to smother her. The towel would have absorbed any tell-tale signs such as blood or saliva which might have suggested she had been suffocated. Later, I suspect, Mrs

125

William Abernetty took the towel home in that needlework bag of hers and destroyed it.

'From Kensington I moved to Clapham where, after a few discreet inquiries, I managed to trace the late Mr William Abernetty's physician to whom I put a few questions, posing as a member of the Abernetty family recently arrived from abroad and anxious to discover the exact circumstances of my cousin William's death which I did not like to ask of old Mr Abernetty for fear of causing him distress. From Dr Martin I learnt that Mr William Abernetty, who you will recall was partially crippled due to a childhood illness, had fallen down the stairs one Sunday morning and struck his head against the newel post. An inquest was held in which Dr Martin gave evidence and, in view of Mr William Abernetty's physical condition, the coroner brought in a verdict of accidental death.

'Three deaths, Watson, all of which led Mrs William Abernetty step by step nearer to inheriting the family fortune! If I could prove those deaths were murder and could lay them at Mrs Abernetty's door, I would willingly retire from practice, satisfied with the knowledge that I had brought that she-devil to justice and cleansed society of her evil presence.'

'Do you intend speaking of your suspicions to Inspector Willard?'

'No, Watson, for they are nothing more than that – mere suspicions with not a scintilla of evidence to prove them. But at least there is enough data to establish her guilt for old Mr Abernetty's murder and for that, I suppose, we should be grateful.'

Rising to his feet, he added, 'Come, Watson. We shall take our leave of Mrs Woodruffe and then call at the police station so that I may make my statement. After that, I suggest we return immediately to Baker Street for I am eager to shake the dust of this accursed place from my feet.'

We had walked part of the way back to the house in silence, Holmes sunk deep in thought, when he came to an abrupt halt and, with a gesture of his hand which encompassed the whole scene, he exclaimed, 'Look at it, Watson! The garden! The trees! The rose-beds! The house itself, so neat and trim, the very image of respectability! I believe I once remarked to you that the countryside presented a more dreadful record of sin than the vilest alleys of London.[14] I am not so certain that my conclusion was correct for I am now more inclined to think that it is in these pleasant, leafy suburbs where we may find lurking the greatest evil, concealing its depravity under the cloak of gentility and moral rectitude.'

In the weeks that followed, Holmes made no further reference to the case. I am not even sure that he followed the newspaper reports of Mrs Abernetty's arrest and subsequent trial at which she pleaded guilty. It was as if he wanted to expunge from his mind all memory of the investigation.

Instead, he flung himself into a variety of tasks and

---

[14] *Vide:* 'The Adventure of the Copper Beeches'. Dr John F. Watson.

diversions, busying himself with his chemical experiments or indexing his papers although there were occasions when he shut himself up in his room for hours on end, playing his violin, or took himself off for long, solitary walks. I had good reason to believe that he was also seeking solace in his old habit from which I had been trying to wean him for years.[15] Although he never openly used the syringe in my presence, there were days when he lay supine on the sofa, staring moodily up at the ceiling.

I was therefore much relieved when Inspector Lestrade called one evening to seek his help in the Grenville Hyde affair, a complex case which occupied my old friend's time and attention over the next few weeks.

It was, I recall, not until one morning in early September that Holmes made any reference to the Abernetty case. I was up later than usual and, when I came downstairs to join him at the breakfast table, I found a copy of *The Times* lying beside my plate, folded back to a news item which was marked with red ink. The report stated that the trial of Mrs William Abernetty had ended and she had been sentenced to hang.

Although expected, the verdict nevertheless caused me some sadness, largely on account of her victims although, remembering her beauty, I felt a small vestige of compassion for the lady herself.

Whether or not Holmes read these thoughts on my face

---

[15] Mr Sherlock Holmes was in the unfortunate habit of injecting himself with a 7 per cent solution of cocaine. He also on occasions used morphine. Dr John F. Watson.

or, knowing my nature, deduced my feelings, I cannot tell. But, taking back the newspaper, he remarked in a loud, firm voice, 'Do not waste your pity, my dear fellow. Let her go to the oblivion she so justly deserves. For that reason, I shall be much obliged if you did not publish an account of the case.'

I gave him my word and therefore this narrative will be placed among my private papers.

Since I completed this account several months ago, circumstances are now a little changed and consequently I wish to add this final postscript. Only last Tuesday, Holmes relented so far as to permit me to make a passing reference to the Abernetty case in one of my published adventures, with the proviso that the lady herself should not be named so that she should remain, as he had wished, in that anonymous outer darkness into which the law had consigned her.[16]

---

[16] In 'The Adventure of the Six Napoleons', Mr Sherlock Holmes speaks of how 'the dreadful business of the Abernetty family' was first brought to his notice by 'the depth which the parsley had sunk into the butter upon a hot day'. Dr John F. Watson.

The Case of the Ferrers Documents

It has always been one of Sherlock Holmes' most strongly held tenets that the successful outcome of an investigation may depend on the observation of trifles.[1] In my opinion, no case demonstrates the wisdom of this axiom more impressively than the inquiry concerning the Dowager Lady Ferrers.

It began prosaically enough with a short, businesslike letter from Mr Alistair Thackery, a partner in the highly regarded law firm of Allardyce, Thackery and Makepeace of the Strand in London. In it, Mr Thackery requested a consultation with Holmes on the following Wednesday morning at 10 a.m. but made no reference to what matter it was he wished to discuss.

Holmes duly replied, confirming the appointment and, apart from remarking that it probably concerned some dry

---

[1] In 'The Boscombe Valley Mystery', Mr Sherlock Holmes informs Dr Watson that his method of deduction is 'founded upon the observation of trifles'. Dr John F. Watson.

as dust legal affair, said no more on the subject. Indeed, I believe he forgot all about it in the urgency of preparing the documents for the Abergavenny murder trial which was shortly to come to trial.[2]

The arrival of Mr Thackery precisely on the stroke of ten o'clock on the Wednesday morning reminded us both of the man's existence. Holmes, who was seated at his desk looking over some of the Abergavenny papers, hurriedly thrust them aside and rose to his feet as Mr Thackery was shown into our sitting room.

He was a tall, distinguished-looking man, impeccably dressed in the sober garb of a lawyer and bearing about him such an air of formal dignity that, after he had shaken hands with both of us and Holmes had invited him to sit down, I excused myself and turned as if to leave the room, assuming he would prefer not to discuss his business in the presence of a third person.

I was therefore greatly surprised when he remarked, 'If you would be so kind as to remain, Dr Watson, I should be much obliged to you for I believe you may have a part to play in the proposition I am about to put to Mr Holmes.'

As soon as I had resumed my seat, Mr Thackery continued, 'I shall come straight to the point, gentlemen.

---

[2] When asked by Dr Huxtable to inquire into the disappearance of Lord Saltire, the only son of the Duke of Holdernesse, Mr Sherlock Holmes remarks that he is 'already retained in this case of the Ferrers documents, and the Abergavenny murder is coming up for trial'. *Vide:* 'The Adventure of the Priory School', which is variously dated between 1901 and 1903, 1901 being the year accepted by most critics. Dr John F. Watson.

My business here today concerns one of my clients, an elderly and extremely wealthy widow whose recent conduct is causing me some concern. She is the Dowager Lady Agatha Ferrers.'

'The widow of the late Sir Cuthbert Ferrers?' Holmes inquired, his eyes kindling at the very mention of the name. 'I believe before she married Sir Cuthbert, her ladyship was a well-known Spanish dancer on the music-hall stage.'

'Exactly so,' Mr Thackery replied, pressing his lips together in disapproval. 'The marriage caused quite a scandal at the time. That, however, does not concern us here. After the death of her husband three years ago, the title, the estate and the bulk of the fortune passed to a nephew, the only direct heir as the Ferrers had no children of their own. Her ladyship, on whom Sir Cuthbert had settled a considerable capital sum of £30,000, was also to receive a yearly allowance of £1000 from the estate which was to cease on her demise.

'On her husband's death, Lady Ferrers moved out of the family house, Kingsmead Hall in the county of Kent, and bought Bryony Lodge, a large property in Blackheath where she is at present residing. I handled the purchase of that house and ever since then I have acted as her legal representative. At this point, gentlemen, I should explain that my client is a difficult and capricious lady to the extent that Sir Randolph Ferrers, the present baronet, and his family have severed all ties with her. I, too, have found her behaviour so exasperating at times that I have myself been tempted to withdraw my services.

'My duties, however, are not onerous. Under the terms of her late husband's will, a solicitor is to visit her every quarter and to report to the trustees on her state of health, both physical and mental. Sir Cuthbert insisted on this clause as her behaviour, even before his death, was becoming a little eccentric. Because of the large financial settlement, he wished to make sure that, if ever she became incapable of managing her own affairs, the trustees could be alerted in good time and could take over the responsibility.

'On these quarterly visits, I always take my clerk with me because Lady Ferrers invariably asks me to make some minor alterations to her will, only to countermand those changes on my next visit and replace them with others.'

Here Mr Thackery paused and for a few seconds a pained expression passed over his face as if the mere recollection of his client's exasperating conduct was enough to distress him. He then continued, 'Lady Ferrers has little to occupy her mind except who shall or shall not benefit from her death. Of course, gentlemen, all of this is in the strictest confidence. I should not have spoken of it had it not a direct bearing on the business which brought me here today.'

Reaching into an inner pocket, he drew out a folded sheet of paper which he handed to Holmes, remarking as he did so, 'I received this letter from Lady Ferrers two days ago.'

Holmes perused it rapidly.

'I see,' said he, 'that the handwriting in the main body

133

of the letter is quite different from the signature. Is that of any significance?'

'No, Mr Holmes. My client suffers from arthritis and consequently is in the habit of dictating her correspondence to her housekeeper, Mrs Donkin, merely adding her own signature when a fair copy of the letter is drawn up.'

'And the signature is her ladyship's?'

'I have no reason to doubt it,' Mr Thackery replied.

'Nevertheless I should be grateful if you would let me keep the letter for the time being and send me another sample of Lady Ferrers' signature with which to compare it.'

'You suspect forgery?' Mr Thackery inquired, looking startled at this implication.

'I suspect nothing at this early stage,' Holmes remarked. 'However, as I assume you wish me to look into her ladyship's affairs, on which this letter apparently has a direct bearing, I should prefer that the question of possible forgery is settled once and for all before I proceed any further with the case.'

'Very well, Mr Holmes. I shall make sure that you receive another example of Lady Ferrers' handwriting as soon as possible, although for my part, it is not the signature which causes me concern,' Mr Thackery replied a little impatiently, as if eager to come to the point. 'It is the contents of the letter which have aroused my suspicion.'

'Then may I read it aloud for Dr Watson's benefit?' On receiving Mr Thackery's consent, Holmes then proceeded.

'"Dear Mr Thackery,"' he began. '"I am exceedingly displeased by your discourteous manner towards me on your last visit over the alterations to my will. Because of this, I have decided that I no longer wish you to represent me. You would therefore oblige me by arranging for another partner in your firm to handle my legal affairs in the future. Yours etc. Agatha Ferrers."'

Mr Thackery, who had listened to this recital with increasing exasperation, now broke in.

'It is an extraordinary letter, Mr Holmes! Quite unjustified! I can assure you that there was not the least incivility on my part. Indeed, I believe I showed admirable patience during my last meeting with Lady Ferrers and we parted on good terms, with no sign from her that she was in any way dissatisfied with either myself or my services.'

'Could it not be simply a whim on her part?' Holmes suggested. 'You spoke of her ladyship's capriciousness.'

'That may indeed be so,' Mr Thackery replied. 'However, I confess I am uneasy at the situation. The visit she refers to happened nearly three months ago. Why has she waited so long before writing to complain of my behaviour? It is this delay which gives rise to my disquiet. Although in all honesty I cannot say I feel particularly cordial towards Lady Ferrers, I have her best interests at heart. It is for that reason I wrote to you, requesting this consultation. I am due to make the next quarterly visit to Lady Ferrers on Friday morning at eleven o'clock. Before I arrange for either Mr Allardyce or Mr Makepeace to take over the duty, I should feel a great deal happier in my mind if you, Mr Holmes, with Dr Watson acting as your clerk, would agree to attend instead. I am sure you, with your wide experience as a private consulting agent, would be better qualified to judge whether or not anything is amiss. I have discussed this with my partners and both agree with my proposal. All you have to do is converse with Lady Ferrers for about half an hour and discuss with her the changes she will inevitably want made to her will on which Dr Watson, as clerk, will take notes. At the same time, you can ascertain the situation.'

'But will not Lady Ferrers think it suspicious that neither of your partners has agreed to represent her?'

'I think not, Mr Holmes. As senior partner, Mr Allardyce will write to her explaining that, because of the short notice of my dismissal and their own commitments, neither he nor Mr Makepeace is free to call on her on Friday morning. Therefore, as a temporary measure only, a colleague of ours, Mr Holmes, and his clerk will take over my responsibilities. At all other times in the future, Mr Allardyce himself will be honoured to act on her behalf. I believe Lady Ferrers will accept the proposal. Indeed, she will have no opportunity to reject it. If Mr Allardyce writes to her tomorrow morning, she will receive the letter only on the day you are due to arrive. Well, gentlemen, will you accept my proposition?'

Holmes glanced across at me, one eyebrow raised quizzically.

'What do you say, my dear fellow? Are you game?'

'Certainly, Holmes,' I replied without any hesitation.

'Then the matter is settled!' Holmes declared with evident satisfaction. 'Now, Mr Thackery, before we call on Lady Ferrers, there are one or two details which I should like clarified. You spoke of her will. Who exactly benefits from it?'

'The bulk of her fortune, including the house and its contents, is left to her niece and two nephews, her late sister's children and her only surviving heirs. In addition, there are several bequests to charities which Lady Ferrers has supported in the past. Her butler and housekeeper, Mr and Mrs Donkin, are each to receive £2000 with a further £5000 if they agree to care for her pet dog, a small black and white terrier called Bonny. I should add that Mr and Mrs Donkin have been in her employment for about thirty years. Her ladyship's dresser when she was on the stage was Mrs Donkin's mother, Mrs Campion, who is still alive. She is also left £2000, that money to be divided between the Donkins should she predecease Lady Ferrers. Further small bequests of varying amounts are left to other servants. It is these bequests as well as those to her niece and nephews which are the ones which Lady Ferrers is in the habit of changing on various pretexts. Either one of her nephews has not written to her as frequently as Lady Ferrers thinks he should or a housemaid has not dusted the drawing room to her satisfaction. On my next visit, these beneficiaries are usually restored to favour and someone else who has aroused her displeasure, the niece perhaps or her cook, is cut out of her will.'

'But not the Donkins, I assume?' Holmes inquired.

'Oh, no indeed!' Mr Thackery declared with absolute assurance. 'They have been with Lady Ferrers for so long

137

that they understand her every mood and anticipate her every wish. Her ladyship has never once suggested that their bequests should be altered.'

'And what of old Mrs Campion, Mrs Donkin's mother?'

'She, too, has always remained in favour.'

'Which leaves only the dog,' Holmes observed with a humorous air.

I saw Mr Thackery's austere features soften a little at Holmes' jocularity and, for the first time during the entire interview, he permitted a small, chilly smile to touch the corners of his mouth.

'Write Bonny out of her will!' he exclaimed. 'Such a thought would never cross Lady Ferrers' mind. It would be no exaggeration to state that she dotes on the creature. It hardly ever leaves her side except for those occasions when Donkin takes it for a walk. It even sleeps in a basket at the foot of her bed. And now, gentlemen,' Mr Thackery continued, rising to his feet, 'I shall return to the office and arrange for Mr Allardyce to write to Lady Ferrers apprising her of your arrival on Friday morning. I shall also send by special messenger that other sample of her ladyship's signature you requested. And may I also thank both of you for agreeing to look into the matter? It has made me much easier in my mind.'

After he had taken his leave and departed, Holmes took a turn up and down the room, chuckling and rubbing his hands with delight.

'A fascinating case, is it not, Watson?' he inquired.

'So you think there may indeed be some irregularity

in Lady Ferrers' decision to dispense with Mr Thackery's services?'

'My dear fellow, how many times have I told you it is a fundamental mistake to speculate about a case until one has collected up enough evidence?[3] No, it is Lady Ferrers herself who interests me the most.'

Striding over to the bookcase, he took out volume 'F' of his encyclopaedia and turned over the pages, murmuring under his breath as he did so.

'Fleming, George, arsonist. Fungu poisoning.[4] Now that was an extraordinary investigation! Fisher, William, the notorious burglar. You recall him, Watson? The bandy-legged little fellow who could scamper up the side of a house like a monkey? Ah, here we are! Ferrers, Lady, formerly Agatha Potts, daughter of William Potts, coal merchant of Stepney, and Mrs Sarah Potts. Made her name on the music-hall stage as a Spanish dancer, under the soubriquet of Juanita Vicario. A famous beauty, known popularly as the Flamenco Queen. Her marriage in 1854 to Sir Cuthbert Ferrers caused a considerable stir in aristocratic circles. Well, are not you eager to meet her?'

'I suppose so, Holmes,' I agreed a little reluctantly. 'But surely she must now be in her seventies?'

'My dear fellow, how you disappoint me!' Holmes

---

[3] In 'A Scandal in Bohemia', Mr Sherlock Holmes remarks that it is 'a capital mistake to theorise before one has the data'. Dr John F. Watson.

[4] Fungu poison, or tetradotoxin, is found in two of the more poisonous species of Japanese globefish. Like curare, it paralyses the central nervous system. Dr John F. Watson.

remonstrated. 'Where is your sense of romance? I had imagined that you, of all people, with your natural inclination towards the fairer sex,[5] would have positively relished the thought of meeting her. Why, in her heyday, she was the toast of London! It was said her admirers stood ten deep at the stage door simply to catch a glimpse of her and the old Duke of Dungeness once sent her five hundred red roses by liveried footmen. I am looking forward immensely to making her acquaintance on Friday. And now, Watson, I suggest we postpone any further discussion of the case until Mr Thackery sends us the second sample of her ladyship's signature.'

With that, he returned to the task of indexing the Abergavenny papers while I resumed my perusal of the *Daily Telegraph*.

The special messenger arrived within the half-hour with an envelope which Holmes eagerly tore open. Extracting from it a single sheet of paper, he carried it to his desk where he laid it side by side with the letter Mr Thackery had given him earlier. I looked quickly over his shoulder at the two documents. To my untutored eye, they looked exactly the same, the main body of both letters being written in Mrs Donkin's small, neat writing with Lady Ferrers' bolder signature scrawled across the bottom of each page.

Sitting down at his desk, Holmes took up his

[5] In 'The Adventure of the Retired Colourman', Mr Sherlock Holmes refers to Dr John H. Watson's 'natural advantages' with the ladies and in 'The Adventure of the Second Stain', he refers to the 'fair sex' as being Dr Watson's 'department'. Dr John F. Watson.

magnifying glass with which he carefully scrutinised the two signatures, remarking to me as he did so, 'The writing is undoubtedly a woman's,[6] Watson, with the right-hand slant showing a passionate and emotional nature. As for the formation of the letters, the upper loop of the "h" as well as the crossing of the "t" correspond. So do the downward strokes on the capital letters, each of which begins with that very distinctive flourish, suggesting vanity and a strong need to dominate.'

To my surprise, he now put aside the lens and took out a ruler which he laid below each signature in turn before, straightening up, he announced, 'The measurements also agree exactly. That is one detail which even expert forgers sometimes fail to take into account. Well, Watson, I think we may safely say that we are not dealing here with a case of forgery. I will stake my life on that. We must now wait until Friday morning to find out what, if anything, it does concern although, in my opinion, Mr Thackery has started up a hare which, at the end of the chase, will prove to be nothing more substantial than a shadow.'

On the Friday morning, we set out for Blackheath by hansom in good time for the eleven o'clock appointment with Lady Ferrers, both of us suitably attired for our roles

[6] Although there is no direct evidence that Mr Sherlock Holmes could determine a person's sex by his or her handwriting, in 'The Adventure of the Reigate Squire', he was able to discern the age and relationship between the two men who had written the letter, a portion of which was found clutched in the hand of the murder victim, William Kerwin. He also remarked that there were twenty-three other deductions he might have drawn from the handwriting. Dr John F. Watson.

of solicitor and clerk, I carrying a leather document case containing a legal-looking notebook in which to write down any changes her ladyship wished to make to her will.

Bryony Lodge was a large, handsome Georgian house of cream-painted stucco, set in well-tended gardens and facing the extensive open area of grassy common land which formed the heath itself. Having paid off the cabby, we mounted the steps of the imposing, pillared porch where Holmes rang the bell. The door was opened by a manservant – Donkin, I assumed. He was a stocky, ruddy-faced man, still bearing about him the horsy, outdoor air of an erstwhile groom or coachman, better suited to tweeds and gaiters than a butler's black apparel although his bearing was solemn enough, even a little melancholy.

As we were ushered into the hall, a middle-aged, pleasant-faced woman, also dressed in black, was in the act of descending the stairs, carrying a tray containing coffee things which she hastened to put down on a table at the foot of the staircase before coming forward to greet us.

'Mr Holmes and Mr Watson?' she inquired, bobbing a little curtsy. 'I am Mrs Donkin, Lady Ferrers' housekeeper. Her ladyship received Mr Allardyce's letter this morning.'

'I trust Lady Ferrers has agreed to the arrangements,' Holmes replied. 'Mr Allardyce very much regretted that, on this occasion, he was unable to act as her ladyship's legal representative.'

'She quite understood,' Mrs Donkin assured us although

I detected a certain nervousness about her manner which made me suspect that Lady Ferrers' attitude on receipt of the letter had not been as sanguine as her housekeeper implied.

'If you would not mind waiting for a few minutes in the drawing room,' she continued, 'I shall return upstairs and inform her ladyship of your arrival.' As she opened a door on the left of the hall, she added, 'Her ladyship's feeling a little unwell today, gentlemen, and has therefore decided to keep to her bed.'

The drawing room into which she showed us was sumptuously furnished with a great deal in the way of painted porcelain, buttoned silk, fringed velvet and crystal glass. But dominating even this lavish display was a huge portrait of Lady Ferrers which hung above the mantelshelf. It depicted her as a young woman of about twenty-five, holding an ostrich feather fan in one hand. She was dressed as if for some grand soiree in a gown of blue satin, her abundant black hair swept upwards and adorned with a magnificent diamond tiara, while her throat and wrists were also hung with precious gems. Holmes had spoken of her beauty and certainly the face which looked out of the gilded frame was very handsome, the features strong and well-cut, the smiling lips a lustrous red and the dark eyes as brilliant as the jewels she wore. I could also see in the imperious lift of her head and the stubborn line of her jaw how she might, with the advancing years, become the capricious old lady whom Mr Thackery had described.

I turned to remark on this to Holmes and saw that he,

too, was studying the portrait intently. Then, to my utter astonishment, he threw back his head and began to laugh.

'What has amused you, Holmes?' I asked, much puzzled by his manner for I could see nothing in the portrait to give rise to such merriment.

'My dear fellow,' said he, clapping me on the shoulder, 'the case is solved.'

'Solved?' I repeated. 'How is that possible? What has made you come to such an extraordinary conclusion?'

'The evidence, of course.'

'In the portrait?' I asked, still mystified.

I glanced back at the painting and, for a curious moment, as I met Lady Ferrers' bold gaze and saw again the painted lips smiling down at me, I imagined that she understood perfectly well the reason for Holmes' amusement and, what was more bewildering, shared in the jest.

'I do not follow,' I said a little stiffly, for I confess I was somewhat piqued at being the only one who could not see the joke.

'Observation, Watson!' said he. 'How many times have I impressed on you the importance of using one's eyes in an investigation? It is the most vital of one's senses. You also have seen the two pieces of evidence on which I have based my assertion – the portrait above the fireplace and the coffee tray which Mrs Donkin was carrying downstairs when we entered the hall.'

'Coffee tray!' I began but Holmes cut me short.

'For the time being, we shall proceed with this little

charade. I need one more piece of evidence, or rather the absence of it, in order to confirm what I have already deduced, which will also supply the missing motive. So you will continue in your role of solicitor's clerk and please, my dear fellow, do take that look of astonished disbelief off your face and replace it with a more suitable expression.'

At that moment, there came a knock upon the door and, on Holmes' invitation 'Come!', Mrs Donkin entered to announce that Lady Ferrers was ready to receive us.

Holmes nodded to me before following her out of the room, while I, with one last backward glance at the portrait, fell in behind them. But whatever Holmes had seen in the painting to convince him the case was solved still escaped me. As for the missing evidence to which he had so puzzlingly referred, I was as much in the dark about this as well.

The housekeeper led us up the broad mahogany staircase and along an upper landing to a door on which she knocked before showing us into a spacious bedchamber.

Like the drawing room, it was furnished in a splendid fashion and it was similarly dominated by Lady Ferrers, not by her painted likeness on this occasion but by the lady herself. She was sitting upright in a large four-poster bed propped up against a great many embroidered pillows, a lace cap upon her head and a fine silk shawl about her shoulders. Although the luxuriant black tresses were now white and the handsome features withered by age, I fancied I could still discern in the dark eyes, which regarded us so directly as we entered, something of the same bold imperiousness which had gazed down at us from the ornate gilt frame. However, I was a little disappointed that she seemed much smaller than I had anticipated for I had imagined her possessing the imposing, statuesque figure of a Juno or an Artemis.

'Mr Holmes and Mr Watson, your ladyship,' Mrs Donkin announced from the doorway. She turned as if to leave the room when Holmes put out a hand to detain her.

'If I may speak to you in private, Mrs Donkin, I shall be very much obliged,' he said.

Her shock and confusion, apparent in her face, were no less than my own. I was also appalled at his discourtesy towards the elderly and distinguished Lady Ferrers. But before I could protest, he had added curtly, 'Come, Watson!'

Left with no choice, I followed him out on to the landing where he came to a halt a few yards from the bedroom door. Folding his arms, he confronted the housekeeper.

'The game is over, Mrs Donkin,' he declared, an expression of utmost sternness on his lean features.

'I do not understand you, sir,' the poor woman stammered in a trembling voice.

'No? I think you do. But since you seem reluctant to give an explanation, then allow me to do so on your account. The lady we have just seen is not your mistress. I am correct, am I not? In fact, I think I may hazard a guess at her true identity. She is your mother, Mrs Campion, whom you have substituted for Lady Ferrers with your husband's connivance. Your motive for doing so is also perfectly plain. Lady Ferrers had threatened to cut you both out of her will.' He paused for a moment as if waiting for the housekeeper to speak and when she remained silent, he continued in a gentler tone, 'What happened to the dog, Mrs Donkin?'

The effect on Mrs Donkin of this simple but to me quite mystifying question was dramatic. She immediately burst into tears.

'Oh, sir!' she sobbed. 'It wasn't my husband's fault. He had taken Bonny out as usual to the heath for her evening walk, when the dog started up a rabbit. Before he could stop her, she bolted into the road straight under the wheels of a hansom. I know he should have had her on the leash, sir, but he only had the dog's best interest at heart. The poor little creature liked to run about free after being shut up in the house for most of the day, not getting the proper exercise she needed. She'd always come to heel before when he called her. Alfie begged her ladyship's forgiveness. He even went out the very next morning to the kennels where Lady Ferrers had bought Bonny and found another terrier of exactly the same size and colour which he paid for out of his own pocket but her ladyship refused even to look at it. Her mind was made up and nothing would change it. "Donkin," she said and her voice was so cold it turned my heart to ice, "you and your wife shall pay dearly for this the next time I see Mr Thackery." Oh, sir, I knew what she meant!'

Pressing her handkerchief to her lips, she broke into renewed sobbing.

'She proposed to cut you out of her will?' Holmes suggested gently. 'But why you as well, Mrs Donkin? The accident was hardly your fault.'

'It was because I spoke up for him, sir. Her ladyship didn't like that. I should have taken her side against him. But Alfie's always been a true and loving husband to me as well as a loyal servant to Lady Ferrers. I couldn't bear to see him cast off by her ladyship without standing by him and that made her angry. "I shall write to Mr Thackery today," she told me, "and inform him of your impertinence."'

'So you assumed she would instruct Mr Thackery to change her will?' Holmes inquired.

'What else could I think, sir? I knew Mr Thackery was due to arrive this morning. I thought he'd bring the new will with him for her ladyship to sign and that would be the end of everything. We'd be left with hardly a penny for our old age.'

'Mr Thackery received no letter from Lady Ferrers instructing him to alter her will,' Holmes told her quietly.

For the first time, an expression of hope passed over Mrs Donkin's grief-stricken face.

'Wasn't there, sir? I knew her ladyship hadn't sent either me or Alfie out to post a letter but we dared not ask the other servants in case it caused gossip. We didn't know which way to turn. And then about four days ago, Lady Ferrers was taken ill and the doctor said she was to keep to her bed and stay quiet; no excitement and no visitors. I was going to write to Mr Thackery on her ladyship's behalf, cancelling his appointment. It was while me and Alfie were talking it over that the idea came to us. If we could find another solicitor to come instead of Mr Thackery, someone who had never met her ladyship, my mother, Mrs Campion, could take her place. That way, we could find out if Lady Ferrers had sent the letter about changing her will and, if she had, then my mother would say to the solicitor that she had thought better of it and did not want her will altered after all. It would give us time, Mr Holmes, as it would be another three months before the solicitor was due to call again on Lady Ferrers. Perhaps by then her ladyship would have forgiven us. We know what she is like, sir; she's always threatening to cut one or other out of her will. It seemed the best way out.

'My mother had served for years as her ladyship's dresser so she knew her ways and could act the part. Besides, she'd been on the stage herself when she was a young woman. So that's what we decided to do. Alfie drove the carriage over to Hackney late last night after all the servants had gone to bed and brought my mother back here. She spent the night in one of the spare bedrooms and then this morning, after I'd got her ladyship up and dressed, I pushed her in her bath chair to her boudoir and my mother took her place in the bed. In the meantime, I had written to Mr Thackery asking for another solicitor to come in his place . . .'

'Signing the letter with Lady Ferrers' name?' Holmes suggested.

Mrs Donkin's pale, tear-stained face flushed a little pink at this implied criticism.

'I meant no harm by it, Mr Holmes!' she protested. 'Ever since her ladyship's had arthritis bad in her hands, it's been her habit to dictate all her correspondence to me to take down and more often than not she would ask me to sign it for her as well. I could write a fair copy of her signature.'

Holmes gave me a brief smile.

'No wonder, Watson,' said he, 'that neither Mr Thackery nor I suspected forgery. We were comparing like with like!' Turning back to Mrs Donkin, he continued, 'And what would you have done when Mr Thackery or his replacement was due to make another of his quarterly visits? You could hardly have gone on substituting Mrs Campion for your mistress without rousing her ladyship's suspicions.'

'I know, sir. Me and Alfie realised that ourselves. We thought the best way round it was for me to write again to Mr Thackery explaining that her ladyship very much regretted her decision to replace him and that she would be much obliged if he would go on acting as her solicitor. I was going to add a little note of my own, asking him not to refer to any of this on his next visit as Lady Ferrers was rather embarrassed by the matter. I knew Mr Thackery would agree to that. He'd seen for himself how much she disliked him mentioning the times in the past when she'd changed her mind over her will.'

'And what would you have done if, after the three months, Lady Ferrers still insisted on cutting you off without a penny?'

'I don't know, sir!' Mrs Donkin again burst into tears. 'Me and Alfie hadn't dared think about that. Of course, we should have gone on serving her ladyship to the best of our ability for as long as she wanted. Me and Alfie have been in her service too long to think of looking for another place and, difficult as she can be at times, we are both very fond of her. And, deep down, I think she is fond of us, too. If only that poor little dog was still alive, Mr Holmes, none of this would have happened.'

Holmes was about to reply when there came the sound of a hand-bell being furiously rung behind a closed door a little further down the landing. At the sound of it, Mrs Donkin gave a gasp and her hands flew up to her mouth.

'That's her ladyship, sir!' she cried. 'She must have heard us talking. I shall have to go to her. But what am I to say to her, Mr Holmes? She will be very angry when she finds out what me and Alfie have done.'

'She is better?' Holmes asked.

'Oh, much better, sir. She's out of bed today.'

'Then give her this,' Holmes told her. Taking out his pocket-book, he extracted one of his business cards which he handed to her. 'Tell her I shall be much obliged if she would grant us an interview.'

Mrs Donkin, who had looked quickly down at the card, raised her eyes and gave Holmes a startled look, as if realising for the first time the significance of his name. But before she could make any reply, there came another violent summons from the bell.

'Go to your mistress,' Holmes said gently, escorting

her down the landing to the door, his lean frame bent solicitously over her. He said something else to her but in so low a voice that I could not catch his words. As Mrs Donkin knocked and entered the room, he turned to me with a smile.

'You see now, Watson, the relevance of that missing piece of evidence I referred to earlier? It was the absence of the pet dog which confirmed my suspicions and provided a motive. Mr Thackery told us that it never left Lady Ferrers' side.'

'Yes, I understand that, Holmes. But how . . . ?' I began.

There were several other questions I wanted to ask him. How, for example, had he been so certain, even before he met the woman posing as Lady Ferrers, that the case was solved? And what was the relevance of the coffee tray?

There was, however, no time. The door had reopened and Mrs Donkin appeared on the threshold to announce that Lady Ferrers would see us and to usher us inside the room.

It was furnished as a boudoir in the same sumptuous style we had already seen elsewhere in the house. But I paid scant attention to the silk curtains or the magnificent Aubusson carpet on the floor. It was the elderly lady sitting bolt upright in a bath chair by the window who caught my attention.

Like her impostor, Mrs Campion, the real Lady Ferrers was white-haired and dark-eyed but there any likeness ceased. The woman who was confronting us was much more strongly featured and bore about her that air of bold imperiousness which I instantly recognised from her portrait.

Raising her ebony and silver stick, which was leaning against her side, she pointed to two nearby chairs.

'Sit down!' she ordered in a peremptory voice. When we were both seated, she continued, 'I see from your card, Mr Holmes, that you are the well-known private detective agent whose exploits I sometimes read about in the newspapers. I assume your companion is Dr Watson. Mrs Donkin has already given me a brief if somewhat incoherent account of what has been going on in my house under my very nose. But even she seemed bewildered by your presence. What may I ask are you doing here, masquerading as a representative of Allardyce, Thackery and Makepeace?'

I must confess I was a little intimidated both by her tone and by the fierceness of the gaze with which she fixed the two of us. I could well understand the Donkins' anxiety about arousing her displeasure. Had I been in their shoes, I, too, would have hesitated to cross her.

Holmes, however, seemed perfectly at his ease. Settling himself comfortably in his chair, he gave a short, succinct account of Mr Thackery's visit to Baker Street and his reasons for asking him, Holmes, to investigate the affair.

'Although,' he concluded, 'the apparent mystery was easily solved.'

'How?' Lady Ferrers demanded brusquely, voicing the question to which I was so eager to hear the answer.

'It was a simple matter of observation, your ladyship,' Holmes replied. 'As we entered the hall, Mrs Donkin was coming downstairs, carrying a tray of coffee things. I noticed it was set for a right-handed person. However, when we were shown into the drawing room, I immediately perceived that in your portrait you were holding your fan in your left hand. The inference was obvious. Whoever the tray had been laid for it was certainly not you, Lady Ferrers. I therefore concluded that someone was impersonating you with Mrs Donkin's connivance. The only question that remained to be answered was: why? What possible reason would your housekeeper, and I assumed also her husband, have for setting up such a subterfuge? The absence of your pet dog, Bonny, suggested a motive which Mrs Donkin confirmed when I questioned her. The dog had been run over and killed and, as a consequence, you had threatened to cut them out of your will, leaving them to face financial insecurity in their old age.'

At this point, Lady Ferrers, who had been following Holmes' account with the keenest interest, thumped twice on the carpet with her stick.

'The woman is a fool, Mr Holmes!' she declared roundly. 'And her husband is not much better.'

I have mentioned before that, when he put his mind to it, Holmes could have a peculiarly ingratiating way with women.[7] He now proceeded to make full use of that ability.

[7] *Vide:* 'The Adventure of the Golden Pince-Nez'. Dr John F. Watson.

Leaning forward, he looked her full in the face and smiled – it was a sincere, disarming smile which crinkled up the corners of his eyes and at the same time appealed to her better judgment.

'Ah, Lady Ferrers!' said he softly. 'You may well be right. I am sure even the best of us have acted foolishly at one time or another. But were I in your place, I should much prefer to dwell on the many years of loyal service the Donkins have given you.'

I saw Lady Ferrers' gaze waver but she was not yet quite ready to succumb to Holmes' persuasive powers.

'They were paid for it,' she snapped back.

'Can loyalty and devotion be bought?' he inquired in a musing tone. 'It has long been my belief that they can only be paid for in kind. Perhaps I am mistaken but I sincerely hope I am not, otherwise life becomes nothing more than a marketplace where all the better qualities of human nature are bought and sold like so much merchandise.'

I saw Lady Ferrers start up in her chair and, for a moment, I thought she was about to order us from the room. And then those hard features softened and a smile came to her lips so that fleetingly she resembled the young, handsome woman in her portrait.

'You are an extraordinary man, Mr Holmes,' she declared.

'Indeed, I have never met your like before. But you are right. Loyalty can only be repaid with loyalty, devotion with devotion. Be so kind, sir, as to ring the bell by the fireplace. I shall speak to the Donkins immediately and put right the wrong I have done them.'

As he crossed the room to carry out her bidding, her ladyship added, 'What is your fee, Mr Holmes?'

'You owe me nothing, Lady Ferrers,' he replied. 'I am already amply rewarded.'

We took our leave shortly afterwards, passing the Donkins coming up the stairs. They had with them a small black terrier with a white patch under its chin which was bounding along eagerly at their heels.

Holmes regarded it with a smile.

'So you have taken my advice and brought the dog with you, Mrs Donkin,' he remarked. 'I have every confidence that it will receive a warmer welcome this time.'

Holmes was correct in this prediction. A few days later, he received a letter from Lady Ferrers thanking him again and confirming that the Donkins had been restored to her good books and Mr Thackery reinstated as her legal representative. Mrs Donkin had added a postscript of her own in which she expressed her and her husband's gratitude to Holmes, as well as stating that not only was her ladyship delighted with the dog but, on meeting Mrs Campion, she had insisted that her former dresser remain in her employment as a paid companion.

The two elderly ladies were now inseparable, regularly playing cards together or reminiscing over their memories of the past.

I was much touched by this last piece of news and said as much to Holmes.

At the time, he was busy at his desk pasting newspaper cuttings in his commonplace book.[8] Looking up, he gave me a brief smile.

'Ah, Watson,' said he, wagging an admonitory finger at me. 'You are an incorrigible romantic. Nevertheless, I am pleased the case ended so satisfactorily, if only for your sake, my dear fellow.

However, I am afraid I shall have to disappoint you over one aspect of the affair. Only this morning, I received a letter from Mr Thackery asking that you refrain from publishing an account of the case as he feels it would contravene that sacred trust between himself and his client and, as he is a solicitor, his word must indeed be the law.'

---

[8] There are several references to Mr Sherlock Holmes' commonplace book in which he pasted any newspaper cuttings he thought relevant. *Vide* among others: 'The Adventure of the Empty House' and 'The Adventure of the Red Circle'. Dr John F. Watson.

The Case of the Vatican Cameos

I

It was, I recall, one morning in June, a few months before Holmes became associated with the lengthy and highly complex inquiry concerning Sir Henry Baskerville,[1] that an unexpected visitor arrived at our Baker Street lodgings.

He was heralded by a frantic pealing at the front door bell, followed by a pounding of feet up the stairs. Seconds later, the door was flung open and a man burst into the room.

'Mr Holmes?' he cried, looking from one to the other of us in great agitation. 'Which of you is Mr Holmes?'

'I am,' my old friend replied coolly, laying aside the *Morning Post* and rising to his feet. 'Pray sit down and

[1] The Baskerville inquiry has been assigned to various years between 1886 and 1900. However, from the internal evidence, the year 1889 seems the most likely. In his account of the case, Dr John H. Watson reports Mr Sherlock Holmes as saying that, although he was aware at the time of newspaper articles reporting the death of Sir Charles Baskerville, he was 'so exceedingly preoccupied' with the affair of the Vatican cameos that he paid little attention to them. Dr John F. Watson.

compose yourself, sir. Watson, I think a little brandy might act as a restorative.'

This last remark was eminently sensible for the man, who was visibly trembling, seemed close to collapse.

He was a tall, rather portly figure in his late forties, I estimated, and was impeccably dressed in morning attire with one or two embellishments about his person in the way of a pearl tiepin and a heavy gold watch chain which, together with a faint accent, suggested he was of foreign extraction. His olive complexion, black hair and small moustache, flicked up at the ends, bore out this impression.

As Holmes settled him into an armchair, I placed a glass of brandy in his hand which he drank quickly, his teeth chattering against the rim. But the spirit seemed to revive him for, by degrees, the trembling stopped and his breathing became easier.

'Now, sir,' said Holmes, drawing up a chair to face him. 'Have you sufficiently recovered to give me your name and state what business has brought you here?'

Holmes' calm manner seemed to encourage the man for, with no further ado, he plunged straight into his account.

'My name, Mr Holmes, is Signor Graziani and I was asked by His Holiness the Pope[2] to bring to London one of the Vatican treasures for display at the exhibition of

---

[2] The Pope at this date was Leo XIII (1810–1903), whose original name was Vincenzo Gioacchino Pecci. He reigned as Pope from 1878 to 1903. Dr John F. Watson.

Renaissance art which is to be held at the British Museum next week. I was chosen for this task because I speak good English and am considered an expert in Renaissance jewellery. In the past I have been called in several times to advise the Vatican on the cleaning and care of some of its collection of precious gems. You see, sir, I have my own jewellery business in Rome, very exclusive and expensive, which caters for only the very richest clients.

'On my advice, the object chosen for exhibition was a set of three fifteenth-century cameos which once belonged to the Medici family.[3] They are exquisite, sir! Priceless!' His voice rose and, in an excess of emotion, he gripped the arms of his chair so fiercely that his knuckles whitened. 'To think that these treasures were entrusted to my care! How am I going to tell His Holiness the Pope that they have been stolen?'

'Stolen?' Holmes repeated abruptly and I saw his head lift, like a gun-dog's scenting game. 'How, sir? From your hotel?'

'No, Mr Holmes. The cameos were kept in the hotel safe until this morning. It happened in the street. I was taking them to the British Museum so that Mr Valentine, the curator who is in charge of the exhibition, could examine them and decide where they could best be displayed. They

---

[3] The Medicis, an immensely rich and powerful family, ruled Florence and later Tuscany from 1434 to 1737. They made their money as bankers and also as silk and cloth merchants. They married into several European royal families, in particular the French. Four members of the family became Popes: Leo X, Clement VII, Pius IV and Leo XL Dr John F. Watson.

were in their silk-lined box which I had placed in a valise. I took a cab to the museum where I alighted at the gates. As I had to search my pockets for money to pay the driver, I put the bag down on the pavement so that I had both hands free. Having paid the cabby, I turned to pick up the valise and *ecco!* it had gone just like that!' he cried, snapping his fingers.

Holmes' features sharpened, his deep-set grey eyes taking on a keener brightness, although when he spoke his voice suggested only a casual interest.

'Did you notice any particular passers-by at the time the valise was stolen?'

'There was a young lady who was walking past me as I was looking for the fare.'

'Would you be able to identify her if you saw her again?'

'Identify her? You are not suggesting she was the thief, Mr Holmes?' Signor Graziani looked horrified at the mere idea. 'She was so beautiful and so well dressed! But I am not sure I would recognise her again.'

'Was there anyone else nearby; a man, this time?'

'Not that I can recall. There were quite a number of people in the street.' Here Signor Graziani paused and, regarding Holmes with a keen glance, added, a note of appeal in his voice, 'Am I right, sir, in thinking that you know who the thief might be?'

'Perhaps,' Holmes replied, with a shrug. 'We shall see. Now, Signor Graziani, pray continue with your account. What did you do next after the valise disappeared?'

'What could I do? I went straight into the museum where I spoke privately to Mr Valentine who is in charge of the exhibition. Both he and I were anxious to avoid any publicity. Think of the scandal, Mr Holmes, if it became known that the Vatican cameos have been stolen! Mr Valentine was of the opinion that the thief might be willing to return the cameos – for a price, of course! – providing the transaction was handled with great delicacy. For this reason, he advised me to come to you as well as informing the police. He said you are by far the best private inquiry agent in the whole of England with many successes to your credit. Will you take the case, Mr Holmes?'

'Indeed I shall, Signor Graziani. It presents some most interesting features.'

'Of course, I must first inform the Holy Father about what has happened and ask his permission for you to undertake the investigation, although I have no doubt he will agree. I shall telegraph him immediately and then report the theft to Scotland Yard. Meanwhile, Sir, will you begin your inquiries so that no time is lost?'

'I shall do so at once,' Holmes assured him. 'But first I shall need a description of the cameos. You said there were three?'

'Yes, Mr Holmes. All of them are portraits of members of the Medici family, cut from agate and onyx. The smaller two are of Pietro and Giuliano, both sons of Lorenzo II Magnifico. The third and largest is of another son, Giovanni who later became Pope Leo X, and is particularly fine.[4] All three are contained in a box, covered with red leather, which has the papal coat of arms stamped in gilt on its lid.'

'Are the cameos framed?'

'Yes, yes, of course,' Signor Graziani said with a touch of impatience. 'The smaller two have narrow, gold settings.'

'And the third?'

'The frame of Giovanni de' Medici's cameo is a little more elaborate. It is also of gold and its upper part is set with seed pearls and a garnet. But the frames are of no great importance. It is the cameos which are the real treasures. They are irreplaceable! Now, Mr Holmes, before I leave for Scotland Yard, is there any more information you need to know?'

'Only your present address in London. Where are you staying?'

---

[4] Lorenzo de' Medici, known as the Magnificent (1449–1492), was virtual ruler of the republic of Florence. A statesman, scholar and connoisseur of art, he was patron of several Renaissance artists including Botticelli and Michelangelo.

Pietro de' Medici (1472–1503), known as Il Sfortunato, the Unfortunate, was Lorenzo's eldest son. He was expelled from Florence in 1494 and died in exile in southern Italy, having failed to reinstate himself in Florence.

Giuliano de' Medici (1479–1516) ruled Florence from 1512 to 1513 after his father's death. He was a cardinal and, after his brother was made Pope, joined him in Rome.

Giovanni de' Medici (1475–1521) was Lorenzo's second son. He later became Pope Leo X. He was the most extravagant of the Renaissance Popes, spending much of the papal wealth. In 1521, he excommunicated Martin Luther. Dr John F. Watson.

'At Claridge's hotel.'[5]

'Then I shall call on you there as soon as I have any news,' Holmes said, rising to his feet. As he escorted Signor Graziani to the door, he added, 'I must congratulate you, sir, on your excellent English.'

Our client's face flushed with pleasure at this compliment.

'I studied it at school, Mr Holmes. It was my favourite subject. It is also good for business for I regularly come to London to attend the sales of jewellery at your two great auction houses, Sotheby's and Christie's.'

'Was Signor Graziani right in thinking you may know who the thieves are?' I inquired as Holmes returned to his chair.

'Oh, there is no doubt about that,' he replied 'Their *modus operandi* gives them away as surely as if they had signed their names at the bottom of a confession. It is one of the curious factors about criminals, Watson: they are creatures of habit, especially thieves and burglars. Time and time again they will break into a house by the same means or tie up their victims using one particular type of knot. It is so in this case. The thieves, whom I shall refer to as Mr and Mrs Armstrong, one of their many aliases, always work together and their method never varies. They operate in public places, usually one of the

---

[5] J. Neil Gibson, the American millionaire, stayed at this hotel when on a visit to London. It was also where Mr Sherlock Holmes arranged to meet his agent, Martha, after the unmasking of the German spy, Von Bork. *Vide:* 'The Problem of Thor Bridge' and 'The Adventure of the Final Problem'. Dr John F. Watson.

railway termini such as St Pancras or Victoria, or in the foyers of large hotels, and their victims are always people carrying some form of luggage. Having chosen a likely person, Mrs Armstrong approaches their target and makes an innocent-seeming inquiry about the time or the location of the nearest cab rank. As she is very beautiful and well dressed, the victim, almost always a man, has no reason to be suspicious. Placing his valise or portmanteau on the ground, he raises his hat, takes out his pocket-watch or points out the direction. It is at this moment that Armstrong, who has been waiting nearby, moves forward and, while the victim's attention is distracted, picks up the bag and walks quickly away with it into the crowd. Mrs Armstrong then takes her leave and, before the gentleman realises what has happened, she, too, has disappeared.

'Of course, they have no means of knowing what is in the stolen luggage but, providing they have chosen a suitable target, it will usually contain something of value even if it is only clothing although occasionally they are lucky and find silver-backed hairbrushes or a pair of gold cuff-links. The contents are then sold either to a fence or a dealer.

'Sometimes there is no need for them to approach the victim directly. He may provide the opportunity himself by putting down his bag to look for a railway ticket or to sign his name in a hotel's register.'

'Or, in the case of Signor Graziani, to pay a cab driver,' I interjected.

'Exactly so, Watson. Now, having identified the

thieves, the next question to be answered is: what will the Armstrongs do once they discover Signor Graziani's valise contains not dress shirts or even cuff-links but a set of cameos? They are obviously not unintelligent. The fact that they have so far escaped arrest proves that, even though the police know all about their exploits. As soon as they see the cameos, they will realise they are extremely valuable. The leather box alone with the papal insignia stamped on its lid will convince them of that. They are therefore unlikely to approach their usual dealer but will look for a fence who handles the better class of stolen property such as antiques or *objets d'art*. The dealer will then sell the cameos to a collector or, as I think more likely in this case, he will, as Mr Valentine suggested, approach Signor Graziani through Mr Valentine himself, offering to return them at a price.'

'But how will the dealer know whom they belong to, Holmes?' I inquired.

'My dear Watson, isn't that obvious?' Holmes replied a little impatiently. 'The bag containing the cameos was stolen outside the British Museum where, as anyone who reads a newspaper will know, an exhibition of Renaissance art is due to be mounted. If the dealer knows his subject, and several of them are as knowledgeable about *objets de vertu* as any expert at Christie's or Sotheby's, he may well realise that the cameos belong to the Vatican collection and that therefore he can charge a ransom for their safe return.'

'Do you have any dealers in mind?'

'There are several operating in London, any one of whom is capable of handling such a transaction. But first I have two calls I must make, one to the nearest post office, the other to the British Museum.'

'Why a post office, Holmes?' I asked in some bewilderment for, although I could see the point of his need to consult Mr Valentine at the museum, the significance of the post office quite escaped me.

'To send a telegram, of course!' he replied, much amused by my obtuseness and, seizing up his hat and stick, he strode briskly out of the room.

II

It was several hours before he returned and, as soon as he entered, I was aware of a change in his demeanour. He was abstracted, as if he had something on his mind. Barely acknowledging my presence, he went straight to the window where he stood gazing down into the street, impatiently drumming his fingers on the glass. It was quite clear he was waiting for someone to call, almost certainly in consequence of the telegram he had sent, but I hesitated to question him in case I interrupted whatever train of thought he was following.

After about quarter of an hour, I heard him give an exclamation of satisfaction and I guessed his expected visitor had arrived. Seconds later there was a ring at the front door bell, followed by footsteps mounting the stairs, and the boy in buttons showed our caller into the room.

He was a short, stockily-built man; a costermonger, I assumed, from his shabby corduroy trousers and the red handkerchief about his neck. But he might have been

Holmes' long-lost brother from the warmth with which he greeted him.

'Sam Wegg!' he cried, shaking him vigorously by the hand. 'I am delighted you could come. Allow me to introduce my colleague, Dr Watson.'

'I 'ave 'eard of you, doctor,' Sam Wegg remarked, smiling broadly. 'I read that story of yours in the Christmas annual. Very enjoyable it was, too, sir.'[6]

I was flattered by his praise and disarmed also by his frank, good-natured expression.

'How is the family, Sam?' Holmes was asking, bustling him into a chair and offering him a glass of whisky and soda.[7]

'Flourishin' like the flowers of May.'

'And the business?'

'Couldn't be better, thanks to you, sir.' Turning to me, he continued, 'It was Mr 'Olmes as set me up as a costermonger. Afore that, I was a dip – a pickpocket to you, doctor.'

'And not a very successful one either,' Holmes interjected at which Sam Wegg laughed heartily.

'You're right there, sir! I've had me collar felt more than once and served me time in gaol. And then one day I

[6] 'A Study in Scarlet', the first of Dr Watson's accounts to be published, appeared in Beeton's Christmas annual in 1887. Dr John F. Watson.

[7] The soda water would have been supplied by a gasogene, an apparatus consisting of two glass globes which produced soda or aerated water by a chemical process. There are several references to it in the canon. *Vide:* 'A Scandal in Bohemia' and 'The Adventure of the Mazarin Stone'. Dr John F. Watson.

'ad the good fortune to try lifting Mr 'Olmes' pocketbook in Charing Cross Road. I say "good fortune", 'cos that's the way 'im and me first got acquainted. No sooner had I slipped me 'and into his coat than he grabbed me by the wrist and marched me into the nearest 'ostelry where he sat me down and struck a bargain with me over a pint of best ale. If I promised to give up dippin', 'e'd give me what 'e 'ad in 'is pocketbook to set me up in a respectable line of business. Ten quid it was, doctor! So, as I'd 'elped an uncle of mine out when I was a nipper on 'is fruit and vegetable barrer, that's the trade I chose. And I ain't looked back since. In return, I said I'd give Mr 'Olmes any information 'e needed about the East End rogues and villains.'

'And that is precisely why I asked you to call here today, Sam,' Holmes said. 'Who among the dealers would be willing to handle high-class stolen property?'

'What line in 'igh-class property?' Sam Wegg inquired.

'Jewellery, small antiques and works of art,' Holmes replied with an airy gesture of one hand.

'Well, there's old Solly Goldman down at 'Oundsditch and 'Arry Best in Poplar. But I know 'oo I'd go to first and that's Monty Gimble.'

'Ah, Gimble,' Holmes said softly as if the name were already familiar to him. 'He lives in Hampstead, does he not?'

'That's right, Mr 'Olmes, in a big 'ouse in 'Azelwood Road, name of Beaumont Grange. 'Is main interest is jewellery although 'e's been known to 'andle other stuff as well. The word got about that Lord Eglinton's table silver finished up in Gimble's 'ands. 'E's also known as Uncle to the nobs.'

'Uncle to the nobs?' I put in, puzzled by the phrase.

'Pawnbroker to the aristocracy, Dr Watson. Say a dook's down on 'is luck or a ladyship owes money to 'er dressmaker, then 'oo can they turn to for a bit of the ready? They can't 'ock the family jewels at the corner pawnshop, like you or me would do. So they takes 'em to Gimble 'oo loans them the cash, 'cept it's generally 'alf of what the sparklers are worth. Or if a client's really desperate, then Gimble takes the jewels out of their settin's and replaces 'em with fakes which 'e cuts 'imself to look so like the real thing that only an expert can tell the difference. They say the Duchess of Bexford's diamond terara is Gimble's work.'

'Is that so?' Holmes murmured with pretended nonchalance which evidently did not deceive Sam Wegg for he glanced shrewdly at my old friend.

'Now see 'ere, Mr 'Olmes,' he said. 'I don't know what you 'ave in mind but if you're thinkin' of tryin' anythin' on with Gimble, then you'd best think again. That 'ouse of 'is is like a fortress – bars on every winder and bolts on every door. Not even a cat could get in. And ever since the Potter gang tried burglin' 'is drum,[8] 'e's taken on a bodyguard, name of Billy 'Obson, 'oo frisks every one afore they're let in. Know 'im do you, Mr 'Olmes?'

[8] A 'drum' is a slang term for a building, such as a house or shop. Dr John F. Watson.

'Battling Billy, the heavyweight bruiser from Bermondsey?'

'The very one, sir.'

'I have seen him in the ring.'[9]

'Then you'll know 'e ain't the sort to trifle with. And it's not just 'is dooks[10] as wants watchin'. 'E's armed as well; a Smith and Wesson, so I've 'eard, which 'e ain't afraid of usin' neither.'

'Thank you for the warning, Sam. I shall certainly bear it in mind. What else do you know about Gimble?'

'Only that 'e lives like a 'ermit in the one downstairs room opening off the 'all; works there, eats there, sleeps there.' Giving Holmes a knowing, sideways glance, he added, 'If you're interested, Mr 'Olmes, that's where 'e also keeps 'is safe.'

If Holmes was indeed interested in this piece of information, he gave no sign, his lean features remaining as inscrutable as a Red Indian's.

'What about servants?' he inquired.

'None 'cept for Billy 'Obson. Gimble's as tight as a clam over 'is business affairs. 'E don't trust nobody. And that's all I knows, Mr 'Olmes. I 'ope I've been of use.'

'You have indeed, Sam,' Holmes replied, rising and holding out his hand. 'I am most grateful to you.'

'I'm only payin' back what I owes you,' Sam Wegg

---

[9] One of Mr Sherlock Holmes' interests was boxing, a sport he took part in while at college. There are several references to his skill as a boxer within the canon. *Vide* among others: 'The Five Orange Pips' and 'The Sign of Four'. Dr John F. Watson.

[10] 'Dukes' is a slang term for 'fists'. Dr John F. Watson.

replied as, shaking hands with both of us, he took his leave.

'Were you thinking of breaking into Gimble's house?' I inquired after the door closed behind him.

'Not any longer,' Holmes replied cheerfully. 'I shall have to devise some other stratagem instead. Perhaps a direct approach might be the best solution. I shall put my mind to the problem. And now, my dear fellow, if you care to pass me the *Morning Post*, I shall continue with the report on the trial of Emily Moorhouse which Signor Graziani's arrival interrupted.'

With that, I had to remain content. For the rest of the day, Holmes made no further reference either to the Vatican cameos or to any plans he might have made for their recovery.

III

It was not until breakfast the following morning that Holmes spoke again of the inquiry and that was only in a negligent manner.

'I suppose, Watson,' said he, rising from the table, 'that before I go any further in the case, I should call on Signor Graziani at his hotel and find out if our little enterprise has the blessing of the Pope.'

'Do you want me to come with you?' I asked.

'There is no need for that,' he replied. 'It will not take long. I should be back within the hour.'

In the event, it was nearly half-past four in the afternoon before he returned with the well-satisfied air of a man who has completed an excellent day's work.

'We have crossed one hurdle, Watson,' he announced, rubbing his hands together with evident relish. 'The Pope had indeed given us permission to proceed with the inquiry. I have also prepared a lure which I believe will draw Gimble into our net.' Taking a small, velvet-covered jeweller's box from his pocket, he placed it on the table and opened back its lid. 'And there is the bait! What do you say to that? Magnificent, is it not?'

Approaching the table, I saw lying in the box a most beautiful brooch in the shape of a butterfly, with sapphires for its eyes and the coloured markings on its wings picked out in an intricate pattern of diamonds, rubies and emeralds.

'It is exquisite, Holmes!' I exclaimed. 'How on earth did you acquire it?'

'Shall we say that a former client of mine, a titled lady of great distinction for whom I was once able to render a small service, has agreed to lend it to me? And here,' he continued, taking a visiting card from his pocket and laying it down beside the box, 'is the hook on which the bait will be hung.'

I picked it up to examine it and saw that it was engraved with the name Sir William Fox Hardy, with an address in Maidstone, Kent.

'I asked a printer I know in Clerkenwell to run it off for me this afternoon,' Holmes explained.

'Who is Sir William Fox Hardy?' I inquired.

'You, Watson,' he replied to my great astonishment. 'On your behalf, or rather on Sir William's, I took the liberty of sending a telegram to Gimble, requesting an urgent appointment with him at six o'clock this evening. As I omitted to include an address to which he could send a refusal, you will duly arrive at Beaumont Grange at the stated time on the assumption that Gimble will see you, as I have no doubt he will.'

'I shall arrive?' I repeated in some alarm. 'You mean I must go alone?'

Holmes gave a chuckle.

'Have no fear of that, Watson,' he assured me. 'In order for it to succeed, my plan involves the two of us. However, you shall take the leading role in the drama. Like Fortinbras in *Hamlet*, I shall be merely a supporting player who arrives on the scene shortly before the curtain falls.

'And now for the play itself and its main character – you, my dear fellow. In view of your predilection for betting,[11] I thought it most suitable to cast you as Sir William who, because of your losses at the race course, are in urgent need of money. Several creditors are pressing you for payment, in particular your bookmaker who is threatening you with bankruptcy if you fail to settle your debts by the end of the week. Having heard that Gimble is willing to lend money, you have come to London this very afternoon, bringing with you your late wife's diamond brooch as security against a loan.

'As for the details of the plot, you will take a cab to Beaumont Grange, dismissing the driver at the front door. Having rung the bell and given your card to Hobson, you will then be ushered into Gimble's presence. It is at this point that we have to improvise for we do not know if Hobson will remain in the room while the transaction is taking place or whether he will retire to the hall and keep guard on the door. The latter seems the more likely: Sam spoke of Gimble's love of secrecy. I am therefore inclined to

[11] See footnote to page 65.

think that he will prefer to conduct his business in private. Although Sam also told us that all the exterior doors are locked and bolted, it seems improbable that, having let you into the house, Hobson will go to the trouble of rebolting the front door behind you when he knows that you will shortly be leaving and he himself is standing guard in the hall. You follow my reasoning, Watson?'

'Yes, indeed, Holmes. But I still do not understand your part in all this. A little earlier you said that you will enter the scene only in the last few minutes . . .'

'And that is still my intention. I shall accompany you in the cab as far as the gates of Beaumont Grange where I shall alight and make my way on foot to the house. Once there, I shall quietly pick the lock on the front door and let myself into the hall.'

'Just a moment, Holmes!' I expostulated, seeing a major flaw in his stratagem. 'As you yourself have just said, Hobson will be on guard. How will you get past him? He will be armed, don't forget.'

'I am well aware of that. The simple answer is he will not be there,' Holmes said coolly.

'Not there? Then where will he be?'

'In Gimble's room, attending to Sir William who has unfortunately collapsed with a heart attack.' Seeing my expression, Holmes burst out laughing. 'Don't look so astounded, Watson! You are, after all, a doctor. It should not be past your capabilities to fake the symptoms. As Gimble, who now must be in his seventies, will not be strong enough to lift you by himself, he will therefore call on Hobson to assist him. While the two of them are thus engaged, I shall enter the house, the scurry and confusion resulting from your collapse covering any noise I might make in doing so. As I do not know what type of lock is fitted to the front door, I may take several minutes to open it. I trust you can keep up your charade long enough for me to do so.'

'You may rely on me, Holmes,' I assured him. Now that he had explained the plan, I felt much easier in my mind. Indeed, I was almost looking forward to the adventure. However, one small doubt remained which I hastened to put to him.

'How will you know when Hobson has left the hall?'

'Oh, that will pose no problem,' said he carelessly. 'Every front door, however stout, has its weak places where one can hear, and indeed see, what is going on behind it. I am referring, of course, to the keyhole and the letter box. The latter gives one a clear, if narrow viewpoint, once the flap is opened.'

'And then, I assume, you will enter Gimble's room and force him to hand over the stolen cameos?' I asked, still unsure about this part of the plot. 'Do you wish me to go armed?'

'Certainly not! Have you forgotten Sam's warning that Hobson searches all visitors before they are allowed to enter? Besides, it will not be necessary.' Consulting his pocket watch, Holmes added, 'No more questions, Watson. There is not time. I must look out my set of pick-locks and then we must shortly set off for Hampstead.'

IV

For most of the journey, Holmes kept me entertained with one of his brilliant discourses on a variety of subjects ranging from the migration of birds to the operas of Herr Wagner, his purpose being, I supposed, to take my mind off the events to come. It was only when the cab was toiling up the hill towards Hampstead that he referred again to his plan, reminding me to keep Gimble and Hobson occupied for as long as possible and to play the part of Sir William, a man desperate for money, to the best of my ability. Soon afterwards, when we were a little short of the gates of Beaumont Grange, he shook me by the hand and wished me luck before, having ordered the driver to stop, he alighted, leaving the cab to go on without him. The last glimpse I had of my old friend was of him vaulting over a fence and disappearing into the shrubbery of the front garden. The next moment, the hansom had turned in through the gates and I saw Beaumont Grange for the first time.

It was a large, ugly house built of dark red brick, with a low roof of grey slates which, despite the sunshine of that June evening, gave it a malign air as if it were crouching there, ready to spring on anyone rash enough to approach too close. The weed-grown drive and the neglected garden, composed entirely of dark-leaved laurel and holly bushes, heightened this impression of glowering suspicion.

As Holmes had instructed, I paid off the cabby and, with a feeling of trepidation mingled with excited anticipation, I mounted the steps to the front door where I rang the bell. Almost at once, I heard the sound of keys being turned and bolts being drawn and the door opened to reveal a huge man with the coarse, battered features of a prize-fighter: Billy Hobson, I assumed. He was incongruously dressed in a butler's sober attire which ill suited his broad chest and massive shoulders. A bulge in his right-hand pocket indicated where he was carrying his gun.

'I am Sir William Fox Hardy and I have an appointment with Mr Gimble,' I said, trying to speak normally, although I was much alarmed, for Holmes' sake as well as my own, by his vast bulk. 'Here is my card.'

He made no reply as he took it, merely indicating with a jerk of his head that I was to enter. No sooner had I crossed the threshold and the door had closed behind me, than he ran his hands expertly over my torso, removing the jeweller's box which held the brooch and which he examined before returning it to me. Then with another gesture, of his thumb this time, he invited me to follow him across the hall to a door on which he knocked. A faint, hoarse voice having called out 'Enter!', he flung open the door and ushered me inside and then departed.

For the first few seconds, I stood there motionless, trying to compose myself after my alarming encounter with Hobson and straining my ears to catch the slightest sound coming from the hall of bolts being closed. At the same time, I looked about me to familiarise myself with both the room and its occupant.

Knowing Gimble's interest in jewellery and antiques, I was surprised to see that the room, though large, was sparsely furnished with a few shabby chairs and a sofa covered in worn brown leather. A wooden bedstead, on which were heaped some rough blankets, was pushed against the far wall. Nearby stood two other items which seemed out of place even in this mean setting. One was a large iron safe, painted green, the other a work bench littered with tools and equipment which I took to be the implements of Gimble's trade as a jeweller.

At first glance, Gimble himself was also a disappointment. He was an elderly, white-haired little man, very hunched about the shoulders from the years he had spent stooped over as he cut or examined precious gems at close quarters. There was a myopic look about his eyes as well which also suggested such skilled and delicate work. Indeed, at first sight, the general impression was of a mild, inoffensive benevolence.

However, as I crossed the room towards the desk where he was sitting, I was aware that behind this benign facade lurked a much more malevolent nature. The pupils of his eyes were as sharp and as hard as needles, putting me in mind of a snake's cold, fixed stare.

'Sir William Fox Hardy?' said he in a low, harsh tone. 'Pray be seated.'

As I took the upright chair facing him, he held out a skinny hand, not to shake mine as I had first supposed, but to take the jeweller's box which I was still clutching. It was quite clear from his abrupt manner that any transaction between us was to be conducted as speedily as possible and I wondered with some alarm how I was to extend these preliminaries in order to give Holmes time to reach the house and inspect the lock on the front door.

Opening the box, Gimble took out the brooch and held it up to catch the light from the window; for a few seconds, his demeanour changed, his features softening and his eyes taking on an unwonted tenderness. But the look vanished as quickly as it had come, the pupils growing small and hard again, his lips clamping shut into a thin line. Picking up a jeweller's eyeglass, he began to examine the brooch minutely stone by stone.

A little unnerved by his silence, I ventured to remark, 'It is very fine, is it not? How much will you offer me on its security?'

'Two hundred pounds,' he said abruptly.

Remembering Holmes' advice that I was to act in character, I decided it would be opportune to protest.

'Is that all? It is surely worth more than that?'

'Then take it elsewhere,' he rasped, thrusting the brooch towards me across the desk.

'Could you not raise it to two hundred and fifty? It belonged to my late wife.'

'I am not in the business of buying sentiment, Sir William,' said he. 'It is a commodity which has no value on any market.'

He had begun to push back his chair as if to indicate the interview was over. I, too, half rose to my feet, my throat dry with apprehension for the moment had come when I had to simulate a coronary seizure. Feeling my heart begin to pound at this prospect, sending the blood racing through my veins, I deliberately succumbed to these giddy sensations and, giving a loud cry, I clutched at my throat and toppled sideways on to the floor.

Lying there on the shabby carpet which smelt unpleasantly of old dust, I kept my eyes closed as part of the deception. I therefore had to rely on my ears alone in order to follow the subsequent events. I heard Gimble give an exclamation of alarm and then the sound of his feet hurrying past my head as he scuttled across the room. Seconds later, the door was opened and Gimble's hoarse voice called out, 'Hobson, come here at once! Sir William is taken ill!'

The footsteps returned towards the desk, a double set this time, Gimble's lighter and less certain tread accompanied by Hobson's heavier gait. Although I still kept my eyes closed, I was aware of the latter's huge frame bent over me and felt his hand fumble clumsily at my neck as he loosened my collar. A little further off, I could hear Gimble's voice, shrill with anxiety, crying out, 'You must fetch a doctor at once!'

As it was imperative that Hobson should not leave the room while Holmes was attempting to pick the lock on the front door, I thought it prudent to feign a partial recovery.

Groaning a little, I opened my eyes and attempted to sit up.

'No, no!' I gasped. 'There is no need for a doctor. It is only a mild attack, such as I have suffered before. Give me a little time to recover and I shall soon be well again.'

With Hobson's assistance, I staggered shakily to my feet and felt about for somewhere to sit down, putting all my weight on Hobson's arm so that he was obliged to support me.

It was while he was bending down to lower me into a chair that the blow was struck although, at the time, it happened so quickly that I was conscious only of a rush of footsteps behind me followed by Hobson's bellow of surprised outrage as he was whirled about to confront Holmes. The next second, Holmes' left fist came flashing upwards to strike Hobson's chin with a dull, sickening thud.[12] He went down like a felled ox, first to his knees before he slumped slowly forwards to lie face down upon the floor.

'Take his gun, Watson!' Holmes cried and, as I hastened

---

[12] Mr Sherlock Holmes used a straight left blow to knock out Mr Woodley, a 'slogging ruffian', who attacked him during his inquiries into the case involving the solitary cyclist. Dr John F. Watson.

to retrieve it from Hobson's pocket, he added, 'Keep Hobson covered, my dear fellow, while Mr Gimble and I exchange a few pleasantries.'

Grey with terror, Gimble sank down on his seat behind the desk, while Holmes, in a leisurely manner, drew up a chair and sat down facing him.

'Now, Mr Gimble,' he began in a pleasant, easy tone, 'you will oblige me by handing over the key to your safe where I believe the Vatican cameos are kept.'

'I know nothing about any cameos,' Gimble protested. 'All I have in there is a few pieces of jewellery which I am holding for clients of mine.'

'Then you will have no objection if I inspect them,' Holmes replied.

'I have every objection!' Gimble, who had recovered a little from the initial shock, retorted. 'Who are you, sir?'

'My name is Sherlock Holmes and I am here on the express invitation of His Holiness the Pope.'

It was evident that Gimble was familiar with Holmes' name for I saw his top lip draw upwards in a snarl like a cur brought to bay. But he was too old a dog to offer any resistance. Taking a key from his pocket, he handed it to Holmes who, crossing the room, unlocked the door of the iron safe. A few seconds later, he returned, carrying a shallow box covered in worn red leather with a coat of arms stamped in gilt on its lid. Setting it down on the desk, he opened it to reveal its white silk interior in which were lying the Vatican cameos, depicting three men in profile, each one cut with superb delicacy from some translucent semiprecious stone. Two of them were framed in a narrow band of gold. But the central cameo, which was larger than the others, was obviously the most valuable for its setting was more ornate, the upper portion of the frame widening out to form an arabesque of fretted gold, ornamented with seed pearls and a single red stone which glittered in the light like a fiery Cyclopean eye.

'Signor Graziani was right,' Holmes murmured. 'They are indeed exquisite.'

He was about to add some other comment when he was interrupted by the sound of wheels drawing to a halt outside the house, followed shortly afterwards by a loud knocking on the front door.

'I believe my visitors have arrived,' Holmes remarked and strolled out into the hall, leaving me to guard Gimble and the comatose figure of Billy Hobson and to wonder who these visitors could be.

The mystery was soon solved when Holmes re-entered the room, accompanied by Inspector Lestrade and three uniformed officers.

'I trust this evidence you spoke about this morning is enough to . . .' Lestrade was in the middle of saying, when he came to a sudden halt and stared about him, his sharp, ferrety features expressing utter astonishment at the scene which confronted him and which to him must have seemed quite bizarre. I saw his eyes dart swiftly from the open safe to the desk on which were lying the diamond brooch and the leather-covered box containing the cameos. From these, his gaze passed to

Gimble, cowering in his chair, and then to the prostrate form of Billy Hobson. Finally, it came to rest upon myself, still standing there with Hobson's revolver in my hand. Made suddenly aware of the ridiculous figure I must be cutting, I sheepishly lowered the gun and placed it on the desk.

'Evidence, Inspector?' Holmes was saying, striding forward. 'Here are the cameos which I have no doubt Signor Graziani will identify as those which were stolen from him outside the British Museum, and which both Dr Watson and I can testify were found in Gimble's possession. If you need further evidence, I suggest you examine the rest of the jewellery in the safe. Most of it was no doubt legally acquired but I am convinced that among it you will also find stolen jewellery which Gimble was proposing either to break up and sell as separate stones or to return to the rightful owners on payment of a considerable fee, as I believe he intended doing with the cameos. They are a priceless part of the Vatican collection, for the safe return of which the papal authorities would have been prepared to pay handsomely. Am I not correct, sir?' Holmes demanded, turning to Gimble.

'I have nothing to say,' he retorted in his rasping voice.

'We will see about that when we get you to Scotland Yard,' Lestrade told him grimly. 'I am arresting you now on the charge of receiving property knowing it was stolen. Reynolds, take him outside,' he ordered, addressing one of the uniformed constables. 'The rest of you deal with the other man.'

As his subordinates hastened to carry out his orders, one seizing Gimble by the arm and escorting him out of the room, the other two struggling to lift Hobson's huge, recumbent frame and drag it into the hall, Lestrade turned to my old friend.

'Well, Mr Holmes, I think I owe you an apology. When you called at the Yard this morning, I confess I was a little sceptical of your story. Me and my colleagues have been trying for years to find the evidence to put Gimble behind bars but he's always proved too fly for us. As for the Armstrongs . . .'

'You have arrested them?' Holmes interrupted eagerly.

'They have been taken in for questioning. I followed your advice and had my men look for them in the places you suggested. They were picked up this afternoon at two thirty in Victoria station. You may speak to them when you call at the Yard a little later, as we have arranged. And now, before I go, I had better make sure this safe is locked. I intend returning later to collect up its contents and go through Gimble's papers. In the meantime, I shall leave Reynolds on duty here.'

Shutting and locking the safe, he pocketed the key before adding with an unexpected twinkle in his eyes, 'I shall leave the task of taking charge of the cameos to you, sir, seeing as how it was your expertise which recovered them.'

'That was magnanimous of him, was it not, Holmes?' I asked as the door closed behind him.

Holmes gave an amused chuckle.

'Oh, Lestrade has his good points,' he conceded. 'As

I have remarked before, he is the best of a bad lot,[13] although when I saw him earlier today, it took a great deal of persuasion before he finally agreed to come here at the time I suggested. It was only when I promised him he would receive all the credit for the case that he consented. He is certainly in need of it after his bungling of the Merrivale affair. As I told him at the time, it was quite obvious the hall porter was the culprit. Come, Watson. It is time we also left. Before we arrive at Scotland Yard, we must first collect Signor Graziani from Claridge's. His evidence will be vital in identifying the cameos.'

'Signor Graziani will be delighted when he hears the cameos have been found,' I remarked.

'No doubt. But I shall keep that particular piece of information to myself until we are at Scotland Yard.'

'Why, Holmes?' I asked, a little surprised at this decision.

'Because I can never resist a touch of the theatricals,'[14] he replied lightly, as he picked up the two boxes containing the cameos and the diamond brooch and slipped them into his pocket. 'I shall merely tell him that the police need a few more facts from him.' Knowing my old friend's love of the dramatic, I assumed he would produce the cameos as a final flourish so that all of us, including Lestrade,

---

[13] Mr Sherlock Holmes makes this comment in 'A Study in Scarlet'. Dr John F. Watson.

[14] There are several references in the canon to Mr Sherlock Holmes' love of the dramatic, among them his own admission that he could not resist a dramatic situation. *Vide*: 'The Adventure of the Mazarin Stone'. Dr John F. Watson.

could witness Signor Graziani's astonishment and joy when the cameos were returned to him.

We left shortly afterwards, walking the short distance to Heath Street where we took a four-wheeler to Claridge's hotel. Here Holmes called briefly to collect Signor Graziani who, as he joined us in the cab, expressed his disappointment that the cameos had not yet been recovered. Although I offered my condolences, I smiled inwardly at the thought of the unexpected surprise which lay in store for him.

V

On our arrival at Scotland Yard, it was evident that, when Holmes had consulted Lestrade that morning, he had also arranged with him in what order the subsequent events were to take place for, when we were shown into Lestrade's office, it was empty apart from the Inspector himself.

After he had invited us to sit down, Signor Graziani remarked, 'I believe you wish me to add to my statement, Inspector. As I have already told you all I know about the theft, I cannot see . . .'

He broke off as there came a knock upon the door and a constable ushered in a man and a woman – the Armstrongs, I assumed. The woman was indeed beautiful, with a delicate cast of features which would persuade most men of her innocuousness. Her companion was more insignificant, his nondescript appearance making it easy for him to slip away unnoticed into a crowd with the victim's luggage.

As they entered, Signor Graziani turned to look at them but I could see no sign of recognition either on their part or on his. My supposition was proved correct when Lestrade, having questioned them on this very point, received positive denials from all three of them. The Armstrongs were then taken away and Gimble was brought into the room in their place. Once again Lestrade asked both Gimble and Signor Graziani if they had ever seen each other before and, once again, each denied it, our client with a shrug of his shoulders which expressed a growing impatience at this apparently useless parade of suspects.

'I really must protest, Inspector . . .' he began as Gimble and his attendant constable turned towards the door.

It was at this point that Holmes interrupted the proceedings to everyone's astonishment, including Lestrade's.

Pulling forward a chair, he addressed Gimble.

'Sit down,' he ordered in a masterful manner which brooked no refusal. As the man obeyed, Holmes drew two objects from his pocket and laid them down on the desk. One was a jeweller's eye-glass, the same one, I assumed, that Gimble had used when he had inspected the diamond brooch and which Holmes must have taken from the man's room. The other was a tiny packet of tissue paper which, when unwrapped, revealed a square-cut red stone, so similar in size and colour to the garnet set into the frame of the largest of the Vatican cameos that for a moment I was utterly bewildered.

How had Holmes contrived to remove it? And to what purpose?

Hardly had these thoughts crossed my mind than he again reached into his pocket and this time produced the leather-covered case containing the Vatican treasures which he also placed upon the desk. Opening back its lid, he revealed its contents.

The effect of this dramatic display, conducted in complete silence, varied from person to person. Lestrade, who knew about their recovery, gave a satisfied smile as if he alone were responsible for their safe return while Gimble, on being confronted once again by the evidence of his guilt, groaned aloud and sank lower into his chair. Signor Graziani was not as jubilant as I had expected. With a cry of astonishment rather than delight, he leant forward to inspect them more closely. For my own part, my bewilderment was only compounded for the cameo depicting Giovanni de' Medici still bore the red stone in the centre of its frame.

What purpose, therefore, was the other single stone meant to serve?

'You have found them!' Signor Graziani was crying out. 'I cannot believe it!'

Holmes chose to ignore these exclamations. Turning to Gimble and handing him the jeweller's eyeglass, he remarked, 'As you are the expert, I should be much obliged if you would examine the two stones and tell me which of them is the substitute. And, I warn you, do not try to trick me. I should not wish you to add deception to your other crimes.'

'There is no need for that,' Gimble replied, waving aside the eyeglass. 'I know without needing to examine them which is which. The single stone is the substitute. I cut it myself yesterday when the cameos were brought to me.'

'By the Armstrongs?' Lestrade put in.

'Yes; I cannot deny it,' Gimble replied, his upper lip once more lifting into that snarl of impotent defiance.

'And therefore,' Holmes remarked, once more taking charge of the interview, 'we may assume that the stone set in the cameo frame is the original? Take care for we can have it examined by an expert jeweller.'

'That, too, is true,' Gimble admitted after a moment's hesitation. Holmes, who seemed not entirely satisfied with this answer, pressed on with his questioning. 'It is a ruby, is it not?'

'I do not know.' Gimble began in a trembling voice.

'Oh, I believe you do, Mr Gimble. Moreover, you know exactly what precious stone it is. Come, sir. Confess the truth. It is the jewel known as the Medici ruby, is it not?'

'The Medici ruby!' Signor Graziani broke in. 'That is absurd, Mr Holmes! It is nothing more valuable than a garnet as all the written records attest.'

'So I understand,' Holmes replied nonchalantly. 'Earlier today I spent several hours in the British Museum's Reading Room researching the subject of the Vatican treasures. As you quite rightly state, the jewel is thought to be only a garnet. As for the Medici ruby, it disappeared after Lorenzo's death in 1492 when his eldest son Pietro took over his father's role as virtual ruler of Florence. But he lacked Lorenzo's courage and, when the French invaded Italy,[15] he tried to buy them off by offering them several fortresses as well as the cities of Pisa and Leghorn. As a result of this treachery, Pietro and the rest of the Medici family were banished from Florence and the mob was allowed to loot their palace. It was then that the Medici ruby vanished along with other priceless possessions. However, we know that Giovanni, who later became Pope Leo X, was in the city at that time because he managed to rescue some valuable manuscripts from the pillage. I suggest he may also have saved other heirlooms, including the Medici ruby. Later, when the Medicis were allowed to return from exile, I believe Giovanni had the stone re-cut so that it could not be identified and had it set into the frame of his cameo, claiming it was nothing more precious than a garnet. On his death in 1521, it passed into the Vatican's possession along with the other cameos.'

'An interesting history lesson, Mr Holmes,' Signor Graziani observed with a smile. 'But what are you trying to prove?'

'I agree,' Lestrade put in. 'Where is all this talk of Popes and Medicis leading to? The Armstrongs have admitted stealing the valise and Gimble has confessed to receiving the cameos knowing they were stolen. As far as I am concerned, the case is over and done with. Nothing

---

[15] The French under Charles VIII invaded Italy in September 1494. Dr John F. Watson.

remains to be done except to charge all three of them and see them brought to trial.'

'No, it is not quite over yet,' Holmes corrected him. 'There is one other person who is as guilty as the others.'

'I suppose you are speaking of Billy Hobson?' Lestrade replied. 'Well, you could be right, Mr Holmes. He must have known Gimble was dealing in stolen property. If I can prove that, he could be charged as an accessory.'

'The person I am referring to is not Billy Hobson.'

'Then who is it, in heaven's name?'

Lestrade sounded both angry and incredulous, as if suspecting Holmes of trying deliberately to confuse him.

'Signor Graziani, of course,' Holmes said calmly.

Signor Graziani immediately jumped to his feet, his face dark with fury.

'This is an outrage, Mr Holmes!' he exclaimed, his voice trembling with rage. 'How dare you accuse me of stealing the Vatican cameos! I have done everything in my power to ensure their safe return.'

'I do not doubt that for a moment, Signor Graziani. It was never your intention to allow such treasures, which you yourself described as exquisite, to pass out of the Vatican's possession. Besides, they are too well known to be sold on. The plan, of course, was to offer to sell them back for a considerable sum of money, a ransom which I am sure the Vatican authorities would have agreed to pay and which would have been shared out between the four of you. That part of the crime was perfectly straightforward.

'But there was another aspect to the theft which was more complex and devious. It concerned the so-called garnet which was set into the frame of the Giovanni cameo. You knew about the Medici ruby, Signor Graziani. As an expert in Renaissance jewellery, you could not have remained ignorant of it. I suggest that when the curator of the Vatican collection asked you to examine the cameos prior to your taking them to London, you realised the gem was not a garnet as was generally believed but was, in fact, a ruby – quite possibly the Medici ruby. Both stones are red although a garnet is of a darker colour. However, anyone who is not an expert could easily mistake the one for the other as I believe happened in this case. And even if it were not the Medici ruby, it is still an extremely valuable precious stone which, with a little judicious re-cutting and resetting, in a ring, say, or a brooch, would fetch a handsome price on the market, money which you and Gimble would divide between you.'

'In your eagerness to expound your theory, you have forgotten to ask yourself one important question, Mr Holmes,' Signor Graziani said, smiling contemptuously.

'And what is that?'

'How I became acquainted with Mr Gimble. Until you can prove that, your accusation is based on nothing more than speculation. I suggest you put it once more to the test by again asking Gimble if he has ever seen me before.'

As he spoke, he turned towards the elderly dealer, directing this last remark straight at him.

Before Gimble could answer, Holmes interjected, 'He may not have met you, Signor Graziani, but he has certainly been in correspondence with you. Why else would he be in possession of this?'

Reaching once more into his pocket, Holmes drew out a small oblong of white pasteboard which he laid face down on Lestrade's desk before turning it over, with the air of a whist player producing the ace of trumps, to reveal the other side. As Lestrade and I crowded close to look at it, I saw it was a business card bearing Signor Graziani's name and address as well as a few words in Italian which I took to mean 'Dealer in Precious Stones'.

At the sight of it, Signor Graziani gave a great cry of mingled horror and rage.

'You old fool!' he screamed at Gimble. 'I told you to get rid of it!'

In his fury, he seemed about to rush at Gimble and strike him but when Holmes stepped forward, he sank down on to his chair, a broken man, and covered his face with his hands.

'That is proof enough for me,' Lestrade remarked, picking up the card and casting a glance of deep disfavour at Signor Graziani who was rocking to and fro in an excess of despair.

Motioning with his head, the Inspector indicated to the constable to take both men away.

When the door had closed behind them, Lestrade turned to my old friend.

'As a matter of evidence, Mr Holmes, where did you find Signor Graziani's card?'

'It was inside Gimble's safe,' Holmes replied. 'No doubt he thought it would be secure there. But I had already begun to suspect Signor Graziani's part in the crime even before I discovered the card.'

'How was that?' Lestrade asked. 'For I must confess it had not crossed my mind he was guilty.'

'Several factors,' my old friend replied. 'When Signor Graziani called on me for help in recovering the cameos, one part of his account immediately struck me as suspicious. It was his statement that the valise had been stolen outside the British Museum. Although the crime was undoubtedly the work of the Armstrongs, I was a little puzzled as to why they were operating in that area when their usual haunts are railway stations or hotel foyers.'

'They may have just been passing the museum, not intending to commit an offence, and simply took advantage of the situation,' Lestrade pointed out.

'Quite so,' Holmes agreed. 'Had that been the only suspicious element in the case, I would, like you, have dismissed it as merely an opportunist crime. However, there were two other factors to consider. Firstly, it was on Signor Graziani's advice that the cameos were chosen for the exhibition, as he himself admitted. Secondly, when I asked him to describe them, he seemed strangely reluctant to give me any information about the frames. Indeed, I had to question him directly. Even then he was dismissive, insisting that two of the frames were not very valuable, being just plain gold, while the third, the one of Giovanni de' Medici, though possessing some artistic merit, was set with stones of no great value either.

'What he omitted to mention, and I discovered for myself when I went to the Reading Room of the British Museum and studied the subject of the Vatican collection, was the fact that the frame of the Giovanni cameo was the work of Andrea del Verrocchio, the Renaissance artist and goldsmith,[16] and a rare example of his genius. For this reason alone, the cameo was considered priceless although, as Signor Graziani himself stated, the stones set in it were described as being merely seed pearls and a garnet.

'But why had Signor Graziani failed to speak of this connection with Verrocchio? As an expert in Renaissance jewellery, he must have known of it. With this question in mind, I read further into the history of the Medici family and discovered those facts I have already mentioned concerning the disappearance of the Medici ruby.

'It was then my suspicions began to crystallise. If Signor Graziani had been so reticent about the real importance and value of the Giovanni frame, was there something else about it he was trying to conceal from me? As neither the

---

[16] Andrea del Verrocchio (1435–1488) was a goldsmith, sculptor and painter. Leonardo da Vinci was one of his pupils. The Medicis, who were his patrons, appointed him curator of antiquities in their palace in Florence. As well as supplying the family with paintings and sculptures, he also designed costumes and decorated armour for their pageants. Among his works are a terracotta bust of Giuliano de' Medici and the magnificent bronze and porphyry tomb of Pietro and Giovanni de' Medici in which Lorenzo and Giuliano were also later buried. Dr John F. Watson.

gold nor the seed pearls had any great intrinsic value in themselves, I was therefore left with the garnet. It then struck me that this so-called garnet could, in fact, be the Medici ruby.

'Once I had come to that conclusion, my suspicions regarding the Armstrongs' presence outside the British Museum had a logical explanation. They were there as part of a conspiracy, set up here in London by Gimble, who had hired the Armstrongs to commit the theft, but organised by Signor Graziani in Rome. The plan was to steal the cameos, remove the ruby and replace it with a garnet before selling them back to the Vatican. As stealing the cameos from the hotel would have been difficult, it was decided the theft would have to take place when Signor Graziani took them to the British Museum.

'As for Signor Graziani's acquaintance with Gimble, I suggest Graziani heard of him when he was in London, attending one of the sales at Sotheby's or Christie's. Although the jewellery trade is international, it is limited to a comparatively few specialists, some of whom, like Gimble, are prepared to deal with stolen gems. Having acquired Gimble's name and address, Graziani wrote to him, enclosing his card. The conspiracy was then set up between them.

'I suggest, Lestrade, that when you question the four of them, you put my theory to them. I am convinced that they will admit its truth.'

In the event, Holmes' speculations were proved correct. When the trial came to court, all of them pleaded guilty not only to the charges of theft and the receipt of stolen property but also to conspiracy to rob. They were sentenced to varying terms of imprisonment, the Armstrongs receiving the shortest as their part in the plot was of less importance while Signor Graziani, who had organised the conspiracy, received five years. Gimble, however, was given the longest term for, as Holmes had predicted, when Lestrade searched his safe, he found other pieces of stolen jewellery, including the Countess of Cleveland's pearl earrings and the Honourable Mrs Ponsonby Foulke's emerald necklace.

Because of the guilty pleas, neither Holmes nor I was required to give evidence at the trial and therefore the part he had played in the investigation was not widely publicised, as he himself preferred. In consequence, Lestrade gained all the credit for its successful outcome.

But he was accorded a personal letter of thanks from His Holiness the Pope which, at the time of my writing this account, he still has in his possession.[17]

As my readers will be aware, not long after the conclusion of this case, Holmes became associated with the Baskerville inquiry, in which I played a not insignificant role.[18]

---

[17] In 1895, Mr Sherlock Holmes was asked by the same Pope, Leo XIII, to investigate the sudden death of Cardinal Tosca, a case of which Dr John H. Watson has left no written account. *Vide*: 'The Adventure of Black Peter'. Dr John F. Watson.

[18] Mr Sherlock Holmes asked Dr Watson to take over the Baskerville investigation when he apparently returned to London. Dr John F. Watson.

For this reason, it was not until much later that I had the leisure to look out my notes on the Vatican cameo inquiry and to expand them into this full-length narrative. By that time, however, interest in the case, accounts of which had been widely reported in the press, had died down and, rather than bring it again to public notice and perhaps cause the Vatican further embarrassment, I have decided not to publish this chronicle[19] but to deposit it among my other private papers at my bank, Cox and Co. of Charing Cross.

---

[19] Dr Watson refers to the case in 'The Hound of the Baskervilles'. Dr John F. Watson.

The Case of the Camberwell Deception

'I see you have received bad news, Watson,' my old friend Sherlock Holmes remarked over breakfast one winter's morning as we examined our respective mail. 'A death, I believe.'

As I looked up from the letter, startled by the accuracy of his statement, he continued with a smile, 'It was hardly a three-pipe problem, my dear fellow.[1] Your expression and the black-edged writing paper were all the facts needed to make the deduction. I trust it is not someone close to you?'

'It is Mrs Cecil Forrester,' I replied. 'Her son, Henry, with whom she was living in Canterbury, has written to tell me she passed away on Tuesday.'

'A sad loss,' Holmes commented.

'It is a break with the past,' I acknowledged. 'Although she was no great age, she had been ailing for some months.

---

[1] Mr Sherlock Holmes considered the case of the Red-head League to be so difficult that it would take him three pipefuls of tobacco to ponder successfully over the problem. Dr John F. Watson.

We had kept up a correspondence over the years but not regularly.'

Holmes, of course, knew of my connection with Mrs Cecil Forrester. My late wife Mary had been employed as governess to her children when the family was living in Lower Camberwell. Indeed, it was through Holmes that I first became acquainted with Mary Morstan, as she then was, during the Sholto inquiry.[2] For this reason, I was considerably saddened by the news of Mrs Forrester's death which brought back memories of that other and much greater personal loss. Mrs Forrester had been my last living link with my dear wife and those happy but all too few years we had spent together.[3]

My mood was not lightened by the weather. It was a bitterly cold morning in January 1901, about a year before I bought the Queen Anne Street practice and moved out of my old lodgings at 221B Baker Street.[4] Although a bright

---

[2] Dr John H. Watson first met Miss Mary Morstan, his future wife, in 1888 when she asked Mr Sherlock Holmes to inquire into the disappearance of her father, Captain Arthur Morstan. *Vide*: 'The Sign of Four'. Dr John F. Watson.

[3] Mrs Watson, née Mary Morstan, died between 1891 and 1894 when Mr Sherlock Holmes was absent from England during the Great Hiatus. The exact cause and date of her death are unknown. Vide: 'The Adventure of the Empty House'. Dr John F. Watson.

[4] Dr John H. Watson bought the Queen Anne Street practice sometime between June 1902, the date of the Three Garridebs inquiry, when he was still living in Baker Street, and 3rd September of that same year when he had already left his old lodgings. Most commentators agree that this decision to leave Baker Street and return to medical practice was linked to his second marriage. Dr John F. Watson.

fire was burning in the sitting-room hearth, the view from the windows was dreary in the extreme. The snow, which had fallen overnight, still lay upon the ground, rutted and dirtied by the feet of pedestrians and the wheels of passing vehicles.

Holmes rose from the table.

'I am loath to leave you on your own this morning, Watson,' said he, 'but I have a pressing engagement with an informant, one of the notorious Stevenson gang, who insists I come alone, and I cannot therefore ask you to accompany me. Will you be all right here by yourself for an hour?'

'Of course, Holmes,' I assured him, touched by his concern. 'I shall reply to Henry Forrester's letter and then I may read the morning's newspapers.'

'Very well then; if you are quite certain,' Holmes replied as he retired to his bedroom to dress.

Shortly afterwards, he emerged, carrying in his hand a small packet wrapped in brown paper which he placed on my desk with the remark, 'I should be most grateful, my dear fellow, if you could spare the time to glance over the contents and give your opinion of them on my return. I should be back within the hour.'

After he left, I settled down to the melancholy task of writing to Henry Forrester. Having done so and sent Billy the pageboy to post the letter, my eye fell on the package Holmes had left for me. My curiosity aroused, as no doubt Holmes had intended, I picked it up and, unwrapping it, discovered it contained two photographs, both studio portraits mounted on stiff pasteboard.

The first was of a young lady of about two and twenty who was standing alone against a painted backcloth of rocks and trees. Although not conventionally beautiful, the features were refined and regular and the general expression was one of a quiet intelligence. But most of all, I was struck by a tragic air about her which was difficult to define. It was particularly noticeable in her large, dark eyes which gazed at me steadily out of the photograph with a grave, unsmiling regard as if searching for some expression of consolation in my own face for whatever sorrow she was suffering. This impression was emphasised by the severity of the dress she was wearing. It was dark, long-sleeved and cut very high in the neck, so that the throat was completely covered, and its plainness was unrelieved by any ornament. It reminded me of mourning apparel and I wondered if she had recently suffered a bereavement.

The other photograph was of a family group, again posed in a studio setting, consisting of a woman seated on a chair, holding a small child aged about three years on her lap. Behind her was standing a pleasant-faced, fair-haired young man in a formal dark suit, smiling a little self-consciously into the camera.

The two women appeared to be related. There was a similarity in their features which suggested they might be sisters, the seated woman being the older of the two.

Puzzled as to why Holmes had requested my opinion of them I turned the photographs over and found written on the back of them in my old friend's handwriting nothing more than the subjects' names: Miss Emma Holland for the lady standing alone and Mr and Mrs George Chapell for the couple with the child.

Holmes returned soon afterwards to find me seated by the fire, still studying the two photographs, in particular that of Miss Emma Holland.

'Have you come to any conclusions about them?' Holmes asked, drawing his own chair closer to the hearth. Taking the Persian slipper which served him as a tobacco pouch,[5] he filled and lit his pipe.

'I believe the two women may be sisters,' I remarked. 'Excellent, Watson! You are quite correct, what else can you tell me?'

Knowing Holmes' insistence on factual evidence rather than mere conjecture, I hesitated a little before replying.

'Miss Emma Holland seems a very sad figure, Holmes. I wondered if she had suffered some tragedy in her life, perhaps a bereavement.'

'That was perspicacious of you, my dear fellow. About a year before that photograph was taken, she had indeed undergone a most harrowing experience, including the death of someone close to her. Did you notice anything else about her?'

'Only that she looks highly intelligent.'

'True again. Watson! You are indeed on capital form

[5] There are several references to the Persian slipper Mr Sherlock Holmes used as a tobacco pouch. *Vide* among others: 'The Adventure of the Empty House' and 'The Adventure of the Illustrious Client'. Dr John F. Watson.

this morning! But what of Miss Holland's hands? Is there anything about those which struck you as remarkable?'

I looked closely again at the photograph, paying particular attention to this detail, but, apart from the fact that they were clasped in front of her and looked very white against the dark fabric of her dress, I could see nothing which was in any way out of the ordinary.

I glanced at Holmes and saw he was regarding me quizzically, a faint smile on his lips.

'Well, Watson?' he inquired, raising his eyebrows.

'Nothing, Holmes,' I confessed. 'What am I supposed to see?'

Without replying, he rose from his chair and, crossing the room to his desk, picked up his magnifying glass which he silently handed to me. Taking it, I looked again at the hands, which were crossed left over right, and with the aid of the powerful lens was able for the first time to discern the narrow band of a ring on the third finger of her left hand.

'She is wearing a wedding ring!' I exclaimed in surprise, more at my ability to see it at last rather than from any real awareness of its significance. Holmes must have realised this lack of discernment on my part for he asked in the tone of a schoolmaster trying to coax a pupil towards the perfect answer, 'And what, my dear fellow, is the name on the back of the photograph?'

'Miss Emma Holland,' I began and then the truth suddenly struck me. 'Of course, *Miss*!' I exclaimed. 'Then why the wedding ring?'

'Exactly so, Watson. Why indeed?'

'Who are these people, Holmes?' I asked curiously. It was evident that he had had some definite purpose in mind when he had asked me to examine and comment on the photographs. 'Are they former clients of yours?'

'Not directly although they were connected with someone who came to see me over twenty years ago, asking for my help, and whose name is very familiar to you.'

'Really? I cannot think who it could be,' I replied, much puzzled.

'If I add that her reason for consulting me concerned a little domestic complication, will that not help you?'

'Mrs Forrester!' I exclaimed. 'I remember my late wife using that very phrase when she first consulted you.[6] You had assisted her employer, she said, over some domestic problem although you always declined to explain its exact nature.'

'I was not in a position to do so, my dear fellow. I had promised Mrs Cecil Forrester that I would say nothing either to you or to your late wife, Mary. However, I feel Mrs Forrester's death has removed that injunction and therefore I am now free to tell you the whole tragic story.

'Mrs Forrester consulted me in 1879, when I was first

[6] In 'The Sign of Four', Miss Mary Morstan explains that she has come to consult Mr Sherlock Holmes about her father's disappearance 'because you once enabled my employer, Mrs Cecil Forrester, to unravel a little domestic complication'. Dr John F. Watson.

in practice in Montague Street.[7] She was concerned about her children's governess, a Miss Emma Holland, whom she had taken into her household about a year earlier. Miss Holland had come to her with excellent references from her previous employer, the Honourable Mrs Frederick Gore Hamilton of Kensington. Mrs Forrester had no complaints about either Miss Holland's character or competence. She was a quiet, efficient young woman, well liked by Mrs Forrester's children. However, a minor mystery regarding Miss Holland had arisen and, being a widow and having no close male relatives in whom to confide, Mrs Forrester had come to seek my advice.

'Her unease arose from the fact that, whatever the season or occasion, Miss Holland invariably wore a high-necked dress of the style you have seen in her photograph. Being curious by nature and on good terms with her governess, Mrs Forrester asked her one particularly hot day about this preference of hers. Miss Holland replied that, as a child, she had suffered from a goitre which had been surgically removed. The high-necked dresses were intended to hide the scar. She seemed, Mrs Forrester added, embarrassed by the conversation and, embarrassed herself at having raised the subject, Mrs Forrester let the matter drop and thought no more about it.

'However, a few months later, Mrs Forrester attended

[7] When Mr Sherlock Holmes first left University, he set up as a private consulting detective in lodgings in Montague Street which is close to the British Museum. He moved to the rooms in Baker Street, which he shared with Dr John H. Watson, in the early 1880s, probably in 1881. *Vide*: 'A Study in Scarlet'. Dr John F. Watson.

a charity bazaar in London on behalf of the Distressed Gentlewomen's Support Society, a good cause to which she regularly subscribed. While at the bazaar, she happened by sheer chance to be introduced to the Honourable Mrs Frederick Gore Hamilton, a fellow subscriber and Miss Holland's previous employer, with whom she had, of course, corresponded when she took up Miss Holland's references. Naturally, they got into conversation in the course of which Mrs Forrester mentioned Miss Holland's goitre. Heaven knows how the topic came up but, given women's extraordinary predilection for discussing matters of health, their own as well as other people's, perhaps the choice of subject matter was not all that unusual.

'The Honourable Mrs Gore Hamilton was astonished. Miss Holland, she insisted, had never to her knowledge suffered from a goitre, bore no scar on her neck and furthermore, in the three years she had been in her own employ, had rarely worn a high-necked dress of the type described by Mrs Forrester.

'In an attempt to solve the apparent mystery surrounding the young governess, the two ladies exchanged further descriptions of their respective employees, the Honourable Mrs Gore Hamilton finally settling the matter by declaring that *her* Miss Holland had light brown hair and brown eyes.

'There was a moment of bewildered incredulity before Mrs Forrester cried out, "But mine has blue!"

'As you may imagine, Watson, this final revelation placed Mrs Forrester in an extraordinary dilemma.

'Who was this young woman, masquerading as Miss Emma Holland, who was clearly an impostor and was, moreover, in charge of her children's education? If she was not Miss Holland, then who was she? And why was she carrying out this deception?

'It was an intriguing little mystery and one which I readily agreed to look into on Mrs Forrester's behalf. I therefore suggested that I be introduced into the household as Clement Stanley, an old school friend of her late husband who had recently returned from America and was anxious to renew the family acquaintance. Mrs Forrester agreed with the plan and the following afternoon I presented myself at her house in Lower Camberwell.

'You will not, my dear Watson, need reminding of Mrs Forrester's drawing room.'

'Indeed not, Holmes,' I replied, recalling that pleasant, comfortable room, overlooking the lawn and the leafy back garden where Mary and I had so often sat together in the weeks leading up to our marriage. Indeed, so strong was the recollection that, for a few seconds, it seemed to flash across that inward eye with such clarity that, had I been asked, I could have described in detail the pattern on the chintz curtains or the collection of porcelain figurines in the display cabinet which stood in one of the chimney alcoves.

'The memory does not pain you too much, my dear fellow?' Holmes inquired a little anxiously. 'If you prefer, I could postpone my account to another day.'

'No, pray go on,' I insisted. 'The story is intriguing and

I should like to know its ending. Besides, it is better, is it not, to learn to come to terms with the past?'

'My sentiments entirely!' Holmes agreed heartily. 'Well then, to continue. It was in that very same drawing room over tea that Mrs Forrester introduced me to the children and Miss Holland. I found her a charming young woman, pleasant and agreeable, and yet, as you so rightly perceived, bearing about her an indefinable air of some past tragedy. Her curious choice of apparel was, of course, immediately evident. Although it was a hot July afternoon, she was wearing a black dress, cut very high in the neck which covered her whole throat almost up to her chin.

'During my consultation with Mrs Forrester the previous day, I had already established that Miss Holland's free day was always a Sunday and that she left the house at about twelve o'clock, immediately after she and the family returned from Matins, taking with her a small covered basket containing a cold luncheon of sandwiches and a flask of lemon cordial. She was out for the whole of the day, not returning to Camberwell until nine o'clock in the evening. Where she went and whom she met during these Sunday excursions was another mystery. Although Mrs Forrester had asked her in a friendly manner what she did in her free time, Miss Holland had told her little, apart from the meagre fact that she visited an elderly relative who lived in the country.

'Thinking that his relative might be a vital clue to Miss Holland's real identity, I had also arranged, with Mrs Forrester's permission, to follow Miss Holland the next

Sunday in order to discover precisely where she went.

'Disguised as an elderly Anglican cleric,[8] I therefore took a hansom to Camberwell, asking the driver to wait a little distance up the road from Mrs Forrester's house.

'Shortly after twelve, Miss Holland emerged and set off up the road on foot, carrying the basket. Paying off the cabby, I followed a little distance behind her. Her destination was Camberwell railway station where she caught a train to Ludgate Hill. I do not propose giving you a detailed account of her journey after that, Watson. It would be tedious in the extreme. Suffice it to say that from Ludgate Hill she made her way, partly on foot, partly by omnibus, to St Pancras station. Fortunately, she was so intent on her own itinerary that she failed to notice that the same elderly, white-haired cleric was following her every move. Indeed, when she bought a second-class return ticket to Banham Cross, the small market town in Hertfordshire, I was standing immediately behind her at the booking office and occupied the carriage next to hers on the train.

'At Banham Cross, she alighted and, having bought a bunch of white roses from a flower seller outside the station, she set off to walk the short distance to St Margaret's church. Once there, she made her way to a grave where she placed the roses in a small marble urn and where she remained kneeling in silent prayer for several minutes, her veil lowered.'

[8] Mr Sherlock Holmes was a master of disguise and, during his career, assumed several different identities, including a 'drunken-looking groom' ('A Scandal in Bohemia') and an elderly Italian priest ('The Adventure of the Final Problem'). Dr John F. Watson.

'Whose grave, Holmes?' I asked eagerly.

Holmes looked pained.

'All in good time, Watson. I am well aware that, as an author, you lay great emphasis on the story, particularly on the complexities of the plot. But do pray allow me to proceed with the account in my own manner by following the logical sequence of events.'

'Of course, Holmes,' I agreed, somewhat abashed.

'To continue, then. While Miss Holland was thus engaged, I remained out of sight inside the porch, apparently intent on studying the times of services posted up on the noticeboard.

'After about ten minutes, Miss Holland rose from her knees and, returning to the railway station, caught a train back to St Pancras from where she travelled by omnibus to Battersea.

'I must confess that I was by now not only perplexed by Miss Holland's peregrinations but a little fatigued by them as well. It was now half past three in the afternoon and I had had nothing to eat all day apart from a very scanty breakfast at eight o'clock which had been cut short by the arrival of an unexpected client who insisted on seeing me at once. In fact, I was only able to persuade him to leave in time for me to take a cab to Camberwell, whereas Miss Holland had presumably refreshed herself with the sandwiches and lemon cordial which I imagined she had consumed in the privacy of the Ladies Only carriage of the train on her way to Hertfordshire.

'I also assumed that the sole purpose of the journey was

to visit the grave at St Margaret's church, not an elderly relative, as she had told her employer. But why had she troubled to deceive Mrs Forrester? And where was she proposing to go in Battersea?

'That last question was soon answered. Her destination was a house, number 19 in Clifford Street, one of those modest, two-storey villas built for clerks or minor tradesmen and their families.

'Having no means of knowing how long Miss Holland might remain inside the house and determined not to give up the chase quite yet, I decided to make a few small changes to my appearance. I could hardly loiter indefinitely in Clifford Street dressed as an Anglican clergyman. My presence would have been too conspicuous. Fortunately there was a public house on the corner which had a gate in its rear wall giving access to a small back yard. Taking advantage of the cover it afforded, I rapidly discarded my wig together with my clerical hat and collar, replacing the latter with a soft collar and a cravat which I was carrying in my pocket in case of need. I then sauntered round to the front of the public house and installed myself in the saloon bar, the window of which overlooked Clifford Street. There I kept watch, fortified by a cheese sandwich and half a pint of the landlord's best ale.

'It was over half an hour before there was any sign of activity and I had begun to believe that nothing further would happen, when the front door of number 19 opened and Miss Holland emerged, accompanied by a man, a woman and a little boy.'

'The family in the second photograph!' I exclaimed.

'Indeed so, Watson. In no apparent haste, they set off on foot to Battersea Park to where I followed them at a discreet distance and where, like other families on that summer Sunday afternoon, they strolled about on the grass, enjoying the sunshine and the fresh air. The man, the father of the child I assumed, had brought a ball with him and he entertained his small son by throwing it to him or kicking it to and fro across the grass.

'They were joined shortly afterwards by a tall, dark-haired young man who shook hands all round and proceeded to accompany them on their afternoon walk. He was particularly assiduous, I noticed, in his attentions to Miss Holland, walking beside her and engaging her in conversation. She, in turn, seemed modestly appreciative of his company, not spurning it but not actively encouraging it either. In short, Watson, I had the impression that while he was strongly attracted to Miss Holland, she was not so certain of her own feelings towards him.

'After about three-quarters of an hour, the second man took his leave and the family, including Miss Holland, returned to the house in Clifford Street where I, too, left them and made my way back to Montague Street. I felt I had seen enough and gathered together sufficient information about Miss Holland's Sunday excursion to follow up my own inquiries at some future date.

'I began at the Battersea end of the investigation. As well as the public house, the Bunch of Cherries, on the comer of Clifford Street, there was also on the other side of the road a small grocer's shop which served the housewives in the neighbourhood. On the pretext of having to deliver a message to the family at number 19 whose surname I had embarrassingly forgotten, I learnt they were the Chapells. The grocer's wife, a garrulous lady, pleased to be diverted from the boredom of weighing out sugar and cutting cheese, added a little more information to this stark fact. So it was from her I learnt that they were a respectable family, the husband being a clerk at Morgan and Whitestone's, the tea importers in Ludgate Circus, while Mrs Chapell had been employed before her marriage as a governess.

'Having found out all I could at Battersea, the following day I retraced Miss Holland's steps to the churchyard of St Margaret's in Banham Cross and there added a few more facts to my growing collection.

'The grave at which Miss Holland had prayed so earnestly the previous Sunday afternoon had inscribed on its headstone the name Henry Charles Grayson and the dates 1847 to 1876 from which I deduced that Henry Charles Grayson had died at the relatively early age of twenty-nine.

'For some reason which I could not then define, the name Henry Grayson seemed oddly familiar to me although I could not recall where I had read it, for I seemed to associate it with a written source. While I was pondering on this elusive reference, I was approached by a middle-aged, strongly built man, a gravedigger I assumed from his attire and the fresh earth on his boots and hands, who was curious to know why I, a stranger, should be interested in that particular grave.

'Thank God for human curiosity, Watson! While one might deplore the habit of neighbours spying on one another's activities, as a private consulting detective I have to confess that on occasions their observations have proved invaluable to my inquiries. It was so in this case.

'"I am an amateur genealogist, interested in tracing my family history," I replied. "I believe Henry Grayson could be a distant cousin of mine. I see he died tragically young."

'"Tragic!" said he. "You're right there, sir."

'In a strong country accent, which I shall not attempt to reproduce, he went on to tell me that Henry Grayson had been a fine, well-set-up young gentleman, a solicitor in the town, who was knocked down and killed by a two-horse van one February morning when he was crossing the road to his office, leaving a widow with one small child. Not long after his death, she took the baby and went to live in London to be near her sister.'

'Holmes!' I interjected. 'That explains everything!'

'Does it, Watson?' he inquired, leaning back in his chair and regarding me with an amused indulgence. 'Pray expound your theory.'

'Well,' said I, warming to the task and thinking that Holmes was being a little obtuse in not coming to the same conclusion, 'Mrs Grayson left the child in the care of her sister, the Mrs Chapell who lives in Battersea. When I examined the photographs, I thought there was a strong

220

family resemblance in the two women. She then reverted to her maiden name, Miss Emma Holland, and took up the post of governess with Mrs Cecil Forrester in order to support the child. It is not an uncommon practice, I believe, for married women to use their maiden names under such circumstances. As governesses, single ladies are usually preferred to married women, even widows.'

'An ingenious theory!' Holmes exclaimed. 'However, you have failed to take into account one important piece of evidence.'

'Have I, Holmes? And what is that?'

'The fact that the Miss Emma Holland who was employed by the Honourable Mrs Gore Hamilton was not the same Miss Emma Holland whom Mrs Forrester appointed as governess to her children. If you remember, Watson, *that* Miss Holland always wore a high-necked dress whereas the first Miss Holland rarely did so.'

'Oh, yes, I see, Holmes,' I said, considerably abashed. 'What then is the explanation? I assume there is one.'

'Of course there is, my dear fellow. All apparent mysteries of human contrivance, however complex, may be solved, providing in this case one has enough evidence and asks the right questions, in this case which Miss Emma Holland was which? The lady using that name had clearly set out to deceive Mrs Forrester about her true identity. The next question was: why should an apparently respectable young lady wish to carry out such a deception? I felt it was not merely her marital status she wished to conceal. Why go to such lengths if that were the only motive? It was not the child either; that was evidently legitimate. It therefore had to be something else in the young lady's past.

'As you know, Watson, I have a retentive memory and can store information, even the most trivial, in my mind on which I can draw later when the need arises.[9] It was so in this case. As I told you earlier, the name Henry Grayson had seemed strangely familiar to me although the exact date eluded me. I suddenly recalled that it had featured in a newspaper report I had read comparatively recently.

'It was my custom then, as now, to keep copies of old newspapers, especially those which contained interesting reports about crime and its punishment.[10] I had the date of Henry Grayson's death which was February 1876. I also knew that his widow had moved to London shortly after the funeral. I therefore deduced this removal had taken place almost certainly in the same year. In addition, Mrs Forrester had told me that the governess calling herself Miss Emma Holland had been in her employment

---

[9] In 'A Study in Scarlet', Mr Sherlock Holmes compares a man's brain with 'an empty attic' which a fool fills with useless lumber but in which the skilled workman keeps only those tools 'which may help him in doing his work, but of these he has a large assortment, and all in the most perfect order'. In 'The Adventure of the Sussex Vampire', Mr John H. Watson refers to Mr Holmes' ability to docket 'any fresh information very quickly and accurately'. Dr John F. Watson.

[10] In 'The Adventure of the Noble Bachelor', Mr Sherlock Holmes claims he read 'nothing except the criminal news and the agony column' in the newspapers while in 'The Adventure of the Six Napoleons', Dr John H. Watson refers to the files of old daily newspapers with which 'one of our lumber rooms was packed' at 221B Baker Street. Dr John F. Watson.

for about a year. As Mrs Forrester had consulted me in 1879, I now had enough information to compute the simple sum and from it to conclude that whatever I had read containing the name Henry Grayson, it must have been in that two-year period between 1876 and 1878.

'A search through my newspaper archives which covered these dates was eventually successful although it was a tedious business. It was in one of the more popular daily papers which I had kept because it contained a report on the arrest of William Carpenter, the notorious bigamist. On the same page was a short report under a general heading of "Life at the Bar", a facetious title for the article contained amusing or sensational snippets about cases heard at criminal courts; I often read it because its contents were sometimes unusual. In it there was an item concerning a Mrs Henry Grayson who on 4th March 1877 was found guilty of attempted suicide and was sentenced to six months in prison.'

'Oh, Holmes!' I exclaimed.

'You may well be horrified, Watson. Although I do not for a moment defend the act of *felo de se*[11] I consider it a blot on a civilised society that any poor wretch who is driven by circumstances to make an attempt on his or her own life should be so hounded by the law.[12]

[11] In 'The Adventure of the Veiled Lodger', Mr Sherlock Holmes tells Eugenia Ronder, who he suspects is considering suicide: 'Your life is not your own. Keep your hands off it.' Dr John F. Watson.
[12] The English law making suicide, or attempted suicide a criminal offence was not repealed until 1961, long after other European countries. Dr John F. Watson.

'Later, I was to hear the full story from Mrs Grayson's own lips. It was a tragic account. After the death of her husband, Mrs Grayson, whose Christian name incidentally was Elizabeth, had decided to move to London where her older sister Emma, her only living relative, was employed as governess by the Honourable Mrs Gore Hamilton. Before her marriage, Mrs Grayson had herself been a governess to a family in Banham Cross which was how she had met Henry Grayson. In London, Mrs Grayson took lodgings in Chelsea where at first she was able to support herself and her child from the money left her by her late husband. However, because he had not been very long in practice, the legacy was not large and Mrs Grayson was soon forced to move to cheaper lodgings and to attempt to earn a living by taking in sewing and giving piano lessons.

'As a society, Watson, we pay too little regard to the Mrs Graysons of this world, impoverished gentlewoman who, left without a breadwinner, struggle to maintain themselves and their children, only to find that, however great their efforts, they are slipping deeper and deeper into poverty and despair.

'It was this despair which drove Mrs Grayson to attempt to take her own life. Leaving the child in the care of her landlady, she took a room in a cheap hotel where she tried to hang herself. Fortunately, in view of subsequent events, she was discovered in time. A chambermaid, who happened to be passing the room, heard a crash as the chair was kicked away and curious to find out what was happening – thank God once again, Watson, for that human inclination to pry into other people's lives! – used her pass key to open the door. Her screams brought the manager running. Mrs Grayson was cut down, revived and taken to Charing Cross hospital where she made a full recovery, apart from a scar left by the rope on the right side of her throat. Hence her custom always to wear a high-necked dress to cover up the mark which she regarded as an indelible stigma of her shame.

'For the manager of the hotel, an officious man who was anxious to keep within the law, had reported her attempted suicide to the police and handed over to them a letter she had written, addressed to her sister. No sooner had she regained her full health than she was arrested, tried and sentenced to six months' imprisonment.

'Her sister was, of course, informed and visited her regularly in prison. It was this same sister, Emma, who made arrangements for the care of the child and found a suitable foster-mother. It was also she who contrived the deception.

'Miss Holland had a fiancé to whom she was secretly engaged and whom she planned to marry a little later in the year. As she did not want to jeopardise her position in the Honourable Mrs Gore Hamilton's household, she had said nothing to her employer about these personal arrangements.

'When Mrs Grayson was released from prison, she would need to find employment in order to support herself and her child. Why not exchange identities? her sister suggested. She, Miss Emma Holland, would give in her notice to Mrs Gore Hamilton and ask for a reference. Mrs Grayson could then, using that reference and the name Emma Holland, apply for a post elsewhere. In the meantime, the real Miss Emma Holland would marry, set up home with her husband and care for her sister's child.

'It seemed an admirable solution to the problem.'

'And you heard all this from Mrs Grayson's own lips?' I inquired.

'Yes; at least those parts of the account which I had not already deduced from my own investigation. On the Sunday following my discovery of the report in the newspaper, I presented myself at 19 Clifford Street at four o'clock, the time I estimated Mrs Grayson would have returned from visiting her husband's grave. Mr George Chapell answered the door and, when I gave my name and asked to speak privately with Mrs Grayson, he showed me into a small sitting room where she soon joined me.

'At that time, I had not been long in practice and the name Sherlock Holmes was not known to her. Besides, when she had first met me at Mrs Forrester's, I had been introduced to her as Clement Stanley, a family friend. Once this confusion had been resolved, I told her the reason for my visit and those facts I had already discovered. She listened without speaking, her eyes cast down and her hands clasped in her lap.

'At the end of my account, I added, "I shall not, of course, pass any of this information to Mrs Forrester without your permission. She came to consult me not out of idle curiosity but from a natural desire to find out the truth in case it affected her children's well-being. If it is your wish, I shall simply tell her that I have made some inquiries and that I can assure her there is no need for her to feel any alarm."

'You spoke earlier, Watson, of the young lady's obvious intelligence. To that accolade, I would add two other qualities: her remarkable fortitude and honesty. After I had finished speaking, she sat for a few seconds in quiet contemplation and then, raising her eyes, looked me straight in the face.

'"Thank you, Mr Holmes, for your offer to keep silent about my past history," she replied. "But I feel it is my duty to speak to Mrs Forrester myself. As she has been so very kind to me during the year I have spent in her employment, it is time I told her the truth, as I should have done at the very beginning. Had I not been so desperate to earn a living, I would have admitted everything and thrown myself on her mercy."

'She then went on to give an account of those aspects of her past life which I had not already deduced, including confirmation of one small detail which I had, in fact, already guessed. The clue to it may be seen in her photograph.'

'The wedding ring?' I ventured.

'Exactly, Watson. As Miss Holland, she could not wear it openly on her finger so she carried it on a chain about her neck.'

'What happened to her afterwards?' I inquired eagerly.

'As she had declared to me, Miss Holland, or rather Mrs Grayson, confessed everything to Mrs Forrester who, being, as you know, a most kind-hearted lady, kept her on as governess for a further year.'

'That is so typical of her,' I said warmly. 'And after that? Did you hear nothing more of Mrs Grayson?'

'I had a letter from her shortly after she left Mrs Forrester's employment. It was to announce her marriage to James Fairclough, the tall, dark-haired young man she had met in Battersea Park on that Sunday afternoon. Fairclough was a fellow clerk of her brother-in-law, George Chapell, at Morgan and Whitestone's which is how Mrs Grayson had made his acquaintance.'

At this point Holmes stopped as if he had come to the end of his narrative. But there still remained one aspect of the case for which he had so far not offered an explanation. I was puzzled by this as Holmes was usually so meticulous in laying out all the facts, however small. Although in this particular instance the omission did not affect the outcome of the inquiry, I nevertheless thought it strange that Holmes had not referred to it.

Moved by the same curiosity which my old friend had himself commented on during his account, I decided to put the question directly to him.

'How were you able to acquire the photographs?' I inquired.

'Oh, those!' he replied in a dismissive manner as if the subject had no significance whatsoever. 'In my letter of congratulations to Mrs Grayson, or rather Mrs Fairclough as she now was, I happened to remark in passing that I would keep her letter as a memento of the case and its successful conclusion. It was meant, of course, as nothing more than mere civility. But Mrs Fairclough must have taken my remark seriously for, by return of post, she sent me those two photographs. I have kept them in my tin trunk[13] along with all the other records of my cases purely as a relic for, as you know, Watson, unlike you. I am not the least romantic.'

'Of course not, Holmes!' I agreed stoutly, suppressing a smile. Although in the past I have had cause to comment on Holmes' lack of emotion, describing him on one occasion as 'a brain without a heart',[14] he was also capable of finer feelings, even of moments of sentimentality for he kept the sovereign Irene Adler had given him as payment for acting as witness at her marriage to Godfrey Norton, and wore it on his watch-chain as a memento.[15]

No doubt, Holmes would claim that this was intended only as a wry reminder of the one case in which he had been beaten by a woman. Nevertheless, I like to think that

---

[13] Mr Sherlock Holmes had a tin trunk in which he kept records and mementoes of the cases he had investigated. *Vide:* 'The Adventure of the Musgrave Ritual'. Dr John F. Watson.

[14] Dr John H. Watson makes this comment in 'The Adventure of the Greek Interpreter'. Dr John F. Watson.

[15] In 'A Scandal in Bohemia', Mr Sherlock Holmes, disguised as a 'drunken-looking groom', followed Miss Irene Adler to St Monica's church in the Edgware Road where he was asked to act as witness to her marriage to Mr Godfrey Norton, a lawyer. In payment for his services, Miss Adler gave him a sovereign which he wore on his watch-chain in 'memory of the occasion'. Dr John F. Watson.

his heart may also have been touched, if only a little, by the former Mrs Grayson's tragic plight and her courage in facing adversity.

Although I never met her, I had my own reasons for feeling grateful to Mrs Grayson for it was because of her retirement from Mrs Forrester's household that Mary Morstan was employed as governess in her place which, in turn, had led to our meeting and subsequent marriage.

When looking back at the past, I have frequently been struck by the thought that, despite our freedom of will, it is often mere chance which is a major factor in determining our fate, whether for good or ill.

Because of the strong link this case has had with my own past, I have decided not to publish my account of it. I have also in mind the people who were involved in the inquiry, in particular Mrs Fairclough and her small son, who I hope have found happiness at last and who deserve to live out their lives in privacy, as no doubt they themselves would prefer.

The Case of the Barton Wood Murder

I

It was a Tuesday afternoon in September 1894 and, lunch being over, Holmes had retired from the table to stand at one of the windows, gazing down at the comings and goings of pedestrians and vehicles in the street below. He was in a restless mood that day. The case of the Norwood builder had not long been successfully concluded and, for the time being, he had no other investigations on hand.[1] But such is his mercurial nature that, instead of rejoicing in this temporary lull in his affairs, he fretted at the lack of activity to occupy his mind.

'London has four million inhabitants. You would think at least one of them would have some pressing inquiry which needs investigating, if only into a servant who has absconded with the family's silver teaspoons,' he was

[1] This inquiry took place in August, 'some months' after Mr Sherlock Holmes' return to England in spring 1894 after the Great Hiatus. Many commentators therefore date the case to August of that year although some prefer to assign it to the following year, August 1895. Dr John F. Watson.

complaining in a half-serious, half-humorous manner when he suddenly broke off to exclaim, 'By jove, Watson, I believe we are in luck after all! A client has at this very moment appeared pat, like the fairy godmother in a pantomime, to grant me my wish.'

'Where, Holmes?' I asked, throwing aside the *Daily Telegraph* and hurrying to his side.

'The portly gentleman over there,' Holmes replied, pointing a little way up the street where a well-built man was indeed in the act of paying off the driver of a four-wheeler before turning away to glance anxiously up at the numbers on the nearby houses.

'How can you be so certain he is a client?' I inquired.

'Gentlemen, dressed as he is for the City, do not usually arrive in Baker Street in such an obvious state of agitation unless something has occurred to cause them considerable distress. A woman in such a condition will cling to her reticule as if to a lifeline. A man will invariably mop his brow. There, Watson! What did I tell you? Off goes his hat and out comes the silk handkerchief!'

'And there goes the front door bell,' I added, amused at this small example of my old friend's close observation of human behaviour.

A few moments later, the gentleman in question was ushered into our sitting room. He was in his fifties and bore about him in his plump, rather florid features and well-nourished figure the unmistakable air of one used to the good things of life. It was also evident in his apparel, from the glossy sheen on his silk hat and the impeccable quality of his shirt front down to his highly polished black boots.

'Mr Sherlock Holmes?' said he.

Although in the short time it had taken to mount the stairs he had recovered some of his composure, his brow, despite the recent ministrations of his handkerchief, was still moist and his eyes, darting from one to the other of us, also betrayed a state of continuing anxiety.

'I am Sherlock Holmes,' my old friend assured him. 'Pray sit down, Mr . . .'

'Wilberforce. George Wilberforce,' our visitor replied, sinking down into the armchair which Holmes had indicated.

'And how may I help you?' Holmes continued. 'I perceive you have suffered some recent shock or some other untoward event which has occurred in the last few hours on which you need help. Am I right, sir? By the way, this is my colleague, Dr Watson. You may speak as frankly in front of him as you may before myself.'

'Of course,' Mr Wilberforce replied, nodding briefly in my direction before plunging into his account. 'I do not know how you managed to deduce it is some recent occurrence which has distressed me, but you are perfectly correct, Mr Holmes. A close acquaintance of mine apparently disappeared earlier today and I am most anxious to trace his whereabouts.

'I should explain that I am the senior partner of Wilberforce and Deakin of Lombard Street. You may have heard of us.'

'The long-established City firm of solicitors?'

'Quite so, Mr Holmes. The business was established by my grandfather in 1811. Many of our clients are wealthy people and part of our duties is to assist them with their financial affairs. Over the years, we have built up a close professional relationship with Mott and Co., the Cornhill bank, to whom we send those of our clients requiring sound advice on their investments. Ever since Mr Algernon Crosby was made one of the directors, I have always recommended him. He is an expert on the stock market and thoroughly reliable. Indeed, I have come to regard him more as a personal friend than a business acquaintance. We share the same club, Aston's, and on occasions have met socially in the evening for dinner or a visit to the theatre, both of us being widowers.

'I had arranged to meet Mr Crosby today for luncheon at our club in order to discuss the affairs of a particularly important client of mine, a titled gentleman whose exact identity I should prefer not to reveal. Suffice it to say that he finds himself financially embarrassed and wishes to obtain a temporary bank loan until he can sell some of his assets.

'Because of the pressing nature of the case, I was considerably surprised when Mr Crosby failed to keep the appointment. Nor had he sent any message to explain his absence, as I would have expected him to do had he been taken ill. He is usually so punctilious over such matters. I made inquiries at Mott's bank where I was told he had not arrived that morning, neither had anyone received any message from him. I therefore took a cab to his house in Chelsea, only to be informed that he was not there either.

However, his housekeeper told me that he had left that morning as usual at 8.30 a.m. apparently for the bank, and she was totally mystified as to where he might have gone. I was by now thoroughly alarmed at the situation and decided to come straight to you, Mr Holmes, to lay the facts before you.'

Holmes, who had listened to this account in silence, the tips of his long fingers pressed together, unclasped his hands and fixed his client with a steely gaze.

'*Some* of the facts, Mr Wilberforce, but not all.'

'I do not understand what you mean,' Mr Wilberforce said stiffly, his florid features flushing even darker.

'No, sir? Then allow me to explain. What you have told me is not the whole of the truth. You are deliberately withholding certain information. Unless you are prepared to tell me every last detail concerning Mr Crosby and his apparent disappearance then I shall have to decline the case. I am not prepared to undertake any inquiry unless I have the full confidence of my client.'

There was a moment's silence in which Mr Wilberforce's expression turned from annoyance to one of shamefaced embarrassment.

'You are quite correct, Mr Holmes,' he said at last, 'although I cannot for the life of me imagine how you found it out.'

'Quite simply, sir. In my experience, senior partners in a busy and highly regarded City law firm do not chase about London inquiring into the disappearance of a business colleague. They would send their confidential clerk. So, sir, what is it about Mr Crosby's affairs which caused you such consternation that you felt the need not only to make your own inquiries but to ask me to look into the case on your behalf? He has, after all, been missing for only six hours, hardly long enough to warrant such obvious and immediate alarm.'

The perspiration had again broken out on Mr Wilberforce's forehead and, taking out his silk handkerchief, he mopped his brow before replying.

'I believe I may rely utterly on your discretion, Mr Holmes, as well as Dr Watson's? I do not ask on my own account but Mr Crosby's, for what I have to tell you was confided in me under terms of the greatest secrecy.' Having received our assurances, Mr Wilberforce continued, 'For the past two months, Mr Crosby has been receiving anonymous letters threatening his life, a situation which I only heard about six days ago.'

'Did he show you any of these letters?' Holmes inquired, sitting up to attention, his deep-set grey eyes kindling at this information.

'Only one, Mr Holmes, the latest he had received. Both the envelope and the letter were written in capitals in red ink.'

'What was the postmark?'

'Guildford. I understood from Mr Crosby that all the letters were similarly franked. He had received seven altogether, sent at irregular intervals.'

'What of the writing? Did you notice any peculiarities about it?'

'It was awkwardly formed, possibly with the left hand, but both the spelling and punctuation were correct.'

'So whoever had sent it is educated?'

'That was certainly my impression.'

'And the contents?'

'I cannot recall them word for word. However, the general gist of them was to warn Mr Crosby that the writer was waiting his opportunity to murder him. He – at least I assumed it was a man advised him to be on his guard day and night. The final sentence was particularly threatening and for that reason I can recall it in detail. It read: "There is a special hell waiting for leeches such as you and it will give me the greatest satisfaction to see you suffering the torments of the damned."'

'The writer actually used the word "leech"?'

'Oh, yes. It was one of the reasons why I took special note of it.'

'Did Mr Crosby know who had sent the letters?'

'No; he said he was totally at a loss as to the writer's identity as well as his motives for threatening his life. I urged him to go to the police but he seemed reluctant to do so.'

'Why?'

'He did not tell me that either, sir,' Mr Wilberforce replied, mopping his brow again. He seemed harassed by Holmes' questions, coming so relentlessly one after the other.

'But you hazarded a guess?'

'I certainly formed an impression.'

'Which was what?'

'I hesitate to put it into words.' Mr Wilberforce began.

'Then allow me to do it for you,' Holmes said coolly. 'I suggest you suspected Mr Crosby had indeed guessed who the writer might be and why he had sent the letters. The word "leech" struck you as significant which was why you could recall that particular sentence so clearly. The epithet denotes a parasite, does it not? A creature which sucks the blood of its victim? When applied to a human being, it describes someone who has misappropriated someone else's money, and is a term often used for blackmailers or moneylenders who charge an exorbitant amount of interest.'

'I must protest, Mr Holmes!' Mr Wilberforce exclaimed. 'Mr Crosby is a man of the highest probity! As a banker . . .'

'Exactly, sir! Mr Crosby is a banker and, while I have no doubt he has always acted honourably, as a banker he must, in the course of his career, have had occasion to refuse a loan to someone whose credit he considered unreliable, or to demand repayment of an overdraft. I am not for a moment suggesting that Mr Crosby took these decisions lightly or irresponsibly but nevertheless such actions could have led to the ruin of one of his bank's clients. Did that not strike you as a possibility, Mr Wilberforce?'

'Indeed it did, Mr Holmes,' the man replied, looking considerably abashed. ''Pon my word, your powers of deduction amaze me, sir! It is as if you have read my very thoughts. However, I do not believe Mr Crosby had any particular former client in mind, only the suspicion that

238

someone with whom he had had such dealings in the past and who might have harboured a grudge against him had, for reasons unknown to him, chosen to seek revenge at this particular time.

'As a solicitor, I could be placed in a similar situation and can therefore sympathise with Mr Crosby's dilemma. Like him, I have had on occasions to deal with a disgruntled client who has felt that I have not done my best by him and have therefore lost him his case. But, unlike him, I have not so far, thank God, been subjected to threats against my life. However, in such a situation, I think I, too, would hesitate to go to the police until I had more information to offer them about the writer's identity. Mott's bank is an old family firm with an excellent reputation. Any adverse publicity could well have harmed its good standing in the City. Now that all of this is in the open, I assume you will take the case, Mr Holmes. Where do you propose to start making inquiries? At Mott's bank?'

'No, not immediately although it may be necessary later. For the time being, I shall start at the place where Mr Crosby was last seen, his house in Chelsea. If I may have his address, Mr Wilberforce?'

'Penrose Villa, Meredith Close.'

'And the name of his housekeeper?'

'Mrs Denton.'

'A description of Mr Crosby will also be useful.'

'He is a little taller than I, about five feet eight inches, but with much the same build. He is also grey-haired and clean-shaven. As he left his house this morning as if to go as usual to the City, I assume he would be wearing clothes very similar to mine.'

'That is all I need to know,' said Holmes, rising to his feet and holding out his hand. 'As soon as I have any definite news, I shall call on you at your office.'

We left soon after Mr Wilberforce had made his own departure and, having hailed a cab in Baker Street, we drove to Mr Crosby's house in Chelsea, a handsome stucco villa set in a quiet, tree-lined cul-de-sac.

The housekeeper, Mrs Denton, a sensible-looking woman in her late fifties, answered the door to us and, when Holmes had given her our names and briefly explained our business, she showed us into her own small, comfortably furnished parlour at the rear of the house where she invited us to sit down.

'I am glad you have come, Mr Holmes,' she said with admirable directness, 'for ever since Mr Wilberforce called on me earlier this afternoon to tell me Mr Crosby had not arrived at the bank and was apparently missing, I have been very anxious about him. He is so regular in his habits that it is quite unlike him to do anything out of his usual routine.'

'I understand he left the house at eight thirty this morning?'

'That is correct, sir.'

'And what would he normally do after that?'

'He would walk to King's Road where he would take a cab to Mott's bank in Cornhill.'

'Tell me, was Mr Crosby still here when the first post arrived?'

'Yes, sir. It came at a quarter to eight. I took the letters to him with his breakfast. There were three, one from his sister in Devon and one from an old friend of his who lives in Cambridge. You must not think I am prying, sir, but Mr Crosby is in regular correspondence with both of them and I am familiar with their handwriting. I did not recognise the writing on the third envelope.'

'Was it addressed in red capital letters?'

Mrs Denton gave Holmes a shrewd look.

'No it wasn't, sir, although Mr Crosby has received letters in the past addressed in such a style. I have never asked who sent them –it was not my place to do so – but whenever they arrived Mr Crosby seemed very distressed. This letter was in longhand and was written in black ink.'

'Did you happen to notice the postmark?'

'I am afraid I did not, sir. I had no reason to pay it any particular attention.'

'What was Mr Crosby's response in receiving it? Was he distressed by it?'

'No, Mr Holmes. He just glanced at it and then put it to one side while he opened his sister's letter.'

'So he appeared not to recognise the handwriting or regard the letter as important?'

'It seemed so, sir, although about ten minutes later he rang the bell and asked me to fetch the gazetteer from his study.'

'And that was unusual?' Holmes asked, his tone casual although his expression was eager.

'I have never known him to do that before.'

'Where is the gazetteer now, Mrs Denton?'

'After I cleared the breakfast things, I found it still lying on the table so I replaced it in the study.'

'And where are the letters he received this morning?'

'I haven't seen them since, sir, although it was Mr Crosby's habit to place all correspondence which needed answering in the top right-hand drawer of his desk.'

'May I examine Mr Crosby's desk?'

'Well, I suppose it is all right,' Mrs Denton replied a little reluctantly, 'although I should prefer you had Mr Crosby's permission first, sir; not that I am casting any aspersions on you personally, Mr Holmes.'

'Of course I understand that, my dear Mrs Denton,' Holmes said suavely, directing at her one of his most charming smiles for, when he chose, he had a winning way with women. 'However, as Mr Crosby is not here and I am as concerned about his welfare as you are yourself, I am sure he would not object under the circumstances.'

'Very well, Mr Holmes,' Mrs Denton agreed. Leading the way back into the front hall, she opened a door on the left and showed us into a square, sunny room furnished as a study with a knee-hole desk under the window, a pair of leather armchairs and two sets of bookcases filling the chimney alcoves.

Opening the right-hand drawer of the desk, Holmes took out two envelopes which he showed her.

'Are these the letters he received this morning from his sister and the friend in Cambridge?'

'Yes, Mr Holmes. Are there no others?'

'No; the third letter appears to be missing.'

'Then I suppose he must have taken it with him.'

With an apologetic glance in Mrs Denton's direction, Holmes looked through the other drawers in the desk but apparently found nothing of significance for, having closed the last one, he turned back to address the housekeeper.

'May I now see the gazetteer which Mr Crosby asked for this morning?'

'Of course, sir,' said she, fetching it from one of the bookcases and handing it to him.

It was a red-covered volume which appeared little used although, when Holmes laid it down upon the desk, it fell open at a page which seemed to have been pressed back on to the spine as if someone had recently flattened it in order to examine it more easily. Peering over his shoulder, I saw that it was a map of the county of Surrey. As I looked, Holmes' index finger came to rest by a place name not far from Guildford which I only then noticed was underlined faintly with pencil.

'Does the name Steeple Barton mean anything to you, Mrs Denton?' Holmes inquired.

The housekeeper shook her head.

'No, Mr Holmes.'

'So Mr Crosby knows no one who might live there?'

'Not to my knowledge, sir.'

Closing the gazetteer, Holmes handed it back to her with the words, 'If Mr Crosby has a Bradshaw, I should be much obliged to borrow it for a few minutes.'[2]

---

[2] Bradshaw's Railway Guide, which was published monthly, contained train timetables. Dr John F. Watson.

Having replaced the gazetteer in the bookcase, Mrs Denton returned with a copy of Bradshaw which Holmes consulted quickly before, thanking Mrs Denton for her assistance, he took his farewell and we left the house.

'We are, I assume, going to Steeple Barton?' I inquired as we set off to walk to King's Road.

'That is certainly my intention, Watson. It would appear that whatever was contained in the third letter Mr Crosby received this morning, it persuaded him to go to Steeple Barton instead of to the bank. The fact that he consulted a map of Surrey and marked that particular place would seem to support such an hypothesis. As he did not also ask for his Bradshaw, it suggests the time of the train he was to catch was provided in the letter. When I looked up the timetable myself, I noticed there was a train from Victoria to Guildford, the nearest station to Steeple Barton, at 9.16 a.m. He would have just had time to catch it which may explain why he failed to send a telegram to the bank or to Mr Wilberforce informing them of his intended absence today.'

He broke off to hail a cab and, once we were inside it on our way to Victoria station, he continued, 'I think we may also assume that, unlike the others he had received over the past two months, this letter was in no way threatening. As Mrs Denton remarked, he seemed unconcerned at its arrival. By the same token, he would hardly have set off alone for Surrey if he felt his life was in danger. Nevertheless, I feel certain misgivings about his safety.'

'Why is that, Holmes?'

Instead of replying directly, he chose to approach the

question from an entirely different point of view.

'Let us put ourselves in the position of the anonymous correspondent. He – and like Mr Wilberforce I shall assume for the time being that it is a man, although that is not yet proved – he, I repeat, is evidently intent on taking Mr Crosby's life in revenge, for some catastrophe in the past for which he, one imagines, regards Mr Crosby as responsible. While his proposed victim remained in London, the opportunity for murder would be severely restricted. Apart from that short walk to and from King's Road, Mr Crosby spent most of his time in the bank where access to him was limited and where there would also be too many witnesses. If you were in the man's shoes, how would you set about ensuring Mr Crosby was alone and with no one else present who might testify against you later in court?'

'I take your point, Holmes. You are suggesting, are you not, that the third letter which arrived this morning was sent by the same man who wrote the threatening letters?'

'Exactly so, Watson. And what pretext would he use to persuade Mr Crosby, a man of regular habits, to break his usual routine and set off by train for a small village in Surrey with which he apparently had no connection?'

Seeing my hesitation, Holmes continued impatiently, 'Oh, come, my dear fellow! Is it not perfectly obvious? He would write to Mr Crosby suggesting a meeting at Steeple Barton at which he proposed naming the person who was threatening his life, giving the time of the train he should catch as well as making some excuse for not meeting him in London. He may also have asked his victim to bring the letter with him thereby covering his tracks when inquiries were made into Mr Crosby's murder.

'Such a letter would present an irresistible lure. Mr Crosby was evidently much disturbed by the threats against him. The opportunity to discover the man's identity and the possibility of seeing his tormentor arrested would have seemed too good to miss. My fear is that he may have gone like a lamb to the slaughter.'

Breaking off, he banged with his stick on the roof of the hansom and, when the little flap door in it opened, he called up impatiently, 'Can the horse go no faster, cabby? We wish to catch the 3.48 train from Victoria.'

As the cab picked up speed, Holmes leant back against the upholstery and lapsed into a brooding silence so intense that I hesitated to intrude on his thoughts with any further questions for I knew that fear over what might have happened to Mr Crosby was uppermost in his mind, as indeed it was in mine. It was a silence he maintained throughout the train journey to Guildford where we alighted and where, much to my astonishment, Holmes made a dash for the station entrance. It was only when I caught up with him and found him questioning one of the drivers of the cabs drawn up on the forecourt that I understood the purpose behind his sudden haste.

'I was anxious to find the same cabby who might have picked up Mr Crosby before someone else claimed the man's services,' he explained. 'I appear to have found him. At least, a gentleman answering Mr Crosby's description who came off the 9.16 train from London this morning hailed his cab.

That is correct, is it not, driver? Where did you take him?'

'The Rose and Crown public 'ouse in Steeple Barton,' the man replied.

'Then we, too, shall be driven to the same destination,' Holmes said, climbing inside the vehicle.

It was a pleasant twenty-minute drive through the open countryside which lay beyond the outskirts of the town. Although it was September and by now late afternoon, the sun still shone with the warmth and brilliance of high summer, flooding the stubble fields and the woodlands, already beginning to assume the russet and gold tints of autumn, with a rich, mellow light.

Even Holmes' sombre mood seemed to lift for from time to time he commented on the beauty of the scenery, an appreciation of nature which had begun to manifest itself more and more strongly since he had returned from his apparent death at the Reichenbach Falls.[3]

However, as we drew nearer to our destination, he again fell silent, averting his head to stare unseeingly at the passing view so that all I could see of him was his profile, his lean jaw as hard as granite with mounting tension at what we might discover there of Mr Crosby's fate.

The village of Steeple Barton was small, a mere half-dozen or so cottages clustered round its two main

[3] Although in 'The Adventure of the Cardboard Box', Dr John H. Watson remarks that 'appreciation of nature found no place among his [Sherlock Holmes'] many gifts', in 'The Adventure of Black Peter', dated July 1895, Mr Sherlock Holmes invites Dr Watson to 'walk in the woods . . . and give a few hours to the birds and the flowers'. Dr John F. Watson.

features – an ancient, flint-built church with a tall steeple, from which the place had no doubt taken its name, and the Rose and Crown tavern which stood immediately opposite.

It was a low, whitewashed building which, when we entered, we found empty of customers, apart from an elderly man, a former farmworker, I imagined, from his attire and weather-beaten complexion, who was sitting alone in the ingle corner, a pint of ale at his elbow and an old, white-muzzled retriever at his feet. Both dog and man seemed to be fast asleep.

The publican, the only other occupant, was leaning with both elbows on the bar counter in an attitude of utter boredom although his face brightened when Holmes and I entered and, straightening up, he regarded us with considerable interest. He was a thin, spry, shrewd-eyed, little man, the very antithesis of the conventional, rubicund image of the landlord of a country tavern.

'You be from Lunnon, bain't 'ee, gen'lemen?' he asked, before Holmes even had time to open his mouth.

'Indeed we are,' Holmes replied, a little taken aback by the man's perspicacity. 'We are making inquiries about . . .'

'Oh, I knows why you're 'ere, sir,' the landlord replied without any hesitation. 'You be askin' about the other gen'leman from Lunnon, the one 'oo called in 'ere earlier this mornin'. A grey-haired, stout man 'e were, with a tall 'at. 'E came to collect the letter.'

'What letter?' Holmes demanded sharply.

'Very free, too, with 'is money. Gave me 'alf a crown for

my trouble, 'e did,' the landlord continued, as if Holmes had not spoken, a dreamy expression softening his foxy-looking features at the memory of this largesse.

With a sideways glance at me of mingled amusement and exasperation, Holmes produced a similar coin from his pocket and laid it down on the counter from where it was immediately spirited away into the landlord's palm with the practised skill of a professional conjuror.

'What letter?' Holmes repeated.

'The letter as was left 'ere earlier this mornin' by a lady.'

'A lady?' Holmes seemed much astounded by this piece of information for it quite refuted his assumption that Mr Crosby's unknown correspondent was almost certainly a man. 'What did she look like?'

'She was tall and slim and dressed all in black, like widow's weeds,' came the prompt reply.

'And her features?'

'Ah, I'm afraid I can't 'elp you there, sir, for she was wearin' a thick veil which covered the 'ole of her face. Spoke soft, though, almost in a whisper. Gave me the letter, she did, and asked me to 'and it to a gen'leman 'oo'd be callin' for it later. Then she vanished.'

'Vanished?' Holmes seemed as surprised as I at this dramatic choice of word.

'I'll show 'ee,' the landlord told us, lifting the flap of the counter and proceeding across the bar to the front door, Holmes and I at his heels. Here he stopped on the threshold to point up and down the road.

'See there, gen'lernen,' he announced.

Following his pointing finger, we saw that, to the left, the road ran straight past the churchyard gate and a row of cottages to continue on into the surrounding countryside. In the opposite direction, having passed two or three other little houses, their front gardens bright with dahlias and Michaelmas daisies, it took a sharp turn to the right to disappear from sight towards some trees, the tops of which, heavy with early autumn foliage, were visible above a hedgerow.

As we looked, the landlord began to give us his account.

'I was curious, gentlemen,' he was saying. 'It ain't often as I gets a woman in my tavern, specially at that time of the mornin', and a stranger, too. Leastways, I ain't ever seen 'er afore. And there was summat queer, I thought, about 'er leavin' a letter like that. So, as soon as I'd propped it up on the shelf be'ind the counter, I came outside to see what way she'd gone.' With apparent inconsequentiality, he asked, ''Ow long do you reckon it took me just now to walk from the bar to 'ere?'

'Two minutes at most?' Holmes suggested.

'Quite right, sir! That's what I makes it. Well, by the time I'd got to the door, she'd vanished off the face of the earth, phut! Just like that!' the landlord exclaimed, snapping his fingers to emphasise the suddenness of her disappearance.

'Curious!' Holmes murmured. 'Is that all you can tell us?'

'Only that when the gen'leman arrived 'alf an hour later to collect the letter, 'e opened it and read it there and then as 'e stood at the bar counter.'

'Did he ask who had left it?'

''E did, sir, and when I said it were a woman, 'e asked what she looked like and I described 'er as best I could, same as I did for you. Anyways, after 'e'd finished reading the letter, 'e put it in 'is pocket and asked me the way to Barton Wood, so I told 'im, down there to the right.' The landlord jerked his thumb towards the distant trees. 'Puttin' two and two together,' he continued, 'it don't take much brain power, do it, gentlemen, to work out where the lady 'ad gone as well? Lovers are they, sir, meetin' in secret? That's what I reckon they were. And 'er recently widowed, too! Well, that's women for you! Off with the old and on with the new!'

'Yes, quite,' Holmes said briskly. 'Thank you for your help, landlord. I am much obliged to you.'

With that, he set off down the road at a fast rate. As I hurried to catch up with him, I glanced briefly back over my shoulder to see the landlord still standing at the door of the Rose and Crown watching our departure with obvious curiosity, one hand shielding his eyes from the sun, until we, too, disappeared round the bend in the road in the direction of Barton Wood.

II

Once we were out of the man's sight, Holmes slackened his pace to a slower walk and, with head bent, began to scrutinise the left-hand side of the road, now little more than a lane, where it ran alongside a grass verge. The dust which covered the surface was generally dry but here and there, where water had seeped through from the adjoining ditch, patches of mud had collected, still damp despite the heat of that September afternoon.

It was these muddy stretches which roused Holmes' greatest interest. Crouching down low over one particular area, he examined it at close quarters before, standing upright, he announced, 'We now know how the lady in black managed to disappear so dramatically, Watson. She was riding a bicycle equipped with worn Dunlop tyres, the pattern of which can be quite clearly seen here in the mud.'[4]

---

[4] In 'The Adventure of the Priory School', Mr Sherlock Holmes remarks that he was 'familiar with forty-two different impressions' left by bicycle tyres. Dr John F. Watson.

'So what are your conclusions, Holmes? Do you suppose the lady in black, as you call her, wrote all the letters to Mr Crosby, including those threatening his life as well as the one he received this morning by the first post?'

'My dear fellow, it is a capital mistake to come to any conclusions so early in a case. Although it would appear that she was the author of the letter left at the public house, whether she sent the others remains to be seen. We may have a conspiracy on our hands between two people, a man and a woman. Or the lady in black may be entirely innocent of the threats made against Mr Crosby and is trying instead to warn or defend him. However, I doubt that. Although Mr Crosby may have been persuaded he had nothing to fear from meeting a woman, this rendezvous arranged to take place in a wood in the middle of the Surrey countryside has about it a most unpleasant whiff of danger. Come! Let us find out if our worst fears have indeed been fulfilled.'

He set off again at a rapid pace, stopping occasionally to inspect other muddy stretches along the side of the road which also bore the marks of tyres until, having reached the edge of the wood and walked about a hundred yards past its perimeter, we came to a green-painted signpost on the verge, bearing the words 'Footpath to Lower Haybrook' and pointing to a broad, grassy track leading off between the trees. A large white arrow chalked under these words also pointed in the same direction.

Setting off along the track, we found other arrows similarly drawn on tree trunks, directing us onwards. They reminded me of the game of Hare and Hounds which, as a boy, I had played with a group of friends and in which one of our number, acting as the hare and using a piece of chalk purloined from the schoolroom, had scrawled similar arrows on the trunks of trees or gateposts, although usually less obvious than these, to lead the rest of us, the hounds, to his hiding place. The memories of this innocent pastime contrasted oddly with the mental picture I had of Mr Crosby, formally attired for a day at his City bank in silk hat and frock coat, picking his way, as we were doing, along this leafy path which led deeper and deeper into the wood.

As the path narrowed and the trees grew more closely together, I was aware of a mounting sense of impending peril, engendered not only by anxiety over Mr Crosby's fate but also by the very atmosphere of the place. It was no longer possible to see the sky. The heavy canopy of leaves had grown more dense, casting deeper shadows occasionally lit by intermittent gleams of sunlight which flickered ominously about the scene like will o' the wisps leading us to heaven alone knew what destination. Even the birds had ceased to sing and the only sound to break the silence was the dry rustlings of unseen creatures in the undergrowth.

We came at last to a beech on the trunk of which was chalked a larger arrow pointing this time not straight ahead but to the right. Following its direction, we set off between the trees, ducking under low branches or forcing a path through thick brushwood. Here and there, other arrows directed us onwards. There were signs, too, that someone else had been this way before us for in places the bracken was already trampled under feet other than ours or a trailing bramble, bearing hard reddish-black berries, not yet softened to full autumnal ripeness, had been bent to one side for easier passage.

The grassy glade took us both by surprise. Because of the difficulty of the terrain, we had been concentrating on the hazards beneath our feet and not on what might lie ahead of us. Our arrival at the edge of the clearing was therefore quite unexpected. One moment we were wading through a particularly dense clump of waist-high bracken, the next we had emerged into the open.

Even now, writing about it several years later, I can still recall in vivid detail the scene which confronted us and the sense of shocked disbelief it aroused even though we were half expecting some tragic outcome. For my part, it was the terrible contrast between the serene beauty of the place and the horror it contained which struck me most forcibly and which remains with me to this day.

The glade was circular in shape, like a natural amphitheatre, ringed about with trees and, like a stage-setting, illuminated with shafts of bright sunshine which fell between the branches giving everything, the leaves, the grass, the soft cushions of moss, a peculiar dappled brilliance as if they were generating their own shifting green light.

In contrast to this natural beauty, the body of a well-built, grey-haired man which lay in the centre of the clearing was shockingly incongruous. It was spread out on its back, its legs together and its feet in their polished black boots pointing towards us, its arms out-stretched at its sides as if it had been crucified. There was, however, nothing reverential in its careful positioning for, in a dreadful parody which was intentional, its black silk hat had been deliberately placed, brim uppermost, by its right hand and the starched white shirt front was torn open to expose the bare chest beneath.

For a few seconds we both stood aghast and then Holmes sprinted forward with me close behind him.

I knew even before I felt for the carotid artery in his throat that the man was dead. The rope pulled tight about his neck and the distorted features, darkened with the effects of strangulation, were enough to convince me that he was past reviving. Rigor mortis was already beginning to set in and the blood from a cut above his left eyebrow had congealed.

I was about to make this comment to Holmes when, for the first time, I was aware of the objects which were set out upon the man's chest, as if on a table, and which Holmes, kneeling at my side, was carefully scrutinising although he made no attempt to touch them. They were an extraordinary collection and, like the positioning of the silk hat, had been deliberately placed there in that particular pattern.

On the left-hand side, just below the breast, was a gold pocket watch, still ticking although the heart which lay beneath it had long since ceased to beat. Over the right breast lay a single white feather while a little lower down in the centre of the torso a number of six-penny pieces had been set out in the shape of a cross. But the most extraordinary object and one which had a gruesome life of its own was a creature about three inches long which, like a large reddish-brown slug, was slowly crawling across the expanse of the dead man's chest, leaving behind it a moist, glutinous trail.

As I stared at it horrified, Holmes, who had risen to his feet, was scribbling something down on a page of his notebook which he tore out and handed to me.

'Give this to the landlord of the Rose and Crown, Watson, and ask him to find someone to take it to the police station in Guildford, preferably by a fast vehicle,' said he briskly. 'Meanwhile, I shall remain here and examine the scene for any clues to the perpetrator of this terrible crime.'

I set off at once to return the way we had come, in my haste leaping over brambles and crashing through bracken, until at last I came to the track and finally to the road where I was able to make better time.

Since our departure, nothing appeared to have changed in the public bar of the Rose and Crown. The old man and his dog were still asleep in the inglenook by the fireplace and the landlord was propped up again on his elbows behind the counter in exactly the same attitude in which we had first found him.

As I burst through the door and gasped out my message, I was relieved to see that my urgency had communicated itself to him for, levering himself upright and going to an inner door which led into the back premises, he shouted

257

for someone called Dick who came ambling into the bar. He was a tall, gangling youth, probably the potboy, to whom I handed Holmes' note with some misgivings for he seemed disinclined to hurry himself.

'And tell the Inspector in charge that it is a case of murder!' I added in the hope of galvanising him into action.

It appeared to have some effect for, having regarded me for a few seconds, his mouth fallen foolishly open, he disappeared through the door with admirable speed, the landlord roaring out after him to take the gig.

'Murder?' he repeated, turning back to me, his sharp, foxy features lively with curiosity. 'I might 'ave guessed no good would come from the pair of 'em meetin' all secret like in Barton Wood. Killed her, did 'e, the man in the tall 'at? Bashed 'er over the 'ead in a lovers' tiff, I wouldn't wonder. You mark my words, there's another man mixed up in all this!'

This last remark was shouted after me as I made for the door and set off again up the road at a run, anxious to return to Holmes as quickly as possible although, despite the dreadful nature of the circumstances, I could not repress a smile at the quite erroneous interpretation the landlord had managed to weave round the few facts known to him. I had no doubt that, even before the police arrived from Guildford, every inhabitant in the village of Steeple Barton would know about the lovers' secret tryst in Barton Wood and its tragic consequences.

III

Holmes greeted my return eagerly, impatient to show me the evidence he had found during my absence. Hardly giving me time to catch my breath, he hurried me to the far side of the glade where he indicated a patch of ground immediately behind a large oak tree.

'Look, Watson!' cried he. 'This is where the murderer and his accomplice waited. You can see how the bracken and grass have been trampled underfoot. And over here,' he continued, pointing to the left, 'is the route by which they left after the murder was committed. While you were away, I traced it back to the footpath which leads to Lower Haybrook.'

'They?' I repeated. 'Then you believe two of them were involved?'

'Having seen the evidence, I am more than ever convinced that this is a conspiracy between a man and a woman, the lady in black who enticed Crosby to this isolated place, and a man who committed the actual murder. See here!' he exclaimed, seizing me by the sleeve once more and dragging me a few feet into the glade where he again pointed to the ground. 'Observe how the grass here is also flattened and even the moss has been torn up in places. It was here that Crosby was strangled after a struggle. You recall the cut over his eyebrow? Well, here and again here you may see where the cut has bled.'

Now that he had pointed them out to me, I could indeed see a few drops of blood staining the grass.

'What else do you notice about this particular location?' Holmes continued.

'Apart from the bloodstains? Why, nothing Holmes,' I confessed.

'Oh, Watson, Watson!' Holmes chided me testily. 'There are times when I despair of you! Do you never use your eyes? Bend down, man, and look again!'

Feeling harassed by his overbearing manner and these orders rapped out in a peremptory voice, but knowing that it was useless to protest, I obediently squatted down while Holmes stood over me, urging me to bend even lower until my head was almost touching the ground.

'Now what do you see?' he demanded.

From this uncomfortable position, I could now make out, faintly marked out across the sward, two parallel lines which led to the body but which were invisible when seen from above.

When I remarked on this, Holmes asked, 'And what does that signify?' But it was merely a rhetorical question for, without giving me time to reply, he hastened on, 'It means the body was dragged into the centre of the clearing, its heels making those tracks in the grass. Like the struggle between Crosby and his murderer, they also suggest it was the work of a man. We have seen for ourselves that Crosby must have weighed at least thirteen or fourteen stones. No woman would have had the strength to drag him that far. And now for the body itself.'

Before I had time to rise, Holmes was off again, striding forward to stand over the corpse where, having regained my feet, I joined him.

His first question seemed utterly inconsequential. 'Do you ever read poetry, Watson?'

'Not since I left school,' I admitted, wondering what possible connection this could have with Crosby's murder.

'But you are familiar with the term "symbol" when used in a poetic sense?'

'You mean the use of a word to convey other meanings, such as "lion" representing the concept of "courage"?'

'Exactly so. Now look at the objects laid out with such precision on the corpse, objects which I believe were deliberately chosen for their symbolic meaning. The pocket watch placed over the heart represents what?'

'Time?' I suggested. This idea had already occurred to me but now, grasping the purpose behind Holmes' question and beginning almost to enjoy this macabre game, I expanded on the theme. 'The heart is stopped but the watch is still going, meaning, I suppose, that it is time for him to die.'

'The white feather?'

'That usually represents a coward.'

'Excellent, Watson! And the money laid out in the form of a cross?'

'I must confess I can see no immediate symbol there.'

'Count it, Watson! How many sixpences are there?'

'Why, thirty,' I replied, hurriedly computing their number. 'Thirty sixpences! Thirty pieces of silver! What does that remind you of?'

'Of course!' I cried, making the connection at last. 'Judas Iscariot was paid thirty pieces of silver for betraying Jesus! The cross must therefore represent the crucifixion as does the way in which the body has been laid out with the arms outstretched.'

'Well done, my dear fellow! You are in scintillating form! According to St Matthew's Gospel, what happened to Judas after the betrayal?'

'He hanged himself, did he not?'

'Indeed he did.[5] Hence the rope which was used to strangle Crosby and which, I believe, represents Judas's suicide. It may have been the murderer's intention to hang Crosby from one of the trees but he chose instead to lay the body out on the ground so that he could display these objects symbolising a timely death, cowardice and betrayal on the corpse itself. And what of this?'

---

[5] According to St Matthew's Gospel, Chapter 27, Judas repented his betrayal of Jesus and tried to return the silver to the chief priests and elders but they refused to take them because it was blood money. Judas then threw down the coins and went away and hanged himself. The money was used to buy a field, known as the potter's field, as a burial ground for strangers. Dr John F. Watson.

Holmes continued, pointing with a long, fastidious finger at the slug-like creature which was still crawling across the corpse's bare chest.

'It is a leech, is it not?' I asked, bending down to examine it more closely.

'Quite so, Watson. You remember, of course, our conversation with Mr Wilberforce earlier this afternoon about the threatening letter sent to Mr Crosby in which he was referred to as a leech? We discussed then the relevance of the word to a blood-sucker. This particular leech is not, however, a *Hirudo medicinalis*, the medicinal leech which was used to draw blood from a patient.[6] It belongs to the genus *Trocheta subviridis*,[7] an amphibious leech which lives on earth worms and can often be found in damp soil. It also has a liking for drains and sewers in which it breeds. I made a small study of the subject when I was attending lectures at St Bartholomew's where I saw specimens of leeches in the pathological museum.[8]

---

[6] Medicinal leeches were widely used in the past not only to draw blood but to treat a number of illnesses including gout, tumours, headaches and skin diseases. Dr John F. Watson. Because their saliva contains hirudin, an anti-coagulant, leeches are again being used by surgeons to drain blood from the restored part of, for example, a severed finger after it has been sewn back using microsurgery. Leech farms have been established for the breeding of medicinal leeches. Aubrey B. Watson.

[7] This species of leech was first recorded in the Zoological Gardens in 1850. It has since spread across the country as far as South Wales and southern Scotland. Dr John F. Watson.

[8] After coming down from University, Mr Sherlock Holmes studied chemistry and anatomy at St Bartholomew's hospital where Dr John H. Watson had been a medical student. Dr John F. Watson.

'We come now to the setting for the murder, which I believe was as deliberately chosen as the objects laid out upon the victim. What may we deduce from that?'

'Well, it is secluded,' I ventured, not quite so sure of my ground in this particular aspect of the case.

'So are many other locations in the vicinity. Had the murderer wished, he could have committed the crime within the depths of the wood itself where there would have been even less chance of the body being discovered. And yet he has chosen this clearing. Why? Have you no opinion on the matter?'

'Not really, Holmes.'

'Then allow me to give you mine. The whole scene of the open glade as well as the disposition of the body in the centre of it suggests a ritual killing, almost like a pagan sacrifice, which in turn tells us something significant about the killer himself. I imagine him as an intelligent man but with an *idée fixe*[9] who has harboured a deep-seated grudge against Algernon Crosby, almost certainly because at some time in the past Crosby, in his capacity as a banker, refused to lend him money or called in a loan already made, thereby ruining him financially and perhaps also causing him acute social humiliation. The killer saw it as an act of betrayal over which he may have brooded for some time but which he has

---

[9] Although the concept of the *idée fixe* (obsession) had been known since the beginning of the nineteenth century, the first serious research into abnormal psychology was carried out by J. M. Charcot at Salt-pêtrière, the hospital for nervous diseases outside Paris. Sigmund Freud was one of Charcot's students in 1885. Dr John F. Watson.

decided only now to avenge. From these deductions, we may picture him as a middle-class man who was once wealthy but is now impoverished and who has recently suffered some further catastrophe, a bereavement perhaps, which is linked in some way with his financial ruin and which, like a match applied to a fire, has kindled an overwhelming desire for immediate vengeance.

'Furthermore, I see him as an educated man with an interest in natural science; his familiarity with the bible and his knowledge of where to find a specimen of *Trocheta subviridis* tell us that. He is also imaginative, as can be seen in his choice of the symbolic objects left on the corpse, and is probably a man with few friends who, had it not been for the presence of the lady in black, I would have suggested was unmarried and lived alone. However, her connection with him is obviously close. She could be his wife or possibly a sister.

'I also suggest that he lives not far away. His knowledge of Barton Wood, and in particular, this clearing in it, supports such a theory as does the fact that the lady in black cycled to the Rose and Crown, which also implies they live at no great distance from Steeple Barton. As for the murder itself, that, too, indicates both the man's intelligence and his need for revenge. It was no spur of the moment decision but the result of careful planning.'

'You astonish me, Holmes!' I exclaimed. 'How is it possible to deduce so much information about a murderer you have never laid eyes on?'

'By interpreting the evidence, my dear fellow. From a few

footprints one may estimate the size of a man's boots and also his height from the length of his stride.[10] By much the same method, one may also determine many factors about a man – or a woman, come to that – by close observation of the scene of the crime. It is simply a matter of using one's eyes and not concentrating all one's attention on the *corpus delicti* although that, too, can furnish the investigator with useful information not only about the victim but also about the perpetrator of the crime. It is an aspect of the science of detection to which I have recently given much thought. I may one day write a monograph on it.[11] Ah!' he concluded, breaking off his disquisition. 'From the sounds of crashings in the undergrowth, I think we may safely conclude that the police from Guildford have at last arrived, having followed the chalked arrows as I directed them in my note. Let us go forward and meet them.'

---

[10] In 'A Study in Scarlet', Mr Sherlock Holmes remarks that 'there is no branch of detective science which is so important as the art of tracing footsteps' and, in the same account, he assures Dr John H. Watson that 'the height of a man, in nine cases out of ten, can be told by the length of his stride'. Dr John F. Watson.

[11] Mr Sherlock Holmes apparently never wrote the monograph. However, in formulating such a theory, he was well ahead of his time for it was not until the 1980s that a similar method, known as 'offender profiling', was first used in a murder inquiry in England. From the data supplied by the police, Dr David Canter, a professor of psychology at Surrey University, was able to provide the detectives with a 'profile' of the murderer, consisting of seventeen points regarding his age, the vicinity in which he lived and so on. This information led to the arrest of John Duffy for the rape and murder of several young women. He was sentenced to seven terms of life imprisonment in 1988. Aubrey B. Watson.

IV

Hardly had he finished speaking than two uniformed officers, an inspector and a constable, emerged from the trees, both looking dishevelled and moist about the brow from their exertions in making their way to the clearing.

The senior of the two, a tall man wearing a thick, heavy moustache which contrasted oddly with his balding head, as if his hair had migrated downwards to his upper lip, introduced himself as Inspector Mumford and his companion, a young, fresh-faced junior officer, as Constable Huggins. Once these formalities were over, Holmes gave a brief explanation of the background to the case and his own involvement in it before leading the two men forward to examine the body and those other areas of the scene which he had already shown to me; he then proceeded to give them a rapid summary of his deductions about the murderer to which I have already referred.

'I therefore suggest, Inspector,' he concluded, 'that you leave Constable Huggins here to keep guard on the body while the rest of us follow the murderer's trail to the footpath which leads to Lower Haybrook, for, as I have explained, the man may very well live in the vicinity.'

Inspector Mumford, who had listened to Holmes' account with an air of intelligent appreciation, agreed with my old friend's suggestion and, leaving Huggins on duty in the glade, the three of us set off once again through the woods.

Although there were no arrows on this occasion to direct us, the route the murderer and his accomplice, the lady in black, had taken was easily discernible by the broken twigs and crushed bracken which marked their progress. Having reached the footpath, we turned right towards Lower Haybrook and, after a distance of about a quarter of a mile, reached the edge of Barton Wood at a stile over which we climbed.

The countryside now lay spread out before us and we saw that the land sloped gently downwards through open meadows to a shallow valley where a cluster of rooftops and a church tower, set a little distance from the houses, indicated the village of Lower Haybrook. Apart from a few outlying farms and cottages, it was a compact place, ringed, as if by a moat or a defensive wall, by a circle of trees towards which the footpath, clearly defined by its stony surface, led its meandering way alongside the irregular field boundaries.

However, three-quarters of the way down, it branched off to the left to take a more direct route through the graveyard of the church itself, another fingerpost pointing the way. Having climbed a second stile, we found ourselves in a newer part of the burial ground, judging by the more recent dates on the headstones and their unblemished condition, for they had not yet become either weather-stained or blotched with lichen. Holmes, who seemed interested in these graves, had dropped back a little to examine some of them, leaving Mumford and me to walk on alone towards the lychgate where we paused to let him catch up with us. As I turned to look back at him, I saw he was bending over a freshly dug grave, little more than an oblong heap of earth, which was close to the path and which was unmarked apart from a simple white wooden cross and a single wreath of withered flowers, to which was still attached a black-edged memorial card.

Seeing us waiting, he stood upright and came striding towards us but, although I looked at him inquiringly, he made no reference either to the graves or to his interest in them, merely commenting generally on the picturesqueness of the scene and the great age of the yew trees which grew either side of the churchyard gate.

Beyond this gate, the footpath finally petered out as it met the road leading directly to the village which we could see at the bottom of the hill about two hundred yards away. As we set out towards it, Holmes again showed an inclination to linger, on this occasion to examine any muddy patches on the left-hand side of the road which, like those we had followed on the way to Barton Wood, were still moist from water draining down from the fields. Mumford, unaware of the significance of these damp stretches, seemed a little impatient at the delay and looked back several times as if to urge my old friend to quicken his pace. But, knowing what Holmes was looking for, I was not at all surprised when he drew to a complete halt at a gap in the tall hedge which ran along the side of the road and pointed down it.

'This way, Inspector,' he called out.

'Why that way?' Mumford asked as we turned to retrace our steps.

'The marks of bicycle tyres,' I said briefly.

There was no time to give a longer explanation for we had reached the opening in the hedge which led on to a narrow path, although Mumford seemed to grasp the meaning for he nodded quickly before setting off after Holmes who was now stalking rapidly ahead of us, head lowered and his whole frame alert like a gun dog scenting its quarry.

The path was only a few feet wide and seemed little used, for the ground was hardly marked either by wheels or by the passage of feet and in places was overgrown with grass. But here and there in the moister soil the distinctive pattern made by the tyres of a bicycle led us as inexorably forward as the chalked arrows on the trees.

We came upon the house as suddenly and as unexpectedly as we had stumbled across the clearing in the wood. It was a small, low, whitewashed cottage which had the same simplicity of design which may be found in a child's drawing of a house – a mere oblong construction with a central door, two chimney stacks at each end and four casement windows, two up and two down, beneath the sloping eaves of a tiled roof. All it lacked to complete the similarity were curling streamers of smoke rising from the chimney pots.

The absence of these signs of life and the neglected state of the front garden gave the impression that the place was unoccupied, although the open front door and a woman's bicycle propped against the wall beside it suggested someone was at home.

Holmes rapidly inspected the tyres of the bicycle, silently drawing our attention to the pattern on them before knocking on the door with his stick and calling out, 'Is anyone there?'

There came no reply. Beyond the open door, we could see a short passageway from which a precipitous staircase rose to an upper landing, and two doors set on either side, both of which were closed.

Having knocked and called again, still with no answer, Holmes stepped into the hall and turned the handle of the door to the right.

His sudden exclamation of horror and the abrupt manner in which he threw the door fully open and rushed into the room warned both Mumford and me that something dreadful lay within but neither of us was prepared for the scene which confronted us as we crowded in behind him.

The room, which ran the full width of the cottage, served as both a kitchen and a dining room, an old-fashioned black iron stove standing in the chimney opening at the rear, two wooden cupboards and, under the window, a pump for water erected over a shallow sink providing its limited equipment.

The front part, the end at which we had entered, contained nothing more than a deal table and three Windsor chairs. Apart from one shabby rug in front of the fireplace, the flagstoned floor was bare.

However, it was only later that I noticed these details. As I entered the room at Holmes' heels, my whole attention was fixed on the dreadful sight which met my gaze and which blotted out all awareness of my surroundings.

It was the body of a woman dressed in black, a veil drawn down over her face, which hung suspended from a rope fixed to a hook in a ceiling beam and which was twisting slowly in the draught from the opened door. An overturned chair lay a short distance from her feet which were also swinging gently to and fro below her black skirts like a ghastly, human metronome keeping time with some inaudible rhythm.

I heard Holmes shout out an order which at the time I failed to register properly although its intention was quite clear. While Mumford rushed off to fetch a knife from a kitchen drawer, Holmes and I supported her weight from below. On the Inspector's return, Holmes took the knife, righted the chair and, having mounted it, cut the rope and between us we lowered the body to the floor.

As with Crosby's corpse, I had no need to feel for the carotid artery in her neck to know that she was dead.

Rigor mortis was already too well advanced for there to be any hope of her revival.

'It is too late, Holmes,' I said, looking up at him as I knelt beside the body. 'There is nothing I can do to save her.'

I was shocked by the expression on his face. Never in our long acquaintance had I seen him look so gaunt and haggard. It was as if the flesh had fallen away from his features, leaving the bony structure beneath pitifully exposed under the thin membrane of the skin so that he resembled a living death's head, ashen in colour, the eyes sunk deep into their sockets.

'Him,' he corrected me.

'Him?' I repeated, greatly astonished.

'It is a man, Watson, not a woman,' he said abruptly.

It was only then I realised that his order to us had been to cut 'him' down.

Kneeling down beside him, he lifted back the veil to reveal the features, terribly distorted by the effects of strangulation. Nevertheless it was still possible to discern under the bloated flesh the lineaments of a young man in his early twenties, handsome if a little over-refined and sensitive, especially about the mouth and chin which gave the lower part of his face a vulnerable quality.

'How were you so certain it was a man, not a woman?' I asked.

'The newly dug grave by the churchyard path which confirmed my suspicions that a recent bereavement could have led Crosby's murderer to seek revenge,' he replied.

'The card on the wreath was inscribed with the words: "To my dearest mother from her ever-loving son, Rupert." There then followed last Wednesday's date and a brief biblical quotation: "To proclaim the day of vengeance; to comfort all that mourn."[12] Her death ten days ago was, I believe, the event which triggered his decision to murder Algernon Crosby.'

'According to this suicide note, you are quite right, Mr Holmes,' Inspector Mumford remarked unexpectedly. He had picked up a sheet of paper from the table from which he began to read out loud.

'"Since my dear mother's death, I have found life intolerable. I have therefore decided to put into action my long thought-out plan to murder Algernon Crosby, the man who brought so much grief and despair to my parents, directly causing my father's suicide and my mother's suffering which hastened her own untimely end. You will find Crosby's body in a clearing in Barton Wood. I have placed all the documents relating to this affair in a deed box in my bedroom." It is signed Rupert Sefton,' Mumford concluded.

There is not much else I wish to add to this account. Inspector Mumford volunteered to walk into the village to requisition a suitable vehicle in which to transport Sefton's body to the mortuary in Guildford. In his absence, <u>Holmes and I</u> inspected the remaining rooms in the house,

[12] The quotation is taken from Isaiah, Chapter 61, Verse 2 which reads: 'To proclaim the acceptable year of the Lord, and the day of vengeance of our God; to comfort all that mourn.' Dr John F. Watson.

all sparsely furnished, including the late Mrs Sefton's bedchamber which was left exactly as it must have been on the day she died, with a bible placed on the night table and the few clothes she possessed hanging in the press or lying neatly folded in the drawers. It was doubtlessly from among this apparel that Rupert Sefton had acquired the mourning dress and veiled hat which he had worn in his role as the lady in black.

Her son's room across the landing was as bare and contained little more than an iron bedstead and a chest of drawers on the top of which was placed a wedding photograph. Both the bride and groom were good-looking, the woman in particular, bearing about her features that sensitive and refined expression which I had discerned in the face of her dead son. The black ribbon pinned to the frame and the little posy of wild flowers placed in a vase before it made their radiant happiness as they smiled at the camera even more poignant.

The deed box, referred to in Rupert Sefton's suicide note, stood beside it but, apart from picking it up and carrying it downstairs to leave in the hall, Holmes made no attempt, then, to open it. He also avoided re-entering the room where Sefton's body was still lying on the floor. Instead, he wandered out into the garden where I followed him, a little anxious about his state of mind, for he had lapsed once more into that brooding silence which always presaged one of his blacker moods. However, a glimpse of his former self reasserted itself when, in the course of his restless peregrinations, he came upon the gully into which water from the kitchen sink drained and called me over to examine what he had found. Lying in the bottom were several loathsome, reddish-coloured leeches of the type which had been placed on Crosby's body, the discovery of which seemed to afford him a sombre satisfaction.

On Mumford's return with a wagonette and its driver, both borrowed from a nearby farm, we laid the body of Rupert Sefton on the straw in the back and, having covered it with a blanket, set out by road for Barton Wood to collect the second body, that of Algernon Crosby, still guarded by Constable Huggins. With his help, we gathered up the objects laid out upon the man's chest and then, between the four of us, we carried the corpse on a hurdle to the road where it, too, was loaded on to the wagonette and covered over. So the two men, who in their lifetime had probably never met, apart from that fatal encounter in Barton Wood, were laid side by side, united in death in a final intimacy.

It was a melancholy journey back to Guildford through that magnificent countryside which but a few hours before I had observed with so much pleasure, its autumn colours now enriched by the glow of the setting sun. Not one of us spoke and the only sound was the creaking of the wheels and the slow, heavy tread of the horses' hooves on the road.

Having left the bodies at the mortuary, Holmes and I accompanied the two officers back to the police station where, in Mumford's office, we read over the contents of the deed box which included old newspaper cuttings, bank statements and letters, among them the last two written by Rupert Sefton to Algernon Crosby which Sefton must have taken from his victim's pocket. The first promised, as Holmes had predicted, to name Crosby's anonymous correspondent who was threatening his life. In it, he suggested a meeting at the Rose and Crown in Steeple Barton and gave the time of the train he should catch from London. The second was a hurried note which the so-called lady in black had left for him at the tavern changing the rendezvous to Barton Wood and directing him to follow the arrows to the meeting place. Both were signed 'Elizabeth Sefton'. Amongst these various documents, we also found a journal of a sort kept by Rupert Sefton over a period of years. From these papers, we were able to piece together the family's tragic story and the events which had led to Crosby's murder and Rupert Sefton's suicide.

Sefton's father, a once prosperous stockbroker, ruined by the collapse of a South African gold-mining company in which he had heavily invested, had indeed been refused a bank loan by Crosby, acting on behalf of Mott and Co. Faced with bankruptcy and inevitable ruin, Frederick Sefton had, as his son was to do later, hanged himself, leaving behind a widow and their only child, Rupert, then aged fifteen.

Forced by penury and the stigma of social disgrace, Mrs Sefton retired to the isolated cottage in Lower Haybrook where the two of them lived like recluses on a small annuity, hardly big enough to pay the household bills. It was then that Rupert Sefton's implacable hatred of Algernon Crosby first took root for, with the emotional illogicality of youth, he mistakenly laid the entire blame for the family's misfortune, including his own, on Crosby's shoulders. A brilliant scholar with every expectation of going up to University to study natural science, he found those bright hopes suddenly dashed when he was taken away from school as his mother could no longer pay the fees. He tried to continue his education as best he could by studying the local flora and fauna, thereby fulfilling yet another of Holmes' predictions about his interest in nature.

From his journal, we were able to trace the development over the years of his one *idée fixe*, which Holmes had also deduced, to avenge his father's death until by a gradual process of deterioration in his mental state, brought to a climax by his mother's death, he was consumed by the one burning desire – to murder Algernon Crosby.

This aspect of his personality was reflected in the coroner's verdict after the inquest which we both attended although only Holmes was called upon to give evidence. It found that Rupert Sefton had first murdered Algernon Crosby and afterwards had taken his own life, the balance of his mind being disturbed.

As I considered the case to be of interest to my readers who, like me, greatly admire Holmes' remarkable methods of deduction, I asked for his permission to publish this account of it. However, he has adamantly refused.

Although I have known Holmes for many years, certain features of his singular personality remain an enigma to me and I can only guess at the reason behind his refusal. However, I am convinced that some aspect of the Barton Wood case, in particular the suicide of the young man, Rupert Sefton, has touched some deep chord in Holmes' memory, of what I cannot say although I strongly suspect it may concern a relation or a close friend who took his own life in a similar fashion.

Until the time when he chooses to confide in me or withdraws his refusal, this account of the case will therefore have to remain in the vaults of my bank, Cox and Co. of Charing Cross, among my other unpublished records.[13]

---

[13] Dr John H. Watson refers to the case in 'The Adventure of the Golden Pince-Nez' in which he states that he has kept notes on 'the repulsive story of the red leech and the terrible death of Crosby the banker'. Dr John F. Watson.

Appendix

An hypothesis regarding the real identity
of the King of Bohemia

Those readers who are familiar with the canon will not need reminding that the King of Bohemia is featured in 'A Scandal in Bohemia', an account which was first published in the *Strand Magazine* in July 1891.

The date on which this particular case began can also be established without difficulty. It was on the evening of 20th March 1889,[1] some weeks after his marriage to Miss Mary Morstan, that Dr Watson, who had returned to private practice as a general practitioner and had moved out of 221B Baker Street to his new address in Paddington, called on his old friend Sherlock Holmes at his former lodgings. It was here that Dr Watson was introduced to a masked man who, at first, claimed to be Count von Kramm, a Bohemian nobleman, although

[1] In 'A Scandal in Bohemia', Dr John H. Watson gives the year as 1888, clearly a mistake as on that date he was still unmarried and living in Baker Street. Dr John F. Watson.

Holmes soon saw through the disguise and established his identity as the King of Bohemia.

The reason for the King's presence in Baker Street is also perfectly straightforward. Five years earlier, on a lengthy visit to Warsaw, he had met and formed a liaison with the American opera singer, Irene Adler, who was then performing at the Imperial Opera House in that city. Although Dr Watson is too discreet to define the exact nature of their relationship, leaving that to the imagination of his readers, it had involved some compromising letters sent to Irene Adler by the King and a photograph of the two of them together which Irene Adler, now retired from the stage and living in London, had threatened to send to the King of Scandinavia whose daughter Holmes' royal client was proposing to marry. Fearing that the resulting scandal might bring about the end of his engagement, the King of Bohemia wanted Holmes to retrieve both the letters and the photograph.

The main problem facing the reader concerning this case is the real identity of the King of Bohemia. Who exactly was he?

Before setting out my own hypothesis regarding this matter, certain background information must first be established.

Bohemia had ceased to be an independent Kingdom in 1526 when, on the death of its monarch, King Ferdinand of Austria had contrived to have himself elected to the vacant throne. In 1889, it was ruled over by the Hapsburg Emperor, Franz Joseph, as part of the Austro-Hungarian empire. Indeed, Dr Watson himself hints at a Hapsburg connection by describing the King of Bohemia as having 'a thick, hanging lip, and a long straight chin', both of which were characteristic physical features of the Hapsburgs.

Because of this description, some commentators have identified the King of Bohemia as Emperor Franz Joseph's son, the Crown Prince Rudolf, who was a well-known ladies' man.

However, by March 1889, Prince Rudolf was dead. Two months earlier, on 30th January, his body was found at the royal hunting lodge at Mayerling, together with that of his seventeen-year-old mistress, Baroness Mary Vetsera. Both had been shot in circumstances which suggested the Prince had first killed the Baroness before committing suicide.

Queen Victoria's eldest son, Edward, the Prince of Wales, later King Edward VII, another well-known womaniser, is another candidate for the role of King of Bohemia. However, in 1889 the Prince of Wales was forty-nine and, although he had married the Danish princess, Alexandra, which might accord with the King of Bohemia's engagement to the daughter of the Scandinavian King, the wedding had taken place twenty-six years earlier in 1863.

Nevertheless, Dr Watson has given us several clues in his account which could point to the King's real identity.

He was German; he was a thirty-year-old bachelor; he was hoping to marry a princess; he was of royal blood and possessed the hereditary title to a kingdom; at the time he consulted Holmes he had some connection with a

Scandinavian monarch which a scandal might compromise and which was causing him acute anxiety. Moreover, despite the mask, Holmes recognised his voice and, once the mask was removed, was familiar with his features. In addition, Holmes openly showed his disapproval of him during the interview. Lastly and decisively, the man was in London in March 1889.

There is one person who, as far as I am aware, has never been suggested as a candidate for the King of Bohemia but whose identity matches the majority of Dr Watson's clues.

He was a German count who, while not of royal descent, was the son of a prince and could be regarded as heir, if not to a royal throne, then to a position of such power and prestige that it far outweighed any regal claim to some minor kingdom. He was also a bachelor who, it was rumoured, was in love with a princess whom he hoped to marry. She was not Scandinavian but German and a member of that other great European dynasty, the Hohenzollern family, to which the Count in question had very close ties. There were also Scandinavian connections but of a political rather than a matrimonial nature. In addition, his identity, if correct, would go a long way in explaining Holmes' cold and dismissive attitude towards him.

As a final and, to my mind, decisive factor, the Count was in London in March 1889 on a delicate diplomatic mission which the least hint of scandal could well have ruined.

The man in question was Count Herbert von Bismarck,

German Secretary of State for Foreign Affairs and the son of Otto von Bismarck, the powerful Chancellor to William II, the young German Kaiser, who had been awarded the title of Prince for his services to the Hohenzollern imperial family.

In March 1889, Count Herbert was forty years old and still a bachelor. Although this makes him ten years older than the age Dr Watson ascribes to the King of Bohemia, this may be a deliberate ploy on the doctor's part to mislead his readers, as may also be his description of the King of Bohemia as a flamboyantly dressed giant of a man, over six feet six inches tall.

The princess whom he was said to have fallen in love with and hoped to marry was Victoria, second daughter of the late Kaiser, Frederick III, and the former Empress, who was herself the daughter of Queen Victoria. A marriage between Count Herbert and Princess Victoria would, of course, have greatly benefited the Bismarcks, bringing them into the Hohenzollern royal family and thus strengthening their ties with the Kaiser.

Count Herbert's mission to London in March 1889 was to promote an Anglo-German alliance, not an easy task as there were deep-seated personal as well as political antipathies towards the Bismarcks in particular and Germany in general. The British royal family resented their treatment of the former Empress, Queen Victoria's daughter, and suspected that they were responsible for conducting a vendetta against her because of her too liberal English views.

On a political level, there was a long-standing disagreement between Germany and Great Britain over the Schleswig-Holstein question. These two duchies had been ruled over by Denmark until 1863 when Austria and Prussia combined to force the Danish King to relinquish them. Britain supported the Danes and the dispute took on a more personal nature when the Prince of Wales married the Danish princess, Alexandra, that same year.

It is in this area of international politics where the Scandinavian connection with Count Herbert von Bismarck, alias the King of Bohemia, had arisen.

The British government was also suspicious of Germany's attempts to form alliances with other European countries, in particular with France and Russia, Great Britain's traditional enemies.

In treating his client with such brusqueness, Holmes may have been expressing this official mistrust or the antipathy may have been due to more personal reasons. Count Herbert was a conceited, overbearing man with an unfortunate habit for someone in his position of German Secretary of State for Foreign Affairs of issuing orders rather than discussing international affairs in a diplomatic manner with his opposite numbers. Holmes' attitude towards him may reflect the private opinion of Mycroft and his colleagues in the British Foreign Office who may well have experienced the Count's high-handed manner during the Anglo-German negotiations.

It is also highly likely that, through his brother Mycroft, who had important government contacts, Sherlock Holmes was introduced to the Count at an official reception which was how he was able to recognise his client by his voice even before he removed the mask.

In the event, Lord Salisbury, the Prime Minister, refused to sign the Anglo-German agreement and the Count returned home empty-handed.

Count Herbert von Bismarck's anxiety to retrieve his photograph and letters from Irene Adler and so avoid any scandal may well have been sharpened by recent events connected with another King and an opera singer.

The King in question was Prince Alexander of Battenburg, second son of Prince Alexander of Hesse. In 1879, with Russian backing, the Prince had been elected ruler of Bulgaria, a newly created state formed from the eastern part of Armenia after the Russians had defeated the Turks and driven them out of the area. In supporting Prince Alexander's nomination to the Bulgarian throne, the Russians assumed he would act as a puppet King and carry out the Tsar's policies.

It was also hoped, particularly by Queen Victoria, that the Prince, a handsome, intelligent young man, would marry her granddaughter, the Hohenzollern Princess Victoria with whom Count Herbert was said to be in love. Naturally, the Bismarcks objected to such a marriage and, using their influence, persuaded certain members of the Hohenzollern family to oppose the match.

Matters came to a head in 1886 when Prince Alexander, who had angered the Tsar by his independent attitude, was kidnapped by Russian secret agents and was forced to abdicate at gun point. In the meantime, he had transferred his affections from Princess Victoria to Joanna Loisinger, an opera singer, whom he secretly married in February 1889, a mere month before Count Herbert's arrival in London. Because of this liaison, Alexander was obliged to give up the title of Prince and, taking the name of Count Hartenu, retired from public life.

It is therefore hardly surprising that Count Herbert, aware of Prince Alexander's fate, should be so very anxious to conceal his relationship with Irene Adler and seek Holmes' help in averting a similar scandal which could have brought about his own public disgrace and ruined his political career.

Dr John F. Watson D.Phil. (Oxon)
All Saints' College,
Oxford.
6th June 1933

ALSO BY JUNE THOMSON

The Secret Notebooks of Sherlock Holmes

In Sherlock Holmes' London, reputations are fragile and scandal can be ruinous. In order to protect the names of the good (and not-so-good), Dr Watson comes to the decision that his accounts of some of his friend's most brilliant cases must never see the light of day. But then a hundred years pass, and the mysteries outlast the memories of those they once could have harmed . . .

An aluminium crutch betrays the criminal who relies upon it for support . . . An Italian Cardinal lies dead in a muddy yard in Spitalfield . . . What do a pair of suspiciously successful gamblers have in common with the Transylvanian mind-reader, Count Rakoczi? And can Holmes and Watson outwit the jewel thief who has the nerve to steal from the King of Scandinavia?